R

"The humour of t
the reader from th
The author, Whitney Dineen, must have a brilliant sense of
humour herself which shines forth in her writing. I love the
way even a visit to a burger bar can engender such hilarity. A
really great read that I didn't want to put down. It make me
chuckle throughout, even in the sad parts. I shall certainly seek
out other work by this author. Watch out Bridget Jones, Mimi
Finnegan is on your tail!"

*-Reader's Favorite*

"Mimi Finnegan is my new hero! A laugh out loud read that I
could not put down."

*-Bestselling Author, Becky Monson*

"A romantic comedy with a lively, funny cast and loveable
main character."

*-Kirkus Review*

"Getting her swan on with irreverent humor, a fab makeover,
and the attentions of not one, but two, dishy dreamboats,
Mimi Finnegan is a heroine you'll love spending time with. I
laughed my way through this entire book!"

*-Author of Twin Piques, Tracie Banister*

"This book made me laugh, cry and want more! Mimi is every
woman. She is approachable, loveable and imperfectly perfect.
I cannot wait to read the sequel!

*-Bookworm*

# The Reinvention
# of
# Mimi Finnegan

Whitney Dineen

Copyright © 2015 Whitney Dineen

Published in the United States by Kissing Frog Publications an imprint of Thirty-Three Partners Publishing.

Library of Congress Cataloguing In-Publication Data.
Dineen, Whitney
The Reinvention of Mimi Finnegan: a novel/ Whitney Dineen
ISBN-13: 978-1511856737
ISBN-10: 1511856734

First Edition

*This book is dedicated to every woman who has ever felt she wasn't enough.*

# Acknowledgments

I am full of gratitude for the many people who made this book possible. First and foremost I would like to thank Melissa Amster of Chick Lit Central for being such a shining star in my author world. Melissa is one of those people who does everything she can to facilitate and share her love of the written word. Lady, you rock!

Tracie Banister, soul sister and fellow author, wow, wow, wow! Where do I start? Enormous thanks for going so far above and beyond for Mimi!

Props to everyone at Chick Lit Chat and Chick Lit Goddesses. You are generous and devoted groups and have saved my chili time and again. More importantly, you make me laugh and that is a gift beyond compare.

I am particularly grateful to my fellow authors Susie Schnall, Becky Monson, Engy Neville, Carol Maloney Scott, Maggie LePage, Celia Kennedy, Geralyn Corcillo and Meredith Schorr. Thank you for your cheers, advice and for not laughing at me when I ask the most inane questions. You are my backbone.

Stephanie Evanovich, cheers to you for being the first NYT Bestselling author to read my first novel, *She Sins at Midnight,* and giving me the encouragement I needed to know I could do this writing thing.

To my darling literary attorney, dear friend and Big Daddy, Scott Schwimer, I adore you!

I would like to thank actor, John Schneider, for sharing with me that no one likes a bone but a dog. I have remembered that all these years and I thank you for that morning on *The Home and Family Show* those many years ago.

Special appreciation to all of my Weight Watchers' leaders over the years, you truly are an inspiration and you're all Marge to me.

To my husband and love of my life Jimmy, you are my rock, my world and the best Barbie chicken wrangler in town!

Much love to my mother, Libby Bohlen, who continues to laugh at my words, even as she reads them for the forty-seventh time and to my father, Reiner Bohlen, for his endless belief in me.

To Kathy Leigh Hancock, up in heaven, life *is* a gift and everyone who had the pleasure to call you "friend," knows that too.

And last, but certainly not least, thank you to every last person who reads my books. Every email and review you take time to construct means the world to me. I couldn't do what I love without you!

# Chapter 1

"A BUNION?" I shriek.

"It would appear so." answers Dr. Foster, the podiatrist referred by my HMO.

"Aren't bunions something that old people get?"

"Yes," he replies. "That's normally the case, but not always. Bunions grow after years of walking incorrectly, or in some instances, not wearing the proper shoes."

Still perplexed, I ask, "What am I doing with one then? I'm only thirty-four."

He says that by the atypical location of my bunion, he can deduce that I have the tendency to walk on the outsides of my feet. He explains that while some people walk on the insides of their feet, giving them a knock-kneed appearance, others, like myself, rotate their feet outward; causing a waddle, if you will. I have a look of horror on my face when he says the word "waddle." I have never been accused of such a disgusting thing in my life. But before I can form a coherent response, he continues, "The extra...weight (and I'm sure he pauses to emphasize the word) that the outside of the foot is forced to endure by walking that way eventually causes it to grow an extra padding to help support the …load." Am I wrong or does he pause again when he says that word?

Playing dumb, I ask, "And I'm getting one so young, why?"

Clearing his throat, Dr. Foster answers, "Well, a lot of it has to do with genetics and the structure of your foot." Then adds, "And a lot of it has to do with the extra weight (pause and meaningful look) you're placing on it."

I am so aghast by this whole conversation that I finally confess, "I have just lost forty pounds." Which is a total lie by the way. In actuality I have just gained two. But I simply can't bear the humiliation of him calling me fat, or what I perceive as him calling me fat.

The doctor smiles and declares my previous poundage did not help the inflammation at all and announces it may have contributed to my bunion. He checks his chart and declares, "I see you're a hundred and seventy pounds. At one fifty, you should be feeling a lot better."

"But I'm 5'11," I explain.

"Yes?"

"I'm big boned!"

He looks at me closely and says, "Actually, you're not." Picking up my wrist, he concludes, "I would say medium, which means one hundred and fifty pounds would be ideal." Of course the photo of the emaciated woman on his desk should have tipped me off as to what this guy considers ideal. She is wearing a swimsuit with no boobs or butt to fill it out and painfully sharp collar bones. She bears a striking resemblance to an Auschwitz survivor.

All I can think is that I haven't been one-hundred-and fifty-pounds since high school. There is simply no way I can lose twenty pounds. I want to tell him he has no idea how much I deprive myself to weigh one seventy. In order to actually lose weight, I'd only be able to ingest rice cakes and Metamucil. But I don't say this because he'd think I'm weak and unmotivated and he'd be right, too. Plus, I just bragged that I lost a record forty pounds, so he already assumes I am capable of losing weight, which of course would be the truth if it weren't such an out-and-out lie.

The doctor writes a prescription for a special shoe insert that will help tip my foot into the correct walking position and then leaves, giving me privacy to cover my naked, misshapen appendage. As I put my sock back on I decide I am not going to go on a diet. I'm happy or happyish with the way I look and that's all there is to it. When I leave the room, Dr. Foster tells me to come back in two months so he can recheck my bunion. In my head I respond, "Yeah right, buddy. Take a good look, this is the last time you're ever going to see me or my growth." I plan on wearing my shoe insert and never again speaking of my hideous deformity.

The true cruelty of this whole bunion fiasco is that I am the one in my family with pretty feet. I have three sisters and we are all a year apart. Tell me that doesn't make for a crazy upbringing. At any rate, the year we were all in high school at the same time, my sisters and I were sitting on my bed having a nice familial chat, which was a rare occurrence as I'm sure you know girls that age are abominable as a whole. But put them under the same roof fighting over bathroom time, makeup and let's not forget the all-important telephone. It was an ungodly ordeal to say the least.

My sisters, to my undying disgust, are all gorgeous and talented. Renée, the oldest one of the group is the unparalleled beauty of the family. Lest you think I'm exaggerating and she's not really all that *and* a bag of chips, let me ask if the name Renée Finnegan means anything to you? Yes, that's right, "The" Renée Finnegan, the gorgeous Midwestern girl that won the coveted Cover Girl contract when she was only seventeen, fresh out of high school. Try surviving two whole years at Pipsy High with people asking, "You're Renée's sister? Really?" The tone of incredulity was more than I could bear.

Next is Ginger. She's the brain. But please, before you picture an unfortunate looking nerd with braces and braids, I should tell you that she is only marginally less gorgeous than Renée. She was also the recipient of a Rhodes scholarship, which funded her degree in the History of Renaissance Art, which she acquired at Oxford. Yes, Oxford, not the shoes, not the cloth, but the actual university in England.

The youngest of our quartet is Muffy, born Margaret Fay, but abbreviated to Muffy when at the tender age of two she couldn't pronounce Margaret Fay and began referring to herself as one might a forty-two-year old socialite. Muffy is the jock. She plays tennis and even enjoyed a run on the pro-circuit before a knee injury forced her to retire. She did however play Wimbledon three years in a row, and while never actually winning, the experience allows her to start sentences with, "Yes, well when I played Wimbledon..." And make pronouncements like, "There's nothing like the courts at

Wimbledon in the fall." Muffy is now the tennis pro at The Langley Country Club. Her husband Tom is the men's tennis pro, insuring they are the tannest, most fit couple on the entire planet. They're perfection is enough to make you barf.

I am the third child in my family, christened Miriam May Finnegan which against my express consent got shortened to Mimi. For years I demanded, "It's Miriam, call me Miriam!" No one listened, as is the way in my family.

While sitting on my white quilted bedspread from JCPenneys, my sisters, in a moment of domestic harmony, decided we were all quite extraordinary. Renée was deemed the beautiful one, Ginger, the smart one, and Muffy, the athletic one. With those proclamations made, they appeared to be ready to switch topics when I demanded to know, "What am I?"

It's not that my sisters didn't love me. I don't think they thought I was troll-like or stupid, it's just compared to them, I didn't have any quality that outshone any one of theirs. So after much thoughtful consideration and examination, like a prized heifer at the state fair Renée announced, "You have the prettiest feet." Ginger and Muffy readily agreed.

Listen, I know you're thinking "prettiest feet" isn't something I should brag about. But in my family, I would have been thrilled to have the prettiest anything, and I am. They could have just as easily said I had the most blackheads, or the worst split ends. But they didn't, they awarded me prettiest feet and I was proud of it. Until now. Now I have a bunion.

As I sit in front of my car in front of the Chesterton

Medical Center, I become undone by the horror of having lost my identity in my family. "Who will I be now?" I wonder. Oh wait, I know, I'll be the spinster, or the one without naturally blonde hair, my true color hovering somewhere between bacon grease and baby poop. Hey wait, I know, I'll be the one who needs to lose twenty pounds!

I turn on the ignition in my Honda and hop on the freeway heading for the Mercer Street exit. Yet somehow, I miss my turnoff and I've hit Randolph before I know it. With a will of its own, my car takes the exit and drives itself to the Burger City a half mile down the road. I demand, "What did you do that for? This is no way to lose twenty pounds." Not that I had agreed to do any such thing. But, I wasn't looking to gain weight either.

Typically, my car doesn't answer back, a fact for which I am eternally grateful. It simply makes its wishes known by transporting me to destinations of its choosing; Burger City, The Yummy Freeze, Dairy Queen, Pizza Hut. I've actually thought about trading it in, in hopes of upgrading to a car that likes to go to the gym and health food stores. But, no, this is my car and as a faithful person by nature, I realize I should do what it's telling me.

As the window automatically unrolls and the car accelerates to the take-out speaker, I hear the disembodied voice of a teenager say, "Welcome to Burger City. What can I get you today?"

Someone, who is surely not me answers, "I'd like a double cheeseburger with grilled onions, two orders of fries and a root beer, large."

He asks, "Will that be all?"

Still not sure who's doing the answering, I hear someone sounding remarkably like me say, "I'd like an extra bun too."

"What do you mean an extra bun?" He squeaks "You mean with no burger on it or anything?"

"That's right." He informs me that he'll have to charge me for a whole other burger even though I just want the bun. I tell him that's no problem and agree to pay $1.75 for it. I'm not sure what causes me to order the extra bread but I think it boils down to my need for carbohydrates. I have either been on The South Beach Diet or Atkins for the better part of two years and I've become desperate for empty calorie, high glycemic index white bread.

You may be wondering how I could have been high protein dieting for two years and still need to lose twenty pounds. The truth is that I cheat, a lot. For two weeks I jump start the diet with the serious deprivation they encourage and then by week three when you're allowed to start slowly adding carbs back into your life, I become the wildebeest of cheaters. They suggest you start with an apple or a quarter of a baked sweet potato. I start with an apple pie and three orders of French fries. I have been losing and gaining the same thirteen pounds for the last twenty-four months.

As soon as my food arrives, I pull over on a side street and inhale the heavenly aroma of danger. The fries call to me, the double cheeseburger begs to be devoured in two bites, but the bun screams loudest, "I have no redeeming nutritional value at all!" So I start with it. And it's pure pleasure. Soft and white, clean and bright… it looks at me and sings, "You look happy to meet me." But wait, this isn't Edelweiss, this is a hamburger bun.

After the bun I eat a bag of fries, then the burger, then the other bag of fries, all the while slurping down my non-diet root beer. My tummy is cheering me on, "You go girl! That's right, keep it coming…mmm hmm…faster…more." From the floor boards I hear a small squeak, "Stop, you're killing me!" It's my bunion. I decide its voice isn't nearly as powerful as my stomach's. While I'm masticating away I start to think about the word bunion. It's kind of like bun and onion. B-U-N-I-O-N. That's when I realize I've just eaten a bun and a burger with onion. I start to feel nauseous. If you squish the words together, I've just eaten a bunion. Oh, no. I think that this may have possibly put me off Burger City forever.

I have a long history of going off my food for various and sundry reasons. For instance in high school, Robby Blinken had the worst case of acne I'd ever seen. It was so bad that his whole face looked like an open, inflamed sore. I felt really sorry for him too because he was shy and awkward to begin with. Having bad skin did nothing for his popularity. Then one day, Mike Pinker shouts across algebra to Robby, "Hey pizza face, that's lots of pepperoni you've got!"

I cringed in disgust, looked over at poor Robby whose face turned an even brighter shade of red due to the public humiliation and bam, I was off pizza for a whole year. And pizza was one of my favorite foods too. It's just that every time I looked at it or smelled it, I thought about Robby's complexion and there was no going back.

Then there was the time I went off onions in college. A girl in my dorm was blind in one eye and there was this white kind of film covering her iris. Whenever I talked to her, I couldn't help but stare right into the blind eye. I was drawn to it by a strange magnetic pull. Then one day it hits me, Ellen's pupil looks like a small piece of onion. I went off onions for three years.

Now at thirty-four, years since I've had a food repulsion, I realize that after my first bun in months I may have gone off them. The onions aren't such a loss as I already have a history there, but buns? I love buns!

Around the second bag of fries, I unbutton my jeans to let my stomach pop out of its confines. Sitting in my red Honda with my belly hanging out, sick at the thought that I just ate a bunion, I do what any reasonable person would do. I drive to the strip mall where the Weight Watchers sign flashes encouraging subliminal cheers to the masses. "Be thin, we'll help!" "We love you!" "You can do it, you can do it..."

So like the little engine that could, I squeeze into a compact spot and walk through the front door before I can come out of my trance. Twelve dollars later, I've received an information package and a weigh-in book. Marge, my group leader, takes me in the back to weigh me. "One seventy-two," she declares. I want to tell her I was just one seventy at the doctor's office but then I remember the bunion I just ate. Marge continues, "You know, you are right inside the acceptable weight for your height.

Are you sure you want to lose twenty pounds?"

I'm sure. After all, I'm single with a bunion. It feels like it's time for some drastic measures. As I have shown up in between meeting times, Marge gives me the basics of the Weight Watchers program and encourages me to come to at least one meeting a week. She also suggests I get weighed at the same time every week as the weight of the human body can vacillate up to six pounds during a twenty-four-hour period. "Consistency of weigh-in times," she claims, "is the answer." I briefly wonder if Doctor Foster would have told me to lose weight if I was only one hundred and sixty-four pounds.

# Chapter 2

I am allowed to eat twenty-nine points a day. I keep telling myself this as I sit at my desk and wait for lunch. With my handy little points app I discover that my forage to Burger City the other day was worth thirty-two points. Thank goodness I ate that bunion. That'll be one less temptation for me while I attempt to lose this weight.

Three days ago after my trip to WWI (Weight Watchers, first attempt, not to be confused with the World War) I stopped by Rite Aid to pick up my shoe insert. I've been wearing it since and am having serious equilibrium issues. I can only wear it with loafers or tennis shoes as it's a foot shaped silicone wedge and won't fit into heels. The whole contraption pushes me towards my proper posture but I swear it's dislocating my center of gravity at the same time. I have never been considered graceful but now I'm downright klutzy, as demonstrated by the five large bruises covering my legs. I seem to tip as easily as a sleeping cow and have not been landing in the softest of places either.

Eleven fifty-eight, eleven fifty-nine, come on noon. I want

to eat. I had a bowl, and by that I mean one cup (which is really only half of a bowl), of raisin bran and half a cup of skim milk for breakfast. At ten, I gobbled up an apple and an ounce of part skim mozzarella cheese. For lunch I'm having a turkey sandwich on the softest white bread on the planet. It's low-cal but has enough fiber to jumpstart a dead person's bowels, ergo giving it the Weight Watcher's seal of approval. I'm also having a salad with fat-free raspberry vinaigrette. When I packed my lunch this morning, I realized how beautiful the food looked, all orange and green and red. It really was a feast for the eyes even though the portions would leave a Lilliputian begging for more.

I'm trying to do what Marge told me and that is to appreciate my food on all levels. Enjoy the beauty of it, the smell of it and last but not least, the taste, which I am supposed to do while chewing the ever loving crap out of it before swallowing. This way it will take me longer to eat and I will start to fill up before overdoing. It's all a load of hooey if you ask me. I'm so hungry by feeding time that I've inhaled my meal before I know it. Yesterday I was crawling around the base of my desk when my co-worker Elaine asked me what I was looking for.

"My lunch." I answered, "I think I dropped it."

Elaine looked slightly alarmed and declared, "Mimi, you just ate your lunch."

"Really?" I asked, more than a little surprised by this knowledge.

Elaine confirmed it was so, but that didn't stop me from picking up and eating a stray peanut I found on the floor from my South Beach days. Tick, tick, tick, NOON! Time to strap on the old feed bag.

I scurry into the break room and fill a glass with cold water. I know I'm blending diet tips here but South Beach recommends a glass of Metamucil before each meal to help fill you up. It works beautifully too, except that with all the fiber I get on Weight Watchers, I find I need to be close to a bathroom at all times. As I munch on my salad, my boss, Jonathan Becker, walks into the break room.

Jonathan embodies all that is right with the world. He is thirty-eight, smart, funny, remarkably good looking and talented. He is also married to my sister Ginger. How you wonder, did that happen when I should have had first dibs on him? I haven't a clue, really. It must have been fate. I mean heaven knows I didn't introduce them. I am not in the habit of trying to help my perfect sisters show me up even more by introducing them to perfect men. That is not my way.

Ginger met Jonathan completely independently of me as she was showing a tour group through the Museum of Contemporary Art. She is the director of the museum, but still enjoys educating the masses by pitching in with docent duties every once in a while. At any rate, Jonathan's parents were in town and he was taking them to the requisite tourist spots when they stumbled into the museum. In front of one particularly abstract painting, Felicity Becker declared, "I suppose the medium here is human feces?"

Ginger smiled, and explained how the artist was trying to express the sepia tonality of his native Cuba; the tobacco and human waste representative of a culture that repressed its own and refused to let it rise above menial servitude. I think she may have quoted Descartes and then conjugated several verbs in Latin for effect. Whatever she did, it was like a mating dance to Jonathan because he asked her out that afternoon and thereafter until they became man and wife a short year later.

When they first started dating, Ginger carried on and on about how smart and funny her boyfriend Jonathan was. Then the day came when she brought him to brunch to meet the family. I had just regained the thirteen pounds I lost on Phase I of South Beach and was not looking forward to meeting the Ken to my sister's Barbie. I remember pulling on my brown skirt with the elastic waist thinking, "Who am I trying to impress anyway? It's not like this guy is coming to see me."

When I drove up to my parents' house, I saw that Muffy and Tom were already there as well as Renée and her husband, Laurent, along with their two kids, Finn and Camille. I walked in and made all the appropriate rounds of kisses and hugs. But the truth was my heart just wasn't in it. Once Ginger introduced her new boyfriend, it would just be me, Mimi Finnegan, spinster.

Ginger and Jonathan walked in the front door as I was filling the water glasses on the dining room table. I heard them before I saw them. Ginger announced, "Hello everyone, we're here!" The whole family tore off towards the entry like a stampeding herd of cattle at the sound of her voice, everyone that is, but me. I wanted to enjoy the last few moments of not being the only sister without a significant other. So I poured water and concentrated on breathing deeply.

They all came into the dining room moments later and I

plastered a smile on my face, prepared to be all that is gracious to Ginger's new beau. When I first saw Jonathan, I was confused and mistakenly thought maybe my Jonathan from work had somehow shown up to be my date so I wouldn't be the family pariah. Then he saw me and I knew that wasn't the case. His face morphed somewhere between total and utter shock and open-mouthed bass. "Miriam, is that you?" Because before Jonathan learned my family nickname, I went by my real name at work. Now they all call me Mimi too.

"Jonathan?" I squeaked.

He strode over and slapped me on the shoulder in a very platonic way and said, "Well I'll be. I didn't know you and Ginger were sisters!"

I countered, "And I had no idea you two were dating." It occurs to me Ginger should have known Jonathan and I work for the same PR firm. You would think that when he revealed that he worked at Parliament, Ginger would have remembered that I work there too. But the truth is while brilliant, Ginger has never been wired for details. For instance, she knows the square root of one million, six hundred forty-two thousand and eight, but she can barely remember her own birthday. She's kind of like Rain Man that way.

The brunch was unbearable and lasted about twelve days. I must have gained three pounds, as the meal became show and tell for the Finnegan family (as I didn't have that much to show or tell, I ate.) Jonathan had never met us as a whole, so we owed it to him to trot out the whole dog and pony show. With circus music running through my head I could see myself as the ringmaster. "If I could have your attention in the center ring, I'd like to introduce you to Renée! Yes, that's Renée "supermodel turned designer" Finnegan and her high profile fashion photographer husband, Laurent Bouvier. But please, before you leave center ring, notice their perfect and charming offspring, Finn, who was recently featured in the Gap Kids ad, and little Camille, the Ivory Soap Baby!"

I drank so many mimosas that day I was forced to stay over at my parent's house and sleep it off. In my drunken haze, I swear I heard my mother say, "Now if only Mimi could find someone to love her." There was laughter and then my dead Grandma Sissy started reciting dirty limericks.

# Chapter 3

I weigh in right after lunch today. It's hard to believe that I've only been on this diet for seven days as I can't remember the last time I was actually full after eating a meal. Well, yes I can. That would have been last week right before I joined up, signed on, and volunteered to go to war for my bunion. It did have a sort of military feel to it. I'm kind of like *Private Benjamin* without being cute, tiny and rich.

I'm discovering that the weekends are going to be a little tougher for me than the Monday through Friday stint. At least during the week, I'm required to actually work, thusly limiting my constant obsession over the next morsel I'm allowed to put into my mouth. When I woke up this morning, I forgot I was on Weight Watchers at all and longed for the cheesy omelet and turkey bacon from my South Beach days. Of course that particular meal translated into six hundred and forty-two Weight Watchers points, so I tried to gear up for more raisin bran. Ugh. I pick up my little red tips booklet and search out a more appealing option. After all, it's the weekend, I don't have to rush. I can plan, execute, and enjoy more complicated fare today. I decide on French toast with fat free syrup. Here's a tip for you on Weight Watchers approved French toast. The bread is so thin that you can't let it soak in the egg for more than an eighth of a second. If you don't heed this rule, the pathetic slice simply falls apart, disintegrating before your very eyes. There's just not enough substance to withstand a normal drenching.

After eight slices of bread and four eggs, I am finally able to salvage three some-what questionable looking pieces. I do as the book recommends and heat my one tablespoon of syrup so it spreads farther, consequently making it feel like more (though it isn't even enough for one piece) and dig in. The problem is I have finished my breakfast in forty-seven seconds. I feel as though I've just had my appetizer and now I'm salivating for the main course. I know! I'll drink another glass of water. That's always so satisfying.

Its 7:43 a.m. and I don't get to eat again for another two hours and seventeen minutes. What to do…what to do… I could always wash my clothes but that would involve going through the kitchen to get to the laundry room and I'm afraid I'm not strong enough for that yet. I could run errands but my car can't be trusted not to take me to Pete's House of Pie against my will. So I decide to go through my closet and try on every garment that I own. This way I can have a full before and after appreciation of how everything fits. I start with the clothes I wear all the time, the size twelves.

Next I pull out the tens. I squeeze myself into the Ralph Lauren jeans, a process involving a coat hanger and lying on the floor (and Crisco if I had any). Once I inhale and fasten the top button, I roll over onto my stomach and attempt to bring myself to a kneeling position. It feels like I'm on the receiving end of a denim enema. By the time I'm in the praying position and leaning against my bed, I'm panting like I've just run a six minute mile. I'm sure if I don't remove the offending garment soon, I'll be on my way to a nasty yeast infection. Pushing up into a standing pose, I goose step over to the full length mirror and check out the final result. Do the words camel-toe mean anything to you?

The last item I try on is my all time favorite black cocktail dress. Working in PR as I do, I'm often required to attend launch parties for books and products we've signed on to promote. So I need to have several dressy options in my closet. I bought this one at Marshalls of all places and while I know the dresses there are crap, this one was the pearl in the oyster. It's a Mui Mui, size eight (my dad calls this designer Mahi-Mahi) and it has tiny spaghetti straps to hold up the plunging neckline and flirty little skirt. The bargain basement price tag of $129.99 is still hanging on it as I bought it too small and have yet to fit into it. I needed to lose ten pounds at the time of purchase. Now I need to lose twenty-three.

I can't wait for the day when I'm finally able to show this little number off at a launch party. For the last seven months I've felt like one of the ugly stepsisters lusting after Cinderella's glass slipper. I slide the dress over my head and realize the nice flowy little skirt is skin tight on me. But I'm not deterred. Inch-by-inch I scooch it down my body until it hits mid-thigh where it finally gives up the ghost. Then I zip the bodice up as far as I can (about an inch), then squinch my eyes so the whole effect won't throw me right into cardiac arrest. Very slowly, I open them, taking in my full reflection bit-by-bit. As I stare at myself, I wonder what I was thinking when I bought this thing. It looks like a sausage casing. One guess who the sausage is.

I have one hour and twelve minutes until my snack. I briefly consider taking a nap to fritter away some time when the phone rings. It's my mom, Maureen O'Callaghan-Finnegan, not a non-Irish bone in her body. While my parents are both one hundred percent Irish, they are also one hundred percent American. It can be a very odd combination at times. While Mo, as her friends call her, has never declared, "Faith and begorrah my wee bairn, tell Father McMurphy all yur many sins." She has demanded that we eat every last bit of our potatoes in honor of the thousands upon thousands that died during the black rot, otherwise known as the potato famine. She is also fully convinced fairies live in the backyard and are responsible for killing her begonias. She's taken to leaving them homemade soda bread in hopes of gaining their favor. I don't know about the fairies but the squirrels love her.

My mom greets, "Happy Saturday, Meems." The only name I hate worse than my nickname is my nickname's nickname.

"Hiya, Ma, what's up?"

"Just checking to make sure that you didn't forget that tomorrow is Camille's second birthday. We're all meeting at Renée and Laurent's at one."

Shit, I had forgotten! The very last thing I needed was to be at a gathering with my perfect family and not be able to self-medicate by eating my way into a coma. So I bluff, "Of course I didn't forget. I'm picking up her present this afternoon."

Mom reminds me, "She's registered at Pottery Barn Kids."

Is it just me or has this registering thing gotten totally out of hand? It used to be something only brides and expectant mothers did as they could logically suppose that a shower in their honor would involve gift giving. But now, everyone does it, for every occasion imaginable, high school graduations, house warmings, bar mitzvahs, first communions, two-year-old birthday parties. Hello, my name is Wanda and I'm an alcoholic and I'm registered at Macy's. When did our society get so greedy we just assumed people should be buying us nonstop booty? Well that's that then. I have to leave the house. I throw an apple and cheese stick in my purse and gulp down a half glass of Fibercon and I'm off.

Camille is the most gorgeous, adorable, lovely, child in the world. Every time I look at her, I feel an egg drop. She is the poster baby for the kids I want some day, as well as being the Gymboree poster child. When I retrieve her list at Pottery Barn Kids, I discover she has impeccable taste for someone whose age, until tomorrow, is still measured in months. I can see the work of her mother here.

Renée has decided it's time Camille's room retires as the nursery and become a full fledged little girl's room. This must be why she's registered for a complete bedroom set including duvet, drapes and lamps. I'm just guessing here, but I can't see Camille performing a clog dance in appreciation of these items, which is why I make the decision to boycott the registry altogether. I pick out the sweetest little white wicker rocking chair and a pretty in pink baby doll. Renée won't be thrilled but it's not her birthday, is it?

In the Pottery Barn Kids parking lot, I inhale my apple and cheese stick, realizing it's almost time for lunch. While I'm out, I decide to drive by Weight Watchers and get my weigh-in over with. Checking my purse to make sure I have my loss/gain chart with me, I take off. Before you can sing Danny Boy, I'm there, but not at Weight Watchers. Burger City, again. "What am I doing here?" I chastise my car and it replies with a rev of the engine.

"Absolutely, not," I tell it. "I'm about to weigh in!" but before I can back out of the line, a minivan pulls up behind me, trapping me in the fast food queue at lunch time. Oh god, the smells are going to undo me. I now feel obligated to order something because I'm in line, but what? What on this whole menu is Weight Watchers approved? I start to drool, the smell of cheeseburgers is wafting through the breeze. My stomach growls like a rabid dog. "Feed me…feed me…feed me…" I've got to get control of myself.

That's when I hear another voice call out, "Don't do it!" It's my bunion to the rescue! It reminds me I'm off Burger City because they serve bunions, delicious smelling, and mouth watering, but bunions all the same. So when it's my turn, I order a large diet coke and keep it for after the weigh in.

Marge declares, "You've lost 3.7 pounds. Good for you!" And while I'm not one who fancies my weight being broadcast in anyway, ever, I find I'm okay with this. This is a loss, baby! Slurping down my large diet coke, I force my car to take me home so I can prepare a healthy lunch. A lunch that feels vastly more satisfying knowing it is going to help the scale go down even more. I'm so euphoric to be on a downward trend I put on my *Priscilla, Queen of the Desert* soundtrack and fast forward to Gloria Gaynor's "I Will Survive."

Standing on my couch, singing into the remote for my DVD player, I belt out, "Walk, walk out the door. Just turn around now, you're not welcome anymore." I'm not singing to an ex-lover that's done me wrong either. I'm serenading my fat clothes and I can actually see them dancing down the steps before they leave the house, never to return.

# Chapter 4

Renée first met Laurent when she was in Paris shooting for Cover Girl. She was only twenty and he was twenty-eight. Their love affair was not a wham bam thank you ma'am kind of situation as Renée was involved with Hot Potty's lead singer, Jeremiah Jones, at the time. Laurent also happened to be married. So for several years, the two shot together, laughed together, and eventually became very good friends. It wasn't until Laurent's divorce at age thirty-four that he began to look at Renée as a possible mate.

At the time she was dating race car driver Lorenzo Fiarenzo (I kid you not, his name rhymed, like Bob Cobb) and had no idea Laurent was about to put the moves on her. Renée actually loved Lorenzo, but did not want to marry him until he gave up the sport. She declared that she didn't want to be a young widow or worse yet, wife of a vegetable. So she left him to consider his options, marry her and retire or lose her and continue racing, while she went back to Paris to shoot a new lipstick campaign.

Her phone rang on her first night at the George Cinq. It

was Lorenzo's manager, Jeffrey Hicks, calling to tell her Lorenzo had just been in a serious accident and he hadn't made it. Renée was not able to digest the information. Cover Girl offered to postpone the shoot, but she declined. On set the next morning, Laurent gave her a big hug and offered his sympathy, secretly feeling guilty that perhaps his newfound lust for Renée was somehow responsible for killing her boyfriend. But Renée just thanked him and proceeded to pose her way to her most popular campaign ever.

Two days later, remarkably dry-eyed, she flew to Florence for Lorenzo's funeral. She greeted his parents and helped to hostess the whole event, murmuring comforting words to the other mourners. When Renée left, she flew home to Pipsy and moved back in with mom and dad. She didn't stop crying for four months. As much as I envy my sister, this one event brought her world crashing so low I decided then and there that she deserved any happiness that life brought her. I still find myself envying her, but now I have a shut off valve if those feelings ever try to take over. It took Renée and Laurent two more years to finally hook up but all signs point to them being the love of each other's lives.

As I pull up to my sister's palatial home in the affluent town of Hilldale, I'm once again awed by the gentrified manor in which she lives. I think of my little yellow house on Mercer Avenue and realize what a far cry it is from the Bouviers' estate. Renée and Laurent decided to move home when they discovered they were pregnant with Finn, as they wanted their kids to grow up close to family. Yet the two of them had amassed such a fortune in their respective businesses they needed a tax shelter for a sizeable chunk of it. That's how they came to purchase a house so far beyond their needs. Even after turning half of the manse into Renée's design studio, they still had room to spare.

I park my Honda next to what seems like dozens of fancy cars in the drive, check my make-up, and grab my gift. My mom opens the front door when I ring and trills, "Meems, you're here, I was starting to get worried."

To which I reply, "I'm only ten minutes late."

"I know darling, but a mother can't help worrying, can she?" Then she leads me through the house, into the kitchen, and out to the back yard where everyone is gathered. The assembly is all very well dressed for a baby's birthday, but it is Sunday. Perhaps they're still in their church clothes. I am wearing a floral print skirt with a sleeveless silk sweater. I feel like I look better than normal and can't tell if it's the weight loss or just a good hair day.

My sisters spot me and advance en masse. Ginger arrives first and she's glowing like she has a nightlight hidden under her skin, "Mimi, we were starting to worry." Then adds, "Your hair looks great!" I can't help but wonder why everyone is all of a sudden so worried about me. Normally, I could arrive three days late and not cause this kind of a hullabaloo.

Muffy arrives next, "There you are!" Then she eyes my outfit and declares, "You look very nice today."

Renée pulls up and concurs, "You do Meems, very pretty."

Staring at all of my sisters I can't help but think that something big is up. While they love me and always greet me when I arrive at a family gathering, they are not prone to making a beeline straight for me, and dumping a load of compliments at my feet. Something is wrong. "Who died?" I ask.

Ginger giggles too loudly and playfully pushes at me as if to say, you silly goose.

Muffy laughs too, and repeats, "Who died? You crack me up!"

I look to Renée and plead with my eyes for her to tell me what's going on. She links her arm in mine and pastes on her supermodel smile before leaning in and whispering, "Look like you're having fun. We're setting you up."

"What?" I screech. Then a bit quieter, I ask, "What do you mean you're setting me up? With whom?"

Ginger reprimands, "Lower your voice Meems or he'll hear you."

My eyes start to dart around the party looking for the elusive "he" that might hear me if I don't quiet down. Yet I cannot seem to find anyone who appears to be single and the potential half to my whole. So I inquire, "Where is he?"

Ginger announces, "Over there." Behind her hand she points across the lawn to the round tables that the caterers have set up. "The table closest to the pool."

I follow her finger and discover the table closest to the pool is surrounded by a bevy of Renée's friends. So I ask, "Is he a she? Have you all decided I'm a lesbian then?"

Renée interrupts, "He's sitting down. You can't see him from here because of all the ladies surrounding him."

To which I comment, "Look, if he is so gorgeous and has already developed this kind of a fan club, there is no way on earth he is going to go for me."

Muffy decides, "He's not really that good looking if you ask me. He's just got charisma."

Ginger demands, "Not that good looking? Muffy, open your eyes, he's distinguished, and refined and very easy on the eyes."

Renée gets a saucy sparkle in her eye and declares, "I'd do him." Then amends, "If I weren't married and so in love with Laurent that is."

I am beyond intrigued by all this fussing and clucking my sisters are doing. But instead of running over to the mystery man I ask, "Have I become so pathetic that the three of you have to find a man for me?"

Muffy answers first, "When was your last date, Meems?"

Ginger intercedes, "It's not that we think you're pathetic, we just want you to find someone to spend your life with. We love you and we want you to be happy, like us."

I'm touched by my sister's declaration, but still bristle at the thought they are trying to set me up. Renée adds, "Plus there just aren't many single men around this area. Its past time we pull together as a family and do our part in finding you a husband."

I laugh nervously, "I'm meant to marry him then?"

Muffy replies "Don't be silly Meems. We just think it's time that you start meeting some single men. He doesn't have to be "the one," but if you're out there looking, you'll eventually find the one."

I announce, "Then you better take me over there so I can fight my way through the throng and throw myself at his feet."

Renée gasps, "Not yet! I need to touch up your make-up and maybe find you a scarf first." My sisters lead me, like a lamb to slaughter up, to Renée's changing room and proceed to have their way with me. I feel like an episode of that old show "What Not to Wear." But instead of two hosts tearing me apart, there are three.

Muffy begins applying lotion to my legs as she declares that they are dry and scaly. Ginger heats up the hot rollers as, this just in, big hair is back! Renée starts to accessorize me. If there was a chance in hell I could have fit into her post-baby curvy size eights, she would have made me change my outfit too. I have to say as irritated as I am that my sisters don't think I'm fine the way I am, I really am enjoying watching my metamorphosis. Stand back caterpillar, the butterfly is on her way!

Just when I think I'm more gorgeous than I've ever been and am ready to go meet the mysterious man by the pool, Renée declares, "You're shoes are atrocious. You're a nine right?"

I mutter that I am. She searches her closet and comes back carrying a pair of gold strappy sandals that must be at least three-and-a-half inches high, "These are perfect for your outfit. Put them on."

Before I remember why I wore the loafers to begin with, I kick off my shoes and slip my feet into her delicate footwear. Muffy is the first to notice and gasps, "Mimi, what is that on your foot?"

Too late, the truth is out. Now my family knows I am no longer the one with pretty feet. I whisper, "It's a bunion."

Renée cringes and in horror asks, "A bunion? But how, when, why?"

There was no way I was going to mention Dr. Foster's theory about extra weight and tendency to waddle so I explain, "Genetic weakness in the structure of my foot."

Renée is in a quandary. The only other pair of shoes in her closet that will work with my outfit and cover the bunion is a pair of Giuseppe Zanotti hot pink Mary Janes. And while they are beyond gorgeous, they also require an advanced degree in cat walking to move in them. She makes me try them on anyway. It's their oohs and aahs and usage of words like divine and perfection that convince me to wear them. Otherwise I would have realized they were an accident waiting to happen. As it is I decide Giuseppe Zanotti is a misogynistic fiend of the worst order.

Once I'm rigged out in all my new gear, the girls lead me toward the stairs. It finally occurs to me to ask, "Who is this guy anyway?"

Muffy answers, "He's an author."

I'm intrigued, "Really, what has he written?" I'm guessing probably manuals for a software company or perhaps how-to books like, "How to Rewire Your House in Five Short Years."

Ginger interrupts my reverie and announces, "He writes legal thrillers."

Intrigued, I ask, "You mean like Elliot Fielding?"

Renée smiles, "Exactly! Because, (drum roll please) he is Elliot Fielding!"

"What? What do you mean he's Elliot Fielding? Elliot Fielding lives in London."

THE REINVENTION OF MIMI FINNEGAN

Ginger intervenes, "He needed a quiet place to work on his next novel and he decided Hilldale was exactly what he was looking for." She adds, "Plus, Jonathan just signed Parliament on to launch his latest novel in America."

To pull an antiquated saying out of my hat, I was gobsmacked. I didn't even know Parliament was up for the job, let alone got it and I'm supposed to be aware of these things. It's my job. Forgetting that Elliot is my potential future husband, I ask Ginger, "When did this happen?"

She answers, "Just last night. It's all been very hush-hush. Elliot didn't want a whole bunch of companies approaching him while he was in the states so he asked Jonathan to keep it on the QT."

I have read all of Elliot Fielding's books and I have loved each one better than the last. For the life of me I can't figure out why my sisters think I have a chance with such a celebrated novelist. Well, actually, I can. They rightly assume I am a product of the same DNA they are which in and of itself makes me spectacular. Unfortunately, they wrongly assume that I have their innate confidence, which I just don't. I go to Weight Watchers and I have a bunion. Elliot Fielding can do a lot better than me.

The next thing I know I'm being led across the lawn in Renée's medieval torture devices. She advises, "Walk on your toes so you won't sink into the grass."

I glare at her, "Easier said than done." I had just started to become used to the insert in my shoe and now I was flying without it *and* my comfortable loafers. Add to that, I am teetering on my tippy toes in drag queen shoes, and I'm pretty screwed here.

As we approach Elliot's table, Jonathan looks up and smiles. He seems genuinely glad to see me and it occurs to me that he has not been made privy to my sister's plans for his new client to join the family. So I smile back and he gives me a nice brotherly peck on the cheek, "Ah, Mimi, you're here! There's someone I'd like you to meet." And just as I start to wonder if he really does know, he gestures to who I assume is Elliot and says, "Elliot, this is my sister-in-law, Mimi Finnegan. She is also my right hand at the office so as the book launch closes in, the two of you will be working together quite a bit."

Elliot pushes his chair out and stands. His eyes slide up and down the length of my body and he smirks as he raises his left eyebrow in a supercilious question mark. I have no idea what that's all about so I simply extend my hand and smile. "It's very nice to meet you, Elliot."

Instead of extending me the same courtesy, he tilts his head to the side, nods it once and declares, "Indeed." Like, "Indeed, you should be happy to meet me."

Well that settles it. I don't care if he was well over six-two or his slightly receding strawberry blonde hair is the most gorgeous color ever or I find him immensely attractive. He's ruined it for himself. I am not going to marry Elliot Fielding.

I rush to lower my extended hand back to my side, where it obviously belongs, when at the last moment he chooses to take it. I try to pull away as if to indicate he has had his chance and the offer is now withdrawn. I'm so peeved by his arrogance that I yank my fingers from his, setting into motion a domino effect I'm sure Renée will later claim ruined Camille's party.

Elliot bends at the waist and gently touches his lips to my reluctant appendage in what I'm sure he assumes is a display of superior English manners, yet my whole body responds in an angry shudder. How dare he think he can "indeed" me and then put his mouth on my person. I yank my hand back, upsetting my very delicate balance, at the same time Elliot takes the hint and releases me. He does not attempt to aid me in any way as I fall backwards, straight into the pool.

As I'm flailing through the air, the world takes on the slow motion effect like a murder scene in the movies. I see everything around me in a series of freeze frame snap shots. Picture one: The smug countenance of one Mr. Elliot Fielding. Snap two: The judgmental faces of Renée's stuck up society friends and number three: Jonathan's wild-eyed attempt to reach out to help me, too late. The fourth picture has sound effects: Renée leaping towards me screaming, "Don't get my shoes wet!" SPLASH!!!

As I hit the water it occurs to me a three point seven pound weight loss is simply not enough to balance the horror of this day. I was feeling so good about myself too. I begin to breast stroke to the shallow end and decide to just go home when I realize that if anyone should leave it's the fancy pants writer. This is my niece's birthday and I'm family. I'm staying!

Renée meets me at the end of the pool and offers her hand to help me out. I gladly accept her aid and give her points for asking if I am okay before inquiring after the state of her shoes. She leads me over to a lounge chair and sits me down before removing the treacherous footwear. She murmurs, "Go on upstairs and dry off. I'll try to come up with something else for you to put on, okay?"

I'm so grateful to her that she isn't berating me for causing a scene or ruining her party that tears start to form in my eyes. Before I can move, my dad hurries over carrying a beach towel. He wraps it around my shoulders and laughingly jokes, "You've made quite a splash my girl!" He thinks he's being funny and I simply don't have the heart to tell him that he's not.

Muffy trails after me as I drag my sopping wet person across the lawn. When she reaches me, she asks, "So what did you think of him?"

I look at her in shock, "I'm fine, Muff, thanks for asking."

She exclaims, "Of course you're fine. It was just a pool, not the English Channel."

Sympathy has never been Muffy's strong suit. Even though she looks like a beautiful country club goddess, the truth is she's one hundred percent tough jock. If a pack of midgets beat me with sticks, she'd declare, "They were just midgets." So I answer, "He's an arrogant, stuck up prig. That's what I think of him."

She asks, "What did he do to you?"

"He tried to kiss my hand." And as soon as the words were out of my mouth I realize how utterly lame they sound. Like a homeless person scolding a shelter for trying to feed them. But Muffy just looks at me with a quizzical smile on her face and announces, "Well, there are plenty more fish in the sea." Then in true smart ass form, adds, "You probably saw a couple while you were in the pool."

Ha, ha, ha, ha, ha, ha, ha, humor at my expense, who

would have thought? I tell her to go back to the party and regale someone else with her wit. I want to be alone.

Back up in Renée's room, I take off my sopping wet outfit and put on one of Laurent's robes, then blow dry my hair. My sister arrives carrying a neon colored, floral caftan with a pair of low healed chartreuse mules. "How's this?" she asks.

I stare in shock and reply, "Absolutely perfect if I were Auntie Mame or Mrs. Roper."

Renée responds in a hurt voice, "Mimi, there just isn't that much in my wardrobe that will fit you."

I want to scream at her not to call me fat, when I realize the truth of her words. My only choices probably are this outrageous bit of drama or Laurent's terry cloth robe which I'm already wearing. So I don the caftan and refuse to look in the mirror before leaving the room. After all, if I don't know how bad I look no one else will either, right? A sorry piece of logic, but I'm grasping at straws here.

As I walk back into the backyard for Birthday Party, take two, my family scurries around me in a show of support, as if to say to all the other guests, "She's one of us no matter how clumsy and embarrassing she is." Eyeing my perfectly groomed sisters and parents, I wonder if there's any chance I could have been adopted. Or maybe my mom cheated on my dad with a circus clown and I'm the result.

After cake and ice cream, both of which I eat (points be damned), Camille opens her gifts. She obviously isn't too delighted by the envelopes with the pictures of bed room furniture that has been ordered in her name. And by the time she unwraps a huge box, containing her brand new duvet, we catch a glimpse of the terrible twos that lie ahead.

Thank goodness my gift is next. Camille opens the rocker first and immediately sits in it and teeters back and forth for about twenty seconds before she tears open the doll. Her eyes light up and she exclaims, "Baby doll, pretty pink baby doll!" Then she plops back into her rocker and serenades the plastic and rubber infant with a heart warming, if not babbling version of "Toora Loora Loora" meets "Frère Jacques."

Meanwhile, I keep the widest berth possible from Elliot Fielding, the demon novelist. He, as I had hoped, did not have the good sense to leave the party before I came down from Renée's bedroom. In fact upon witnessing my return, he smiled at me and arched that god-damned eyebrow again. The arch said, "You silly, clumsy buffoon, I didn't even want to kiss your hand."

I merely glared at him and showed him my back. My screamingly loud floral back, which countered, "You are so far beneath a fool like me it isn't even funny."

Happily I manage to avoid Elliot until the time of my departure. As I'm leaving, I wonder why he's still here. Doesn't he have other damsels to distress? When I hug Ginger goodbye, I ask, "What is *he* (said with the same disdain I might utter the word slug) still doing here?"

Ginger replies, "He came with us." Then adds, "You have to give him a chance, Meems. He really is a wonderful man. I just don't see how he's responsible for you falling into the pool."

I lean into my sister and lie, "He pushed me." Then I walk out the front door. That'll show those nosy broads to leave my love life alone. Or I hope it will anyway.

# Chapter 5

I manage to avoid Jonathan for the better part of two days when he finally corners me and asks, "Isn't it great news about Elliot Fielding? What do you think of him anyway?"

Ignoring his second query, I counter, "Why did we get the account instead of the New York office?"

He answers, "New York will still take care of some of the press, but we'll be responsible for hitting all of the Middle America markets. You know, we'll book him on shows like *Good Morning Tulsa* and *Wake Up Chicago*."

I pretend, "Wow, that's great!" and suggest, "You should have Riley work with him."

"Riley?" Jonathan disagrees. "She's a junior coordinator." He continues, "No way Meems, you're the one for the job."

Here's the rub. While I would rather eat a whole bowl full of bunions than work with Elliot Fielding, I don't have that option. Jonathan, might be my brother-in-law, but first and foremost, he's my boss. I can't refuse to work with Elliot because he's a cocky British prick. Most of the clients I labor for are a million times more egregious. Like the night club owner who actually stuffed a sausage down his pant leg to make himself appear better endowed. Therefore I simply declare "I'd be delighted to work with him." Adding as an afterthought, "When the time comes."

My co-worker, Elaine, is unintentionally responsible for making my whole week. Just yesterday she asked if I was losing weight. She said she noticed my clothes were fitting a lot better. Now while you may normally think this is a backhanded compliment, as though she were insinuating I'm normally stuffed into my wardrobe like manicotti, I don't care. Backhanded or not, a compliment is a compliment and I'm not going to turn my nose up at it.

My clothes *are* fitting a lot better. And while I'm in no danger of changing sizes any time soon, I can once again wear panty hose without feeling like I'm being cut in half at the waist. Between you, me, and the fencepost, I stood naked in front of the full length mirror last night without even the slightest urge to become a bulimic.

Bulimia is a dieting trick that I've tried on occasion during my adult life with absolutely no success as I have the gag reflex of a porn star. You could ram a tree trunk down my throat and I would simply try to eat it, not throw it up. I have never told anyone about the attempted bulimia. I mean, my entire well-intentioned family would pile into a string of cars to drive me to the Betty Ford Center if they knew.

The day sails along beautifully until four-thirty when Jonathan calls a staff meeting. I have just finished my afternoon snack and begin the process of deciding which Weight Watchers entrée to microwave for dinner when he rings me to say that he needs to meet with the entire staff in the conference room, ASAP. I do my part and gather up the masses and ten minutes later we are assembled, nervously waiting to find out why he's called this meeting. The last time Jonathan held an unscheduled meeting was to inform us that a senior member of the New York branch of Parliament was going to be observing us for three days. And while we weren't to worry, that person did have it in his power to fire any of us, including him, our boss. Yes, thanks, we won't worry. You have never seen so many hyper-animated press dealings in your life. I personally took twenty-three imaginary calls and even had time to avert six potential, fictitious disasters. The good news, no one lost their job on that trip, but it didn't keep us from worrying over future visits.

Our fidgety group of fourteen doesn't so much as breathe until Jonathan arrives four minutes later. Unfortunately, he isn't alone. With my eyes glued to his companion like I am witnessing the beginning of the apocalypse, Jonathan smiles and announces, "I would like you all to meet Elliot Fielding. Elliot has just signed on with Parliament to cover the press relations for his next book that is due out in the spring." The group glows in anticipation of meeting an international celebrity. Normally speaking, we work with fame at a more local level, restaurant and nightclub openings, resident children's book authors, Bebe's House of Hair launching another location. Okay, so maybe we were a little fancier than that but still, Elliot Fielding is most certainly our biggest client to date.

Jonathan continues, "Elliot is staying in Hilldale while he

finishes his latest book and will occasionally be coming into the office to observe our work. You see," he pauses for dramatic effect, "his new novel is set in a PR company!" The crowd oohs and aahs their excitement and pleasure. I do not.

After Jonathan's announcement, the staff of Parliament rushes at Elliot in a massive wave of excitement. Brenda from payroll exclaims, "Oh Mr. Fielding, I just love your books!"

Edgar from accounting asks if Mr. Fielding would mind signing his hard covers and Elaine bats her eyes and offers, "If there's anything I can do to make your stay more comfortable, please let me know." Then, for good measure, she rubs up against him like a cat in heat. Me? I leave the room.

At my desk I decide to retrieve all of the change out of my purse in order to buy as many Ho Ho's as I have the cash for. The vending machine was just filled this morning so my hope is that I find enough coins for at least seven double packs. But before I can leave my office, my bunion lets out a small cry of pain and I'm forced to rethink my position on raiding the snack machine. Instead, I dig through my purse for my Weight Watchers book and call the hotline number. I need a meeting and I need it now.

Luck is on my side. If I leave the office right now, I'll be able to make the 5:30 meeting in Hilldale. The Pipsy branch doesn't have a Tuesday meeting after two in the afternoon. I quickly grab my purse and attempt to flee the premises at the same time our new client walks by my office. As I scurry out the door with my sights on the elevator, I run smack into the knave that caused my unexpected swim over the weekend. Elliot reaches out instinctually to keep me from falling before he realizes who he's caught.

I let out a loud, "HMPH!" on impact and then notice the owner of the arms that surround me. I want to scream, "Unhand me, you brute!" but against my will I realize how nice it feels to be in the embrace of someone I'm not related to. I pause for several seconds too long, simply enjoying the sensation when Elliot leans down and whispers in my ear, "I did not push you into the pool."

Coming to my senses as though doused in cold water, I accuse, "Nor did you attempt to help me."

Elliot retorts, "My dear Miss Finnegan, you yanked your hand from mine, I didn't have the opportunity to save you from your folly."

I just stare at him thinking, "My folly? My folly, you bastard? I'll show you my folly." And while I want to rip off my loafer and beat him senseless with it, I opt to just walk away.

# Chapter 6

I miss Marge. The Hilldale Weight Watchers leader looks like she's had a face lift, liposuction, and a fake tan. I feel she's guilty of false advertising. It's like she's saying, "Do what I tell you and your wrinkles will disappear, your cellulite will evaporate and you'll glow like a bronze statue." All Marge's countenance says is, "If I can lose thirty pounds on Weight Watchers so can you." No false promises, no expectation of immortality. As I listen to Cheryl drone on about the importance of fiber, I want to raise my hand and tell her too much fiber makes you gassy but I'm afraid the good ladies of Hilldale will run me out of the meeting.

Surprisingly, there is one man in the meeting. He looks to be about my age and has a lovely, round face that reminds me of one of the contestants on that TV show, *The Biggest Loser*. Maybe this is the reason I feel like I know him, so I send him a smile. I applaud the folks on that show. I mean, they go on national television seriously overweight and let the world watch as they compete to see who can shed the most poundage. They are subjected to the most monstrously cruel temptations too, plates of cookies and doughnuts, pizzas and steaks. I know I could never do it. Shoot, I've been known to hide in my car during work hours and eat chocolate chip muffins until I can feel the beginnings of a diabetic coma coming on.

The only good thing I learn in the meeting is Weight Watchers has come out with a new product, The Double Fudge Bar, and it's only one point! That's right, one point. In my calculations, if these things are any good, I could eat twenty-nine of them a day. Of course I wouldn't be able to eat anything else, but still. Cheryl stresses that they contain five grams of fiber as well. There goes my plan to eat twenty-nine, but I'm still going to pick up a box on my way home.

As I'm collecting my purse and new hand-outs, the nice, round-faced man from across the room approaches me. He smiles and asks, "Mimi Finnegan, right?"

I answer, "Yes. Do we know each other?"

"Kevin Beeman," he answers, "from Mr. Phips' chemistry class junior year?"

Ah, so this is why he's so familiar. "My gosh, Kevin, it's been years. How are you?"

Shaking his head, he answers, "I've been better." Then with a mischievous glint in his eyes, he adds, "And thinner."

"Oh don't I know it. I tried on my ski jacket from high school the other day and looked like a tic about to pop."

He laughed, "But you look great now. Have you just lost a whole bunch of weight?"

"If you call three point seven pounds a whole bunch of weight…"

Kevin looks confused, "But you look as gorgeous as ever. What are you doing at Weight Watchers?"

I want to throw myself at him and kiss him with tongue in appreciation of such a spectacular compliment. Instead, I suggest, "Hey, you wanna go to the store and pick up a box of those fudge bars. I'm dying to see if they're any good."

Kevin says it sounds like a plan and off we go. We buy a box of six and then walk over to the park to eat one. "Creamy," I declare.

"Not gritty like some," Kevin adds.

Having decided they are well worth one point each we have another. I learn that Kevin and his wife Megan were recently divorced. Kevin explains that Megan had been cheating on him with his business partner, David, and she announced it one day over breakfast. She added she was pregnant with David's child, so if he had any crazy ideas of trying counseling or something, he could just forget it.

Kevin was devastated and went on a six month bender of eating everything he could get his hands on. He gained fifty pounds, lost his wife, his business partner, and his self-respect. He's been back in Pipsy for a month and has been a member of Weight Watchers for the same amount of time. Then he asks me what I've been up to.

I answer, "I work at a PR company, I'm still the least attractive sister in my family, and I have a bunion."

He counters, "What do you mean you're the least attractive sister in your family? You're gorgeous!"

Then I look him dead in the eye and say, "Thank you, Kevin, but do you by any chance remember what Renée,"

Ginger, and Muffy look like?"

He grimaces, "Do they still look like that?"

"Better."

Like a true friend, Kevin stands by his words, "You're prettier than you used to be in high school and I had it bad for you back then."

"You did not, you big liar! You were dating Helen Bishop for all four years."

He laughs and answers, "Only because I knew I couldn't get you."

In mock anger I declare, "Well, thank you, Kevin Beeman. You mean that I didn't have to be dateless through four years of high school, but was, thanks to you?"

He smiles sheepishly and asks, "Any chance I can make up for that now?"

I'm totally surprised Kevin is asking me out. I mean, just so we're perfectly clear, the last guy who propositioned me had a bratwurst in his pants. I can't help but think that Kevin is not my dream man. I mean, he's pudgy, divorced, and a little depressed, but what the heck. I still have to lose sixteen point three pounds, and I have a bunion. So I say yes. We decide to go out Friday night. He'll pick me up at seven. He laughs and says, "Hey, you know what? It's going to be great to go out with someone who has to count points the same as I do."

I add, "We can force each other not to cheat." On that note we eat our third double fudge bar (only three points total) and enjoy the feeling of being with a kindred spirit.

# Chapter 7

The phone is ringing as I walk through my front door. I run to grab it but my answering machine has already picked up. I hear, "Meems, it's Ginger, are you there? Pick up the phone if you are. MeeeeMeeee, pick up the phone."

So I do, "Heya, I just walked in, what's up?"

"Who were you eating ice cream with in the park?"

Pipsy is a small town and word spreads like a forest fire doused in gasoline, but still, I've only just left the park. How could Ginger already know I was there with a man? I cautiously answer, "That was my friend, Kevin, from high school, why?"

She demands, "Are you dating him?"

"Oh for Pete's sake, Ginger, we just ran into each other and decided to catch up. We aren't dating." I don't know why I don't tell her we have a date on Friday night, but I don't. I guess I'm secretly hoping she'll still try to set me up with other men. I mean, I like Kevin, but I just can't see us getting romantic.

"Good," she declares. I'm having a dinner party Saturday

night and there's someone I want you to meet."

Woohooo! She is going to introduce me to someone else. I tell her I'll be there without tipping my hand about how excited I am. She informs me it starts at seven sharp and not to be late. I hang up with her and dance around the living room singing, "It's raining men, hallelujah it's raining men!" I feel like Bridget Jones. Now if I could only get a couple of hunks to fight over me in a knock-down-drag-out brawl. The last ten days of my life have brought a slew of changes, a bunion, a diet, and dates. I decide to zap a W.W. Mac and Cheese in the microwave and then go out in search of a new outfit. I had promised myself no new clothes until I was a size ten, but I just can't seem to help it. I haven't purchased a new dress since Linden.

Linden Fairbanks was my last real boyfriend. While he shared the same last name as Douglas Fairbanks (and Jr.), the similarities end there. Lin was a real mama's boy. He would ask his mother to come over to his house every Saturday morning to lay out his clothes for the week. She always set out a couple extra outfits too, in case something like a squash game or opera opening came up at the last minute and she wasn't able to get to him in time. When I spent Friday nights at his house, I would have to leave by ten the next morning so his mother wouldn't know I had slept over. If he stayed at my house, he had to leave by the same time so he could get home and make his bed look slept in.

I have no real defense for dating a man like this except for plain loneliness. Certainly when we are seventeen and full of hope and potential, it never occurs to us we will one day settle for anything. But when enough empty years pass, it's only human to try to convince yourself something is better than nothing. Linden was my something. I met him at an opening for a restaurant in Hilldale. Parliament was promoting it and Linden was funding it. As a fourth generation trust fund baby, Lin was always looking for ways to invest his inheritance as he didn't actually have a real job. He simply handled the money that was his birthright.

In retrospect I don't think I would have broken up with him if he didn't turn on me. But the truth is, Mrs. Fairbanks never approved of me. I was a middle class Catholic from Pipsy who didn't even belong to the Junior League. So when she decreed it was time for her son to wed and breed, I was deemed inappropriate. Like the white Anglo-Saxon protestant he was, Linden listened to his mother and cut me loose. I can't claim to have been exactly devastated by the experience, but I was hurt. I just couldn't imagine anyone thinking my stock wasn't good enough for them. I had spent my whole life thinking the exact opposite. Linden married a cousin just far enough removed for the union to be legal outside the state of West Virginia and is now the proud, pussy-whipped father of twins.

Do you know for only two extra points you can add more cheese to your Weight Watcher's Mac and Cheese? I've done this both times I had the entrée and I'm astounded by how delicious it is. I don't savor my dinner tonight though as I can't wait to drive over to the Ann Taylor at the mall. They have some stunning new dresses in the window and now that I've decided to pry open my wallet long enough to buy one, I want the shoes and accessories to go with it. I am simply high on the possibility Saturday night holds.

The first dress I try on is a black cocktail number that hits just above the knee. It's not unlike the Mui Mui in my closet except this one is a substantial size twelve and not a skinny eight. The next dress I try on is a sleeveless form fitting red sheath dress, again hitting just above the knee. The astounding feature on this garment is that the back drapes down to the waist, showing off a good deal of skin. It will require a special bra, but I'm leaning towards it as it's so very eye catching. And really when you think about it, three hundred -forty-seven dollars is a steal for a show piece like this. Once the saleslady assures me it can be taken in should I lose weight (which I am going to do,) I hand over my debit card.

Next stop is DSW, a.k.a. Discount Shoe Warehouse. The store is the size of a football field and carries no less than five thousand different styles of ladies' shoes in every price range. After trying on fourteen pairs, I discover I need to go up a half-size in order to fit my friend, the bunion. I stuff the toes on the left shoes so they don't fall off and prance around the store. I finally settle on a pair of daring gold backless numbers that buckle at the ankle. I have no idea how Ginger's man friend is going to be able to resist me. I can barely keep my hands off myself when I think of how gorgeous I'm going to look on Saturday.

The rest of the week drones on like the last three days of Lent. Work is work and would have been a complete breeze if I didn't keep running into that bastard Elliot. He's everywhere. For a guy who "might be popping in once in a while," he seems to have become the guy who moved in with no hope of ever leaving. Today he even walked into my office during a phone call with an important client and sat down in the chair across from me. What did he want, you ask? I have no idea. He just kept staring at me and taking notes. I finally got so self-conscious I crawled under my desk for privacy.

Kevin called me twice today to confirm our date and I'm getting concerned this evening means more to him than it does to me. I vow to keep an open mind though. I know better than anyone that surprises can be waiting around every corner. For a good deal of my adult life, I was convinced it was closed fists that were waiting, but now, who knows.

I'm in my car and on the way home by 5:30 P.M. I do not say goodbye to anyone, pass Go, or collect two hundred dollars. I'm just gone daddy gone. As I pull up to the house I notice that a package is waiting on my doorstep. I pick it up and see that it is from the Podiatric Wellness Center. It's the new silicone demi foot wedge that I sent away for. I'm very excited to try it out and decide to wear it on my date. Poor Kevin, some stranger I've never met gets the sexy red dress with strappy sandals and he gets stuck with the orthopedic foot pad. Oh well, I promise I'll do my makeup nicely for him.

Weight Watchers suggests actually eating a meal before going out to dinner so you aren't tempted to cheat on your diet with warmed rolls and butter. The problem is I only have seven points left for the whole day which won't allow me to do this and I'm starving. Plus I have PMS for a small village and nothing within six inches of my mouth is safe. As a matter of fact, I ate two pencils and an eraser this afternoon. So I drink three glasses of water, with a wedge of lemon (trying for an extra calorie or two to sustain me.) I change from my work dress into a pair of khaki capris and throw on a red sleeveless sweater. I slide my new gel pad into my red espadrilles and voilà, I'm ready.

By the time Kevin picks me up and we get seated at the restaurant, I'm so famished I'm ready to eat my napkin. Instead, I point across the room and say, "Look, doesn't that girl look like Becky Brady from high school?" And as he turns to take a gander, I grab a roll and stuff it into my purse. I try the trick once more and by the time I have secreted away two rolls with pats of butter, I excuse myself to use the ladies room. I sit on the toilet and devour them both in seconds. They are the best thing I've ever eaten and I would kill to have the remaining two here in the bathroom with me. Yet once the initial euphoria of my crime wears off, I immediately feel guilty. I must have eaten at least nine points worth of bread and butter and now I don't have any left for dinner.

As I walk back to the table I spy Kevin brushing crumbs off the table trying to hide the evidence of what I'm assuming is the same transgression as my own. I sit down and smile at him fondly noticing that the bread basket is empty. "How were your rolls?" I ask.

Guiltily he answers, "Good, yours?"

"Truthfully," I confess, "they would have tasted better if I hadn't eaten them on the toilet in a public restroom."

We giggle as easily together as two naughty children and both order the grilled vegetable plate with no oil (zero points.)

Kevin and I have a lovely dinner and we laugh more than

I've laughed in years. It's so nice to talk to someone who knew me when, back in the day when I was a blank slate waiting for the world to make its mark on me. Back when I was young and hopeful and one hundred and fifty pounds. Kevin tells me all about the hopes he had for his life and confesses that sometimes in the middle of the night he's so full of regrets he feels like his chest is about to explode.

I reach across the table and hold his hand (as a friend, not date) and ask, "You still love your wife, don't you?"

Kevin's eyes fill with tears and he asks, "Why do I still love her? No one has ever treated me as badly as she has and yet I still dream that one day she'll wake up and realize I'm the one for her." He continues to bare his soul and adds, "Even in my most secret fantasies I don't turn her away. I simply open my arms to her and welcome her home." At that point I get up and scoot into the booth next to him and put my arms around him. I let him cry on my shoulder and I recognize that it's too bad I'm not interested in him in any romantic way. Kevin Beeman is a man that any woman would be proud to call her own.

After dinner Kevin takes me home. I tell him I had a lovely time and more than anything, I'm delighted to have a new friend. He laughs, "Not much of date, huh?"

"Kevin," I tell him. "I had a better time with you tonight than any man in the last ten years. You are wonderful."

He kisses me on the cheek and suggests, "Who knows, maybe one day I'll finally get over my wife and you and I might have a chance."

I assure him one day he will be over his wife and when that

time comes he'll meet the perfect woman for him. He smiles and before I get out of the car reminds me, "Call me tomorrow and tell me how much you lost, okay?"

I agree as it's nice to have someone else to be accountable to as well as having a partner in crime

# Chapter 8

"One point two pounds," Marge declares. I am absolutely speechless.

And when I do find my voice, it's only to say, "Tell me I did not just suffer through an entire week of self-denial for a one pound weight loss?"

"One point two," Marge corrects.

To which I counter, "Marge, the point two doesn't mean a hill of beans. I'm starving and I've only lost a pound."

She asks, "Have you cheated at all this week?"

I recall the cake and ice cream at Camille's birthday party. I reflect on the two buttered rolls in the ladies' room last night. And I say, "Not one bit."

"Well honey, that sometimes happens." Then she suggests, "Maybe your Great Aunt Flo is coming soon."

It takes me a minute to figure out what she is suggesting. I mean I'm conversant in euphemisms like period, the curse, being on the rag. But my Great Aunt Flo? That's a new one for me. But Marge is right. My period is only about four days away. A fact of which I am sure, due to my increased agitated state, tender boobs, and craving for all things deep fried, salted, and iced. I'm so deflated every muscle in my face relaxes to the point where my mouth is hanging downward like an upside down crescent roll (buttered, salted, and drizzled with chocolate icing).

Marge notices the sure fire signs that one of her camp is about to lose it and asks, "Have you been exercising?"

"No. No time."

She encourages me with the pep of a varsity cheerleader, "Honey, there's always time to exercise! Even if you have to quit cleaning, doing laundry and going to work, there is always time to exercise. Plus," she confides, "the more you exercise, the more points you get."

She has my attention now. You see, apparently Weight Watchers works on the same system I do, the reward system. If I go for a nice long walk, I get two extra points. Marge shares that I don't have to use those points. Because if I don't I'll just lose the weight that much faster. Yeah, yeah, yeah, it's like I can't hear her. After all, not use the points? I'm starving here! I consider taking a leave of absence from work and doing nothing but walk all day just so I can double my points to fifty-eight. I briefly fantasize about how I would spend them. I'd include a glazed raspberry donut at breakfast. At lunch I'd have a large order of fries and for dinner, I'd eat three Weight Watchers meals and sprinkle extra cheese on all of them.

Marge notices the smile creeping onto my face and recognizes the look of a potential cheater. She says, "Remember honey, I'm here every day between eleven and six. You call me if you feel like you're about to go off the wagon."

That's when I realize Marge is like my very own AA, NA, GA leader; whether its alcohol, narcotics, gambling or food, we are a society out of control.

I call Kevin from my cell phone in the parking lot and give him the news. He's thrilled for me, "Mimi, that's great! Remember it's a loss, not a gain."

"A gain?" I demand. "How could anyone gain weight on this Nazi diet?"

He confesses, "I gained two point four pounds last week." And before I could ask

how, he tells me. "Cocoa Puffs. It's like the box leapt into my grocery cart and then forced itself on me. It was a rape by cereal."

I believe him. I tell him my car has a tendency to take me to fattening destinations without discussing it with me first.

Kevin believes me too which is a sure sign this friendship is on the right track. I ask him about exercise and he says he hasn't tried it yet. We decide to meet in the park for some jumping jacks and a walk. Already I feel a lot better.

Later as I lay on my back in the tub with my feet as far up the wall as they'll go, I realize my legs look great upside down. Too bad dinner tonight won't be in an anti-gravity chamber. I am still very excited about Ginger's party despite the bad start to my day. In fact I've only eaten eight points so I can reward myself with a glass of wine and perhaps some kind of starch, drenched in fat (then deep fried, salted, and drizzled with icing.)

The red dress looks killer on me and that old song from the eighties pops into my head; "Lady in red," I sing along, "I've never seen you looking so lovely as you do tonight, I've never seen you shine so bright. The lady in red is dancing with me, cheek to cheek." I remember hearing that the artist, who composed the song, wrote it for his wife. I get all choked up. Imagine someone who's already married to you thinking those wonderful things. It's just so romantic. Now I'm seriously about to come undone and realize a good cry might be just the thing. Plus, if you cry just enough without going overboard, your face can take on a very youthful appearance. So I envision that right after he writes the ballad, he gets killed in a grizzly car accident and his wife finds the lyrics after it's too late to tell him how much she loves him too. Oh god, sobbing. Now, I'm about to swell up past the point of redemption so I start to tell myself some jokes to counter the overpowering grief. A horse walks into a bar and the bartender says, "Why the long face?" I have to do better than that, I'm starting to fill with snot. Quick, where's the remote? I flip to Comedy Central and in the nick of time I find an episode of South Park. Cartman is saying, "Punch and pie, punch and pie."

Whew, crisis averted.

I strategically apply my makeup and notice that the minute facial swelling caused by my tears has filled in some of the lines on my face, as well as giving my lips a provocative bee stung appearance. Lord, I'm hot. I have to leave right now so that my mystery date can meet me before my features revert to their normal size. I take one final look, spritz my key pulse points with Annick Goutal and I'm out the door.

Even though Ginger and Jonathan live in Pipsy, their house is on the North side of town which is closest to Hilldale, hence the homes in their neighborhood are a good bit fancier than the ones in mine. They have been married for two years and made the decision to try to have a baby right away. I just assumed Ginger would conceive the minute she set her mind to it as everything else has always come so easily for her, but this has not been the case.

The doctor says she can't find anything wrong with either of them so there is no reason why they can't get pregnant, except for the small fact that they aren't. While I would dissolve into a puddle of self-pity and bitterness, Ginger and Jonathan have looked at it as an opportunity to give an unwanted child a home. They are on three potential adoption lists and are just waiting for one of them to call.

Ginger answers the door within seconds of my ring and exclaims, "My word Meems, you look gorgeous!"

This is just the kind of greeting I need to calm any nerves about meeting the mystery man she has invited. Ginger looks fabulous too. She has on a very simple black cocktail dress. She barely looks like she's wearing makeup, and the only jewelry she's sporting is her wedding set. Her silky golden hair is hanging straight down her back and the front is fastened with a plastic barrette. Yet, she'll easily be the most gorgeous woman at the party, as long as Renée isn't invited. I forgot to ask.

As I walk into her house, the gentle flicker of pillars and tapers is the only apparent lighting. I fully appreciate this as my thirty-four-year-old skin can stand the mystery that candlelight lends. My sister announces my arrival to the group and I see she's invited her friends Jeremy and Liz, Donald and

Cassandra, her newly single friend Trinny, and the mystery man, wherever he is. After introductions, Ginger whispers in my ear, Robert isn't here yet. Cue the doorbell. Ginger's eyes light up and she goes to answer it.

I hear his voice before I actually see him and I want to cry. Robert has not arrived, but another mysterious guest has. Ginger leads Elliot Fielding into the living room. He looks absolutely stunning in his dark suit and silver tie. In the candle light he looks like the hero in a romance novel. But all of that is just between you and me. I'll deny it to the death if word ever gets out that I thought those things. Ginger introduces Elliot, much as she did me. There is a substantially greater buzz upon his arrival than mine. By the time she gets to me, she concludes, "Of course you know Mimi."

Elliot arches his god-damned eyebrow, tilts his head, and then the bastard takes my hand. Before I have a chance to retract it, he has it clamped in his own and is kissing it. He leans in and whispers, "There's no pool here so it's a good thing you let me kiss you." Then adds, "Otherwise you might fall back and get a concussion."

In my head I reply, "You filthy scum sucking British worm." In reality I whisper back, "Yes, well I'm going to help Ginger in the kitchen lest the temptation to push me overcomes you." As I walk away I hear the warm timber of his laughter and a delicious heat runs through me, but only just a little.

I stride towards my sister and pinch the skin on the back of her arm causing her to jump. I interrupt her conversation with Trinny and say, "Ginger, I smell something burning, you better come with me to the kitchen." Ginger casts Trinny a helpless look and follows in my wake.

When we arrive in her newly designed gourmet kitchen, complete with fireplace large enough to roast a boar, she asks, "What's wrong?"

Calmly, very calmly, I answer, "Elliot Fielding."

"Oh for heaven's sake Meems, he swears he didn't push you into the pool. Plus I invited him for Trinny, not you."

My heart sinks slightly, "For Trinny?"

"Yes," she answers, "You know her divorce just became official yesterday and she's feeling a bit low. I thought Elliot would be perfect for her."

While I know she's right, I can't help feeling, what's the word, jealous? No, that's not it. But if I'm truthful with myself, it's an emotion not too far removed. So I answer, "Well then, fine, as long as I'm not sitting next to him at dinner or anything."

Ginger smiles as my drama seems to have resolved itself and concurs, "Of course not, you'll be sitting next to Robert once he gets here."

Yes, Robert. I forgot all about him. I imagine that he's about seven trillion times better looking than Elliot and a small smile creeps over my face. Okay then, Robert. Bring on the wine. I'm ready to blow a few points.

By seven-thirty, there is still no sign of Robert and I'm feeling on the happy side of tipsy. My empty stomach sucked up that glass of Chardonnay like a thirsty sponge. Ginger takes a phone call and announces that Robert has been sidetracked at the hospital with an emergency, but he'll get here as soon as possible. Then she instructs us to find our places at the dinner table.

While I'm totally disappointed my date hasn't arrived, I'm also delighted to discover he's a doctor. So on the way to the dining room, I sidle up next to Elliot and whisper, "Hear that? Robert's a doctor."

He looks down the length of his patrician nose at me and replies, "That should come in handy if he ever tries to kiss you."

I'm not even the tiniest little bit ruffled by his ill-mannered comeback. I merely ask, "Jealous?"

Again with the eyebrow, "I am an internationally acclaimed novelist, you know."

Before we separate to find our seats, I ask, "Ever saved anyone's life?" Then I punctuate my question by turning my back on him and walking away. Take that, you stuck up wanker.

Ginger has prepared all the food herself but has asked her cleaning lady to come in and serve. We start out with delectable lobster bisque, of which I only eat six bites because it's made with cream. I decide to spend a few more points on another glass of wine instead.

Our main course is grilled Atlantic salmon with wild rice and braised asparagus. It's delicious. I'm half way through and onto my third glass of wine when the doorbell rings. It has to be Robert. I'm peeing myself with excitement when Ginger gets up to answer the door. She comes back to the dining room with a thoroughly pleasant looking man in his forties.

Robert is tallish (maybe six feet), dark hair, happy crinkly laugh lines around his eyes, no alarming features, just very pleasant looking. While I'm disappointed he's not better looking than Elliot, I console myself that he is a doctor. Everyone at the table seems to already know him except for Elliot and me. The stuffy novelist takes the opportunity to ask, "So Robert, what kind of doctor are you?"

"Obstetrician," he answers.

I raise my eyebrow at Elliot as if to ask, "Brought any babies into the world lately?"

Elliot isn't done and gambles on the question, "Ever save anyone's life?"

Robert laughs, "No, no, real life isn't always like television. I've never had any close calls like that."

I, in turn, refuse to look at Elliot and ask Robert about the baby he delivered tonight. When Jonathan interrupts and suggests, "Elliot, tell everyone about the time you gave that baby CPR after it choked on a carrot stick."

Oh for crying out loud. I look at Elliot with such disgust and loathing that he has deigned to save the life of a child that he demurs, "Oh, it was nothing, really."

Trinny stares at Robert, all dewy eyed, and asks, "How have you been, Robert?"

My date, emphasis on the "my," looks across the table at her, with what appears to be longing, and answers, "I've been okay, Trin, how about you?"

She smiles shyly and announces, "I'm doing great," then quietly adds, "the divorce became final yesterday."

You have got to be kidding me! I went out and shelled out nearly five hundred dollars on a new dress and shoes and my date is all hot to trot for the divorcée sitting across the table. Yes, thanks, I'll have another glass of wine. The rest of the night passes in a blur. Ginger serves her famous flourless chocolate cake with crème anglais. I eat my whole piece and wash it down with a tawny port.

I have often thanked God I'm not a sloppy drunk. This quality comes in handy tonight as I am positively shit-faced. I've also fallen off the diet bandwagon with such abandon that Elliot catches me in the kitchen stuffing the remains of someone else's dessert in my mouth. He quips, "I was coming in to do the same thing. Anyone else leave leftovers?"

I look at him miserably and point to another plate sporting a couple bites of cake. He shrugs his shoulders and declares no one at the table appeared to have had cooties as he stabs a fork into the remains and digs in.

I have to smile that he's not too stuck up to miss a great opportunity like eating off of other people's plates and ask, "Where's Trinny?"

Elliot clears his throat and declares, "She's just left with your date."

"Oh for fuck's sake, are you kidding me?" I roll my eyes and proceed to lick the dish that I've been eating off of. "God damned lousy blind dates." Elliot just stares at me in what is either amusement or horror or a bit of both. "Son of a bitch! Miserable do-good doctors." I am unclear as to what happened at this point in the evening because the next thing I know, I'm waking up the following morning in Ginger's guest room still wearing my red dress and shoes.

# Chapter 9

My head feels like it's caught between two cymbals desperately trying to be reunited in a thunderous clang. They are striving valiantly to reach each other but my stubborn skull refuses to get out of the way. Oh lord, I'm hung over. Not in the feeling a little queasy sense either. I am still drunk. I try to sit up but soon realize the bed is trying to buck me off and I have to hang on for dear life. I try to discern what time it is but the clock is facing the other direction and the mere thought of expending the energy to turn it towards me exhausts me to the point I fall back asleep.

The next time I open my eyes, it's to discover Ginger sitting on the bed next to me. She's brought a tray of buttered toast and coffee. She trills, "Hello sleepy head! How do you feel this morning?"

Even though my mouth is full of cotton balls, I still manage to tell her to quit shouting at me. She smiles in an irritating fashion and asks, "Feeling a little worse for wear this morning?"

I reply, "Ugh, frmph, shlunk, mmmph gggrrrr."

Translation, go away and leave the food. But she doesn't go away. She tells me she has a hot bath running for me and that I need to sit up and drink my juice and take a couple of aspirin. What I need is an anesthesiologist to knock me out until tomorrow when the alcohol has been metabolized through my system.

Sitting up involves the kind of excitement normally reserved for riding roller coasters. While I'm not suffering from full blown vertigo, I am suffering. Everything in the room is so bright and clear I swear I can see individual molecules dancing through the air. If only I could vomit.

Ginger unbuckles my shoes and tells me how pretty they are. Then she helps me out of my dress and asks where I bought it as she thinks she might like one just like it. So I tell her I got it at Ross. That ought to keep her from ever finding it and getting one just like it, only two sizes smaller. She leads me into the bathroom like one would lead a crippled grandmother with one leg and only two toes on the remaining foot, which is exactly how spry I feel. Once I'm in the tub, she submerges a washcloth in the hot water, wrings it out, and drapes it across my eyes. It's heavenly. If I could only die right now I would go marginally happy.

Ginger sits on top of the toilet and apologizes, "I'm so sorry about Robert. I didn't know until last night that he and Trinny had gone out before." I grunt in response. She continues, "Apparently he had a problem with her still being married and told her that he couldn't see her again until the divorce was final." Grunt, grunt, to acknowledge I heard her. "But still. I'm not going to rest until I find you a man."

I actually moan in response to this, and beg, "Please stop. No more men. Not for a while. Please."

While she doesn't actually concede to my wishes, she does comment, "That Elliot's really something isn't he?"

"No," I reply.

"Why Miriam May Finnegan, that's not the way you were acting last night."

These words have the same effect on me as a glass of ice cold water poured over my head. No longer do I feel drunk. The sensation has been replaced by sheer panic. "What do you mean that's not the way I was acting last night?"

Ginger laughs and recounts, "Don't you remember how you got up to bed last night?"

Her prompting starts the beginning of a foggy outline forming in my mind. In what is surely a fabricated memory, I vaguely recall a tall British man carrying me up the steps with my worried sister trailing behind, telling him where to take me. Then I seem to recollect him gently laying me on the bed and then…oh please, make it stop. I did not say, "Come on big boy, want to join me?" Did I?

If this is truly a memory and not the nightmare I'm hoping for, Elliot quirked that eyebrow again, right before declining my gracious offer. He did however agree to rethink his position should I ask him when I've sobered up. Oh please, kill me now.

By the time I feel well enough to leave Ginger's it's four-thirty on Sunday afternoon and I've already consumed another hundred and eighty-seven points. As soon as I walk through my front door, I go straight to the phone to confess my sins to

Kevin. He picks up after the third ring and I tell him everything that happened last night. Then I ask, "Should we try to calculate how many points I ate?"

"Absolutely not," he declares. "Just start over fresh tomorrow and don't continue to eat everything you want tonight."

I tell him I'm weak and I can't be trusted in a house with a refrigerator. He decides to come over and baby-sit. When he arrives, he's carrying a box of double fudge bars and declares, "First, we exercise!"

"No," I beg. "I can't, I might still be drunk. I could hurt myself." Kevin will not take no for an answer and instead searches my shelf for the obligatory workout videos, the ones every woman over the age of sixteen owns. He finds them right next to the complete works of Jackie Collins. He chooses, "Buns of Steel," with that annoying creature, Tami Lee Webb, and we're off, squeeze, squeeze, pinch, lift, hold, repeat. By minute twelve, I'm starting to feel a little better. The workout endorphins are taking over and by the time the video ends, I want to do "Arms and Abs of Steel" too.

Now its Kevin's turn to demure. "Jeez, Mimi, there's working out, then there's killing yourself." So we opt to think about it over our first fudge bar. I tell him all about Elliot Fielding and he exclaims, "I love that guy! Once I pick up one of his books, I can't put it down until I'm finished."

I roll my eyes, "Kevin, you are obviously not fully aware that as my new girlfriend you are supposed to hate Elliot. Furthermore, no matter what you really think, you are to tell me his writing is drivel and an epileptic monkey could do a better job."

Kevin looks surprised, "Really? That seems like a lot of work. Can't I just like him and console you?"

"No." I tell him. "You cannot."

We decide to do the Abs portion of "Arms and Abs of Steel." Then after five trips around the block, I microwave Weight Watcher meals for us. I have the Fettuccine Alfredo and Kevin has the pepperoni pizza. We both add extra cheese.

Over dinner, Kevin confesses he ate half of a box of Cocoa Puffs last night. I ask, "What were you thinking about when you ate them?"

"Megan. I was thinking that Megan will probably be having her baby any time now."

I reach across the table and take Kevin's hand, "You have got to start thinking more of yourself, my friend. Megan has taken enough away from you. Don't give her all of your power too."

"Oh, Mimi, I know. It's just that it should be my baby. I should be the one coaching her through it."

Frustrated, I demand, "She's not worthy of you Kevin. You need to develop some revenge fantasies." Then before he can respond I ask, "Who is your favorite model?"

Without missing a beat, he answers, "Gisele Bündchen."

"Okay," I say, "when you start to feel the cocoa puff urge overtake you, I want you to visualize yourself all trim and thin, walking down the street with Gisele. Close your eyes," I demand. "Now, you and your supermodel are holding hands and laughing. Suddenly you stop on the street corner and you kiss. It's not a simple little peck either. It's a full blown passionate assault. You with me?" Kevin groans in the affirmative. "Just as Giselle runs the tip of her tongue over your earlobe, you hear, "'Kevin, is that you?'" You look up and it's Megan. But she's gained like sixty pounds and her hair is gray and she's got a pimple the size of Detroit on her upper lip." I pause to appreciate the look of contentment on my friend's face. "You look at this woman and say, 'I'm sorry, I don't think I know you.' Megan answers, "'Kevin, it's me Megan, your wife?' at which point Gisele faces Megan and she relates, 'No, I'm his wife.' Because you see, she's left Tom Brady for you, Kevin Beeman."

Kevin is beaming like he just won Publishers Clearing House. "Holy cow, that was good. You've got talent Mimi!"

"Yes, well, I've been dumped before. I know how to get even."

# Chapter 10

Everything is going fairly well at work today with one major exception. That rat Elliot is in the office, again. He keeps looking at me like the cat that swallowed the canary. And while yes, I know that I propositioned him while lying on a bed on Saturday night, I was also drunk at the time. Everyone knows proper party etiquette dictates you immediately forget embarrassing proposals made when one or both of the parties is under the influence. Yet it doesn't seem like the high and mighty Mr. Fielding knows the rules. He keeps grinning at me like we share a dirty little secret.

After a twenty-four hour all-you-can-eat bender, I feel surprisingly in control of my food consumption today. I have discovered tic-tacs, tiny little nuggets of spicy-sweet that help to keep my mind off of say, cheesecake. At three twenty-six on the nose, and I know this as I am staring right at the clock when it occurs. His Highness, Elliot Fielding, walks through my door and simply stands there. I am sick of the looks he has been shooting at me all day so I demand, "What Elliot? What do you want?"

Marginally taken aback by my combative tone, he quirks his damn eyebrow again and says, "I wanted to ask you something about Saturday night."

Well now I've had it! Not only does he not possess the good manners *not* to bring the incident up, but he is actually daring to speak of it in the light of day. So I stand up and shout, "Do you want to take me up on my offer? Is that why you're here?" And then horror of horrors I start to unbutton my blouse. "Because if that's what's brought you here, big boy, come and get it!" And I stand before him, completely topless with just my lacy pink satin bra for protection. My arms spread like Jesus Christ himself about to bless the bounty at the last supper.

Elliot just stares at me, then at my chest as it heaves up and down in expended fury, then at me again. But he doesn't move. There are sparks shooting between us at an alarming rate and I feel like I've just been electrocuted when he takes a step towards me. I want to scream "Don't dilly dally, get over here and take me!" when who should walk into my office behind Elliot? Yes, that's right, my brother-in-law, Jonathan.

Jonathan strolls in and asks, "What did she say about Saturday night?" It occurs to me at that moment that Elliot must have had a legitimate query and may in fact be talking about next Saturday instead of last Saturday night. My gaze is drawn to my boss who is slack-jawed at the image of his sister-in-law standing partially undressed in front of his most important client, apparently offering him the smorgasbord that is her body. He looks shocked, confused, and a little faint all at once. He asks, "Mimi?" his tone begging for a reasonable explanation.

At first I can't think of what to say as I have hormones raging through me at the speed of food poisoning. As inexplicable as this reaction is, I still want to jump Elliot Fielding's bones, even though we are no longer alone. Look out, I've become kinky. I had no idea I had this in me. Just as my thoughts segue to rubber boots and whips I answer, "Oh hi, Jonathan. I um," indicate the blouse in my hand, offer, "I just spilled diet coke on my blouse before Elliot walked in."

Jonathan visibly relaxes and averting his gaze says, "Well, my goodness then, we should leave you alone."

He turns to exit the room but Elliot doesn't move an inch. He just stands transfixed by the sight before him. After giving himself a little shake, he uncomfortably declares, "Right then. Well, I'll ask you later, how's that?" And he turns and walks out the door.

I drop to my desk and vaguely wonder if God has put a team of Vaudeville writers in charge of my life's script. I can see them now, "You know what would be funny, Stan? Make her rip her blouse off." "No kidding, Ollie, that's your best idea yet!" I dig into my closet for any spare tops that might be lurking about as I can no longer put on the blouse with "a diet coke" stain on it. The only thing I have is a sweatshirt that we used as a promotional gimmick for a canned cheese product. It says, "Think of Us When You Gotta Whizzzzzz!"

My main concern at the moment is how I am going to leave the building without running into Elliot. I mean this is shame like none other and I have known shame. I pick up my phone to call Elaine and ask if she's seen Elliot anywhere. She snootily tells me *Mr. Fielding* went into Jonathan's office and they've just closed the door. Without as much as a thank you for being such a nosy, pain in the ass bitch, I hang up on her and run out my own door. I am about to take a very late lunch that will extend into a very early dinner.

Ginger calls me at six-thirty to commiserate over the scene at work to which I naively inquire, "Scene, what scene?" I wrongly concluded there was no way that my boss would rat me out to my sister.

Ginger says, "Jonathan told me all about it, Meems."

"Oh," I sigh dejectedly. "Well then yes I would have to agree that it was one of the most embarrassing moments in my life. But happily it ended all right."

"You have to be careful with those cans of soda, you know. They always spray at the most inopportune times."

I'm thinking soda, what soda, when I remember my fabrication to Jonathan explaining my state of undress. I take a moment to offer a silent prayer of thanks that I didn't get so mad that I whipped my bra off too. I mean, there would be no way of talking my way out of that mess, would there? So I change the subject and ask Ginger, "What did Elliot want to ask me about Saturday night? Do you know?"

"Yeah, actually, I do. But first off, I want to apologize again for trying to set you up with him. If I had known then what I know now, I never would have, I promise."

What? What's she saying? It sounds like code for "Elliot is a mob boss" or "Elliot is an ax-murderer." So I demand, "What are you talking about?"

"Elliot wanted your opinion on the perfect restaurant to

propose to his girlfriend. She's coming in town from London on Friday and he wants to ask her to marry him on Saturday."

I start to hear this bizarre whirring sound in my head like I'm in the middle of a washing machine. So I ask Ginger to repeat what she just said. She does and the sound gets even louder. I fake call-waiting and hang up before I faint or scream or both. I plop down on my sofa to wait out the spin cycle in my brain and catalogue the facts about my brief association with Elliot Fielding. Elliot Fielding has never been interested in me. Elliot Fielding is about to become engaged to another woman. I have taken my shirt off and propositioned Elliot Fielding in my office when Elliot Fielding only wanted my opinion about which restaurant to use to propose to his girlfriend. While I should be relieved Elliot Fielding is not longing for me or planning an assault on my womanhood, I am left with an alarming realization. I want Elliot Fielding!

My life has become a farce, a Greek tragedy, it's become the sole reason that I let my car take me to Burger City, no questions asked. While I wait in the long dinner hour line, I inhale the bunion aroma and let it soothe me. I don't know about napalm in the morning but bunions during times of crisis are it for me. And speaking of bunions, mine has developed a very irritating voice. It has taken on the tone and inflection of Edith Bunker from those *All in the Family* reruns on "Nick at Nite." You remember how Edith used to pester, "Aaaarrrrrchhieeee?" My bunion nags, "MeeeeeeeeMeeeeeeee, what are you doing? You've been so goooooooooood. What about meeeeeee?"

I scream at it, "Shut up, you dumb bump, this is no longer

about you. It's bigger than you. Elliot Fielding is in love with another woman!"

My car revs its engine in sympathy but my bunion just won't shut up. Now she (I've decided to just name her Edith Bunker) says, "I was there when you were talking to Ginger and she just said he was about to get engaged, not that he already was. Go after him, win him over, and don't eat bunions!"

Good lord, did Edith Bunker have a point? Should I really try to win Elliot over after that alarming display in my office? Was there still a chance for me? When it's my turn in line, I order a diet coke and drive over to Kevin's to see if he has any ideas how to go about this. He is a man after all.

Kevin's advice is sexy clothes. He says men are extremely visual and cites Elliot's inability to speak while I stood before him in my pink bra. Kevin encourages plunging necklines, lots of leg, high heels, and sexy hair. "Jessica Rabbit," he declares, "when all else fails, think Jessica Rabbit."

So I say, "Fine, Kevin, I'll turn myself into a walking pin-up girl, but there's one problem. What do I say to him about jiggling my girls in his face and demanding that he ravish me in my office?"

Kevin cringes at the image, "There's only one excuse that he'll buy. And you're not going to like it."

I'm up for any justification that'll get me out of this jam so I ask, "What?"

Kevin puts his arm around my shoulder and announces, "You my dear are suffering from PMS. Now here's the important part, okay? You cannot have this man think you behave this way every month because lord knows, it'll get him to wonder if you're worth it." Becoming a little flustered, he clarifies, "I mean of course you are worth it, but he doesn't know that, yet. So anyway, you must tell him that your gynecologist has just put you on a new kind of birth control pill and its wreaking havoc with your hormones. This way, you have an excuse for your truly bizarre behavior *and* (stress the "and") you have just told Elliot that you're on the pill. He will subconsciously start to see you as a sexual creature. Then when you start looking extra hot, it'll lower his guard towards you and you will have a chance to shift his love from the cold English fish to the hot-blooded American. What do you think?"

I conclude, "Kevin, you're a genius. I'm in. Now so long as I don't freeze up and swallow my tongue while I'm blaming my crazies on Aunt Flo, I think I might have a chance." What I don't tell Kevin is I truly am suffering from PMS and if I don't get home and get my bra off immediately, my aching nipples are going to go on strike.

# Chapter 11

Elliot, who has been at the Parliament office every single day since he came to town, is not here today. Why, you ask? Because I was going to apologize of course and Stan and Ollie don't think this makes for very good comedy. I imagine if I were planning to knock him on the head with an anvil and laugh, knuck, knuck, knuck, knuck, followed by a "soytenely!" he would be here with bells on. But he's not and I am, looking like sex on a plate, I might add, with no hungry diners in sight.

With nothing else to do, I call Renée and ask her if I can come over to her workshop later this afternoon and check out her summer/fall line. I explain that now that we, as a sisterhood, have decided I need to trap me a man, I should start dressing for the hunt. She's delighted and exclaims, "Oh, Meems, I'm thrilled! Of course you can come over, anytime. Pick out whatever you want and I'll have the boys measure you and make the clothes right away!"

Renée doesn't have a haute couture line like most designers. She claims to not have the stomach for the drama. The world of super high fashion is one she knows well and was happy to leave behind when she stopped modeling. When she decided to create her own line, she did it with the thought of snazzying up the common woman. While I have no idea how the common woman affords her prices, her clothes are scrumptious to behold. They tend towards classic feminine lines and are made in the most decadent fabrics imaginable. She's been after me for years to let her dress me, but I have always declined. The only reason I can give for not taking advantage of her bounty is that I spent my childhood as one of her Barbies and the experience was painful at best, psychologically damaging at worst.

Instead of doing my work, I daydream about Elliot. Why did I never realize how thoroughly and utterly gorgeous he is? And smart…my gosh, the man has written fifteen *New York Times* bestselling novels. I close my eyes and see his tall, lanky, British form and sigh. I've always liked dark-haired men, but not now, mister. Now I like them strawberry blonde, and slightly receding at that. I've just started wondering how Elliot kisses, when Elaine walks in carrying the most gorgeous vase full of hot pink flowers. I gasp, "Did someone send you flowers, Elaine?" I sound a bit incredulous as I can't imagine anyone sending her a bouquet of vibrant blooms, snakes, yes. Flowers, no.

"No," she declares and puts them on my desk, "They're for you." Yet once she unhands them, she doesn't leave.

I ask, "Is there something I can help you with?"

"Aren't you going to read the card?"

I am curious who they are from, but the last person to send me an arrangement was Linden and they were my consolation prize for being dumped. Hence, I have no intention of opening the card in front of Elaine, so I answer, "I'll open it later." She still doesn't leave, so I ask, "Anything else?"

She looks at my blouse and answers, "It looks like you've slipped a couple of buttons there." And while she is wrong, they didn't slip, they were pushed, I quickly fasten them and thank her for drawing my attention to them.

Elaine, while probably not the devil incarnate, is at least his first cousin. She's worked at Parliament two years longer than I have, even though I have been promoted above her. She has told anyone and everyone who will listen that it is because the boss is my brother-in-law. The truth is, that I exceeded her standing long before Jonathan and Ginger became an item. This doesn't stop her from spewing her venom though. As soon as she leaves the room, I pick up the card and notice it has been sealed shut instead of the flap just being tucked in, as is the norm. No wonder Elaine had to ask who they were from. Normally, she would have just looked before bringing them in.

As soon as I pull out the heavy card stock note, I wonder if Stan and Ollie have dozed off. What other explanation could there be for me receiving something as lovely as flowers? No bouquet of dynamite, no ticking bomb, but actual peonies. The note is from Elliot and he apologizes for any misunderstanding between us. He hopes that we can start anew and have a very nice working relationship. He signs it, Elliot Fielding

I pick up the phone and call Kevin. I know he has a job interview today but I'm hoping to catch him before he leaves, and I do.

Kevin declares, "This Elliot is a class act. You make an ass out of yourself and he apologizes for it. Wow."

"Yes Kevin, but what do I do? Should I call him at home? Should I find out where he's staying and show up to thank him? What's my next move?"

Kevin answers "Wait for him to come back to work. Don't call or stop by. Right now you're on his mind and that's a good thing. You don't want to push it and have him think you might be a stalker."

"But I've scared him away from work. He may never come back."

Kevin suggests I talk to Jonathan and give him a restaurant recommendation for Elliot. Then Jonathan will tell Elliot and then Elliot will realize I have returned to normal and he in turn will feel comfortable coming back to Parliament.

I counter, "It will also help him propose to his girlfriend."

Kevin replies, "He'll find the perfect restaurant with or without you. But if he finds it without you, you won't know where he's going."

"What good is it going to do me if I know where he's doing the deed?"

Kevin chuckles, "You want to have dinner with me Saturday night?"

Missing his point entirely, I answer, "Yes, Kevin fine. Let's eat together Saturday. But you didn't answer my question."

Kevin says, "Ask me where we're going to eat."

I play along, "Where are we going to eat?"

"Wherever Elliot is taking his girlfriend."

I'm shocked and thrilled at the same time and ask, "You mean we're going to crash his engagement?"

I hear the smile in my friend's voice when he answers, "We might even invite ourselves to join them."

I want to hug Kevin and then reward him with a box of fat-free, sugar-free, point-free Cocoa Puffs, but no such animal exists. So instead I tell him he's brilliant and I'll talk to him later.

I spend the rest of the afternoon trying on my new sex-pot persona. I brush up against the copy machine like it's a virile Viking looking for a good time. I lick phantom spills off my fingers and even practice the "bend and snap" I learned about many years ago in *Legally Blonde*. I think I'm really getting the hang of this vixen thing when Bob Meyer from promotions corners me in the elevator and asks if I want to have dinner with him. I answer, "Thank you for the offer, Bob, but don't you think your wife will mind?"

"We won't tell her," he purrs, all the while licking his lips.

Shocked by this side of my squat little co-worker, I answer, "Sorry, Bob, I'm gonna have to say no."

"But you've been begging for it all day! I've watched you sucking on your fingers and rubbing up against the office supplies. I know you want me." Then he grabs his crotch and adds, "Come on, baby, hit the stop button. We can do it right here."

My answer to Bob is to lift the twenty pound manual I'm carrying and hit him over the head with it. For good measure, I add, "Snap out of it, Bob!"

He yelps his displeasure but the elevator door has already

opened and I just walk away. While totally revolted by his antics, I am also very proud of myself. Who knew I could drive a man into a frenzy like that? The power I feel is positively intoxicating! I can't wait to try it out on Elliot.

On the way to Renée's I decide to walk everyday at lunch and to try my darndest not to exceed twenty-five points a day. I also call my hairdresser and book an appointment for Saturday morning. I schedule highlights, a trim, and a blow dry. I am going to leave nothing to chance.

# Chapter 12

By the time I get home from my sister's house I feel like I've been run through a food processor. I've been measured, pinned, judged, and then measured some more. LeRon (pronounced just like her husband, Laurent) and Fernando simply cannot believe my hips are forty-two inches around. This bit of news causes a great deal of excitement with their delicate constitutions. There are gasps, semi-hysterical hand wavings, and re-measuring just to make sure. The fifth time they measure me, I am forty-three inches around. That's when they decided to accept forty-two. Once they grasp that I am not my sister, they really start to have fun with my curves. LeRon even confesses, "When we dress in drag, I pad and pad but I can never quite attain your degree of womanliness."

I thank him for the compliment and suggest he might be packing a few things I'm not, hinting that might work against the whole "woman" look.

He laughs and shrieks, "I strap that down, girlfriend!" Then he playfully smacks my hand and declares, "You're so bad!"

Fernando confesses that women in his native Argentina are

very curvy and he claims to be delighted to help dress me. Once it's all over, I'm not sure how many outfits they are planning to sew, but I'm not to worry my pretty little head over it. They swear to have a spectacular dress finished by Saturday morning and send me on my way.

As I fall asleep I dream about Saturday night. While I do not get a clear vision of the gown I'm wearing, I know its silver-blue and floor-length and it flows. Every time I move I virtually flutter through the air as though I'm about to take flight. There also appears to be some kind of a sumptuous boa around my neck. I'm gorgeous. Elliot can't possibly resist me like this. Especially as his girlfriend is wearing an atrocious brown tweed getup circa World War II, and she's fat. Not curvy and Marilyn Monroey like me, but seriously corpulent and those ankles! I've seen hundred-year-old tree trunks with less girth. I break for a moment of sisterly concern and hand Philomena Snood (as that's what I name her) Marge's business card. Poor Marge is going to have her hands full with this one.

As soon as Elliot sees me, he stares at me longingly and rises in slow motion. He looks to Philomena with regret and declares, "I'm so sorry, Phil, but I simply can't go on seeing you. This (gestures to me) vision of perfection is the one for me and I love her beyond all reason. Then somehow Philomena evaporates and I am the one sitting with Elliot. The waiter brings us ice water with lemon wedges and two frozen dinners, Weight Watchers Swedish Meatballs, my favorite. And only six points. I can't remember what else I dream, but I wake in the morning with an aching jaw and my teeth hurt like I've taken direct hits to the mouth.

The week flows by with alarming speed and I do not lose the thirteen pounds I'm hoping for. According to Marge, I've only lost point two pounds. Two tenths of a pound? I demand to know how this could be as Kevin and I have worked out three times and not once did I consume more than twenty-six points (not the twenty-five I had hoped for but still.) My peppy leader assures me that my losses will get smaller and smaller as I approach my goal and that I should soldier on. She also mentions something about muscle weighing more than fat and I grab onto that bit of information like a life boat. In fact, that has to be it. I am simply that much more muscular than I was last week.

After weighing in and reporting to Kevin, I drive over to The Gates to get my hair done. The salon is aptly named as there is a pair of truly intimidating iron doors blocking the entrance to the building. You don't get buzzed through until you announce yourself into the intercom. Somehow the whole experience makes the three hundred dollar expenditure feel justified. I used to pay nothing for the first year after the grand opening as I had been in charge of their PR. But once my freebies ran out, I was seriously hooked on all the attention I got and started to shell out the bucks myself. After all, when was the last time Supercuts offered me a glass of wine? Courtesies like that are priceless.

Francoise declares it's time for a change and I bow to his obvious excitement and skill and think, "Why not?" The same old, same old hasn't gotten me anywhere, its time to try something new. He asks if I want to know what his plans are but I say no. I've obviously been watching too many episodes of *Extreme Makeover* where the participants never have any idea what's happening to them until it's all done. I do request a five point, 6 oz. glass of white wine though, for courage.

As my fearless hairstylist dry cuts my hair, Edith Bunker starts carrying on again. She has not shut up all week. Apparently she's mad that I haven't worn my silicone wedge everyday like the doctor advised. But I keep reminding her it was her idea for me to go after Elliot and there's simply no way I can take him away from his intended in loafers. I assure her that the heroines in big Hollywood movies never get the guy while wearing sensible footwear.

Edith Bunker declares as soon as I realized that Elliot wasn't coming into the office, I should have switched shoes. I counter that he could have surprised me at any moment so I had to be prepared. On and on we go until I wonder why Archie never divorced this bitch. I mean, honestly every time she opens her bunion mouth I just want to get a knife and cut her off.

Francoise asks me one more time if I want to know about the color, but at this point I'm so preoccupied with Edith Bunker I wave him away. Not in the least concerned he might be dying it hot pink with purple highlights. There are two steps to my coloring process instead of the normal one and I finally begin to get a little nervous. Francoise assures it's simply because I have a good deal more gray than normal and he has to obliterate it before tending to the highlights.

I close my eyes while the color brews and visualize how I will look when I'm done. Somehow the dye is magical and once it's washed out and my hair is styled, I look just like my supermodel sister. With a smile on my face, I continue the fantasy all the way to the alter, where Elliot awaits me in regal anticipation.

Francoise nudges me and croons, "This way mi amore, meine liebchen, bonita..." He throws international endearments at me all the time, but today I eat them up like a starving castaway. Once I'm rinsed and scrubbed, he leads me back to his station and finishes off my miraculous transformation. Thirty-five minutes later he spins me around and announces, "Voilà!" That's when I gaze into the mirror and realize I look nothing like Renée. Because I'm a redhead!

Francoise asks me to close my mouth and really look at myself before saying a word. Ten minutes pass before I can speak. As a rule, I have a very delicate apple cart, easily upset by subtle change, yet alone dramatic ones. During this time of silence my apple cart tips, and tips, threatening a spectacular spill, but it never actually falls over. Francoise can't take it a moment longer and demands, "What do you think of it already?!"

As a slow smile creeps over my face, I finally realize that I love it. I have the mysterious, sexy, almost wanton look that only a redhead can achieve. I look individual and unique and thoroughly stunning. I want to kiss Francoise right on the mouth but am afraid he wouldn't be able to handle the shock as I'm sure that that one smooch from me, looking like this, would catapult him straight into heterosexuality. I am woman, hear me roar!

It's two-thirty before I leave the salon as I decide to have my makeup done while I'm here. After all, I don't know how to do a redhead's makeup. Charlene sits me down and starts to enumerate key tips to remember but I can't hear a word she's saying. The applause in my head is drowning her out.

The boys meet me at Renée's workroom at three to make sure the dress fits appropriately. I've asked them not to tell my sister that I'm wearing it tonight because I don't want my family to think there's someone special, yet. Once they find out that I've staked out a man, they'll make me miserable with constant demands to know how it's going. Plus, they can never know I'm after Elliot. They now view him as off the market, due to this alleged girlfriend.

When I arrive, LeRon sees me first and almost succumbs to a fit of vapors. He lets out a squeal that nearly shatters the windows as he calls for Fernando. Once both boys are assembled they begin to dance around me like I'm their high priestess. LeRon declares, "But you're gorgeous! Who would have ever known?"

Fernando simply sighs, "Dios mio, you're as beautiful as your sister." I know I look good, but as beautiful as Renée? Yet if a gay man says it, it must be true, right?

LeRon brings out the dress and it is without a doubt the most stunning creation I've ever seen. It is turquoise green with a plunging neckline that exposes a fair amount of my 36Cs. The bodice is as form-fitting as my own skin, and the skirt only offers enough extra room to sit. Normally, I'm super self conscious of my curves and do everything in my power to conceal them. But this is a revelation! The boys tell me it's so perfect because it was sewn to my exact measurements. "Off the rack," they declare, "only looks good on the fit model the garments are sized on."

Happily, Renée and Laurent are out with the kids so I don't have to explain my dramatic new hair color and the dress quite yet. On the way home I'm tempted to call Kevin and give him a heads up on how I look but then decide to just surprise him. I want to see an honest reaction so I can gauge the kind of effect I'm going to have on Elliot.

# Chapter 13

Kevin arrives fifteen minutes before we need to leave so that I can help choose the right tie for him to wear. When I answer the door, his mouth drops open and he stammers, "Mimi, is that you?"

I twirl to show myself off, front and back, and demand, "What do you think?"

"Holy shit, you're hot!"

I throw my arms around him in grateful appreciation and pull him into the living room. I pick out a tie that complements my dress without making us look like a couple on the way to prom and we're off. We have eight o'clock reservations at La Petite Maison, the same restaurant where Elliot is taking Philomena. I know this for a fact as I called to confirm his reservation this afternoon. Elliot's reservation is for eight-fifteen which is why Kevin and I are arriving at eight. I want to be settled by the time he gets there so I can get an eyeful of the fiancée before we "bump into each other."

A soon as we get into the car that pain in the ass Edith Bunker starts yammering about how I'm wearing the wrong shoes again, but I just tell her to shut up. I'm bursting with too much excitement and hope to let her ruin my night. She punishes me for ignoring her by stabbing me with needles of piercing pain.

Kevin and I are seated by the very admiring maître d' at a corner table as requested. We sit side by side so that we can mutually scrutinize the entrance. We have both been banking points all week in anticipation of really enjoying our night. A bottle of champagne gets ordered to celebrate our renewed friendship and Kevin raises his glass to me as he toasts, "Holy fucking shit, it can't be!"

Perplexed, I toast back, "Holy fucking shit to you too, buddy."

"No," he whispers, "It's Megan. She's here with David, you know, the father of her child?"

I look in the direction he's pointing and gasp at the sight of who I assume is his very pregnant ex-wife. "What in the world is she doing in Pipsy?"

He answers, "David's parents live here. Oh Mimi, what do I do now?"

My heart positively aches for him and I reply, "Leave it to me."

As Megan and David are led past our table I declare rather loudly, "Kevin Beeman, you have made me the happiest woman in the world. Thank you for a wonderful first year together!"

Megan hears my toast and whips around as fast as a nine month pregnant woman can and asks, "Kevin? Is that you?"

Taken completely off guard by my declaration, Kevin

manages, "Megan, how are you?"

Megan pats her stomach and says, "Fine. We're fine." She's clearly considering my toast. Because she asks, "You're celebrating your first anniversary, are you?"

As Megan confessed her affair eight months ago, she is realizing that Kevin must have cheated on her first and she seems to be having quite an interesting time absorbing this bit of information.

Kevin has pulled himself together enough to answer, "Would you like to meet Mimi?"

Megan stares at him and simply replies, "No," before turning to waddle back towards the front of the restaurant. (I wish my podiatrist were here so I could show him what a real waddle looks like.) David, who has had the good sense not to utter a word, trails after her. As Megan turns to take one last look at Kevin before stalking out the front door, I lean in and kiss him for all I'm worth, which after my transformation is about eighteen hundred million dollars and change. That'll show her for breaking my friend's heart! Unfortunately, it also showed the Fielding party as they walked in at the same moment.

"God damn it," I whisper into Kevin's mouth.

Stunned by my attack, he replies "Wow, that was some kiss!"

"Elliot walked in just in time to catch it too."

Kevin pulls back and declares, "NO! This is not our night."

Stan and Ollie are up from their nap just in the nick of time to ruin all my hard work. How do I explain this to Elliot without appearing to be on the make for him? Those miserable old vaudevillians would get the ass-kicking of their lives if I knew how to get my hands on them.

The first thing that I notice about Elliot's fiancée is that she isn't obese at all. In fact she's slim and elegant and every inch a lady. All of a sudden I feel like a call girl with my boobs hanging out like an all you can eat buffet. As they walk by our table I notice that she is not gorgeous though. Her features are as plain as her mousy brown hair, which is the same color as mine used to be; which leads me to wonder why I let Francoise transform me. Obviously Elliot likes that shade of bacon grease. As they pass our table, Elliot smiles, and nods in our direction, as though he has no intention of saying hello. So I blurt out, "Hello, Elliot."

He stops mid-stride and stares at me. Then asks, "I'm sorry, have we met?"

I'm about to scream at him for being such a ruthlessly stuck up prig when I realize he truly doesn't recognize me. Shit, if I had just kept my mouth shut, he would have never known that I, Mimi Finnegan, kissed another man. Of course I wouldn't have been able to foil his attempt at engagement, but still. My head is pounding with the reverberating hilarity of Stan and Ollie.

I muster up, "Mimi Finnegan, we met at the office?"

Elliot gasps, "Mimi? My goodness, you look nothing like yourself. I mean you look great..." he continues to stammer, "Not that you didn't before..." then declares, "This is Beatrice (pause), my friend."

Beatrice, with all the warmth of an iceberg murmurs, "Hello." She nods her head like Elliot does and I briefly wonder if the English are unfamiliar with our custom of shaking hands.

There is an awkward pause before Kevin loses all of his marbles and takes on the persona of his gay alter ego. He flamboyantly declares, "Beatrice! What a positively gorgeous name! And look at you, all the grace and style of the queen herself! Why you are the epitome of class!" Beatrice, the little mouse, is eating this up and she beams adoringly at Kevin.

I open my mouth as if to say something but have no idea what that would be so I close it again. Elliot looks shocked and amused and asks, "So Kevin, have you and Mimi been dating long?"

"Dating?" Kevin asks as his eyes roll into his head. He snaps his wrists forward, "Good lord, no! What would make you ask that?"

Uncomfortably, Elliot replies, "I thought I saw you kissing when we walked in. I must have been mistaken."

With a belly laugh and a slap on the table, Kevin confides, "Oh, Meems was just helping me out." Then he points, "See the bartender over there? He and I just broke up and I'm trying to make him jealous."

Elliot turns around to look at the very buff, very black bartender and asks, "You mean the one that's holding hands with the blonde woman?"

Discovering a new depth of homosexual drama, Kevin blasts, "That Nancy bitch, how dare he?!"

I still haven't said a word when Kevin asks, "Elliot, why don't you and this rose (indicating the delighted Beatrice) of feminine pulchritude join us for a drink?"

Elliot replies, "No thank you," at the same time that Beatrice sits down next to Kevin and accepts.

So there we sit four fish so far out of water that we might as well be in the desert. Kevin is completely monopolizing Beatrice, trying to give me time with Elliot and while I'm sure I must be grateful, I still have an immense desire to smack him. We are not at all following our script, but then again improvisation *was* in order after our lip-lock.

I finally lean towards Elliot and apologize about the other day. He smiles and assures me the whole incident has been forgotten. Then I ask, "Is Beatrice in town for long?"

He clears his throat and answers, "No, just a long weekend."

He doesn't embellish so I say, "She's lovely." What am I thinking? Maybe I should suggest he propose to her. What I should say is, "Don't marry her! Marry me!"

He looks at me with a pained expression and utters, "Yes, well."

The Englishman and I appear to have nothing to say to each other and I could just cry at our awkwardness. After all, Kevin is doing a bang up job entertaining Beatrice and I am totally blowing my opportunity. I hear Kevin ask Beatrice to dance and almost spit out my champagne.

Elliot takes that moment to try to get Beatrice to go to their own table but she insists she wants to dance with Kevin first. She seems to have developed a crush on him as a result of the extravagant attention he's paying her. It occurs to me she is the ultimate fag hag.

As soon as our dinner partners leave, Elliot leans a bit closer to me and says, "You look lovely this evening, Mimi. I like your hair." While the compliment is not exactly delivered with an excess of passion, I still get chills.

I thank him and tell him he looks very nice as well and then we just sit there in painful silence. After the next song starts and Kevin and Beatrice still don't appear, Elliot offers, "Would you like to dance?"

I shake my head and before I can stop the words, I say, "I'd love to but Edith Bunker won't let me."

Elliot stares at me like he's sitting with a schizophrenic who's gone off her meds and responds, "I see."

I am beyond appalled at myself for blurting out such a thing and try to make it better by clarifying, "No, you don't. Edith Bunker is my bunion." I look at him like, see, now it makes sense. But of course it doesn't.

Peering from side to side to see if there's a butterfly net within arm's length, Elliot asks, "Your bunion is named Edith Bunker?"

"Yes," I try to explain, "but only because she sounds just like Edith Bunker."

"Ahh, your bunion is a girl and she talks to you?"

I want to lay my head on the table and cry! Elliot Fielding is never going to want to spend the rest of his life with me now. After all, how many personal ads have you read that specify "mate with talking bunion preferred?" I slowly look up at him and announce, "I'm making such a fool of myself." Then grabbing the bull by the horns, I add, "But only because I like you so much."

Elliot looks at me as though I've just thrown my drink in

his face. He cocks his head to the side in an endearingly obtuse manor and says, "Mimi, I don't know what to say. I mean..." and before he can say what he means Kevin twirls Beatrice back to the table.

She is flush with excitement and actually has a rose between her teeth. Kevin declares, "The lady dances like a dream!" Elliot begins to excuse himself and his date claiming that it's time they go find their table but Kevin announces, "Don't be silly, you're dining with us."

Beatrice pats Elliot's hand and says, "That's right, Elliot. Kevin asked us to join them and I said we'd be delighted to."

It appears Elliot and I would both rather lie down in front of an oncoming train than continue this unbearably awkward evening. But our dates have decided for us, so we can do nothing but try to make the best of it. The one ray of good news is there is no way Elliot is going to propose while we're sitting here. The bad news is I've just told him I like him and have no idea in this world what he thinks of me. Other than I'm a crazy, stripping weirdo with a talking bunion.

While searching out menus, Kevin asks me how many points I think are in the Coq au Vin. My guess is thirty thousand but I can't be sure. Beatrice asks, "What are points and what do they have to do with food?"

I send Kevin a "don't you dare, under the penalty of death tell her about Weight Watcher's look." But he is already gazing at her in an adoring fashion and declaring, "Meems and I are on Weight Watchers. Our food gets broken down into points and we can only eat so many of them a day."

Beatrice exclaims, "But Kevin, you're perfect the way you

are! In fact, I think you're cuddly."

Beatrice using the word "cuddly" surprises me more than my mother saying the word "masturbate," a word she uses every Thanksgiving when she declares that she's bought a self-masturbating turkey. The first time she announced this, I went off turkey for six months. But now I know she means self-basting and I'm back on the bird. But Beatrice, cuddling? I can't see it.

While the dynamic duo chats away, Elliot leans towards me and says, "You don't need to be on Weight Watchers. You look fabulous just the way you are." I'm torn between asking him if he likes me too and jumping into his lap and declaring myself when I realize I can see inside his jacket pocket. What I spy is a definite ring sized box and my heart hits the floor. I'm no longer worried about how many points are in the food as I'm certain I can no longer manage to swallow with the huge lump forming in my throat.

Elliot and I spend the rest of the meal casting furtive glances at each other as we try to make polite conversation. Beatrice and Kevin carry on like Siamese twins separated at birth. And while Kevin is supposed to be the Great Gaydini, I notice that he is acting just like his normal self. By the time the night is over, I have a pounding headache, a throbbing bunion, and a pit in my stomach. I just want to go home, take a bottle of aspirin and wake up next week.

# Chapter 14

My teeth are killing me when I wake up this morning. Actually none of me really feels great. I think over the events of last night and suddenly realize that my life has taken on the subtext of a romantic comedy gone horribly wrong. Because in this movie girl does not get boy because boy thinks girl has fallen off her rocker and sustained serious cognitive damage.

While I'm lying in bed trying to make deals with Stan, Ollie, and Edith Bunker, my doorbell rings. I have no idea who has come a knockin' at eight a.m. on a Sunday morning but I promise myself to be extra careful lest I encounter any whipped cream pies in the face.

I have the foresight to ask who it is because even Stan and Ollie wouldn't let me answer should the reply be, "Ted Bundy, just hoping to borrow your phone ma'am."

But it's not Ted, its Muffy. You might be wondering why I haven't mentioned Muffy that often and the truth is while I love her very much, the two of us are not the closest in our quartet of sisterhood. I think it has to do with the fact I was always looking for my big sister's approval and felt like I was

99

competing with Muffy to get it. When I brought home first prize in the glitter and macaroni art competition, Muffy began jumping hurdles over the couch. When I won third place in the All-Pipsy spelling bee in the eighth grade, Muffy went to state in track. You see what I mean. While my accomplishments were impressive by normal earthling's standards, they were not such a big deal in the Finnegan family. I used to dream about being adopted out to a family that would appreciate me.

I open the door to my little sister, not full of concern as I'm certain nothing bad could or would ever happen to her. In fact I'm pretty sure my parents are destined for immortality because I cannot imagine Muffy ever being orphaned. I do however have a shadowy vision of her attending the funeral of her slightly older sister someday, so I am aware I will not be spared the grim reaper's visit. In this hallucination I am the only one who ages too. I'm about one hundred and eight to everyone else's thirty.

So I greet my little sister, "Morning, Muff, come on in." Muffy walks through the front door and heads straight for my kitchen where she starts to make a pot of coffee. I ask, "What's up?"

After several moments, she says, "I need to tell you something." I'm expecting something like, "My knee is all better and I'm off to Wimbledon."

What she says is, "Tom is cheating on me with Victoria Witherspoon from the club."

I have no idea what to say, but I mumble something like, "Are you sure? Maybe you're just imagining it."

Tears form in my sister's eyes and she answers, "I'm sure. I even have the photographs to prove it." Apparently Muffy hired a private investigator several months ago to put her suspicions to rest. Six months ago Tom was sleeping with Leesia Houghington, three months ago it was Isabelle Rentworth and now, Victoria Witherspoon.

I don't know what to say or what to do, so I do the only thing that even vaguely comes to mind. I wrap my sister in a huge embrace and let her cry on my shoulder. Once the initial waterworks subside I ask, "What are you going to do, Muff?"

She answers, "I'm going to leave his sorry ass, but right now, I need to not see that Mrs. Robinson gigolo for awhile." What I didn't know, not being a member of the country club circuit, is that Victoria, Leesia, and Isabelle are all in their late forties, perhaps fifties. They are all married to much older men and apparently Tom is their man whore.

I ask, "What do Ginger and Renée think? I mean, if they want to pass the hat for a hit, I'm in.".

Muffy looks at me slightly panicked and answers, "I haven't told them, yet."

"Why?"

She mumbles, "Because they'll judge me. They'll think I did something wrong, or I haven't handled the situation right, or that I should try marriage counseling."

I want to ask if she's ever met her other sisters because they would never do any such thing. They would rally around her in righteous indignation and champion her cause above all else. What I do ask is, "Then why did you come to me?"

She answers, "Because you're the sensitive one, the one

with the big heart. I knew you would support me no matter what."

Excuse me, what? I'm the one with the big heart? When did this happen? What I say is, "I thought I had the prettiest feet."

"Don't be ridiculous, you have a bunion."

I declare, "No, no, I mean when we were kids we decided that Renée was the pretty one, Ginger, the brain, you were the jock, and I had the prettiest feet."

Muffy looks at me with a furrowed brow and responds, "I don't know what you're talking about. You were always the one with heart, you were our rock."

I'm feeling faint. I mean, I know my sister is suffering a grave hurt, but I feel like my whole world has been based on wrong assumptions and I need a little more clarification. "Muffy, what are you talking about?"

She answers, "Hello? Every time something has gone wrong in one of our lives, who was the first person we went to? You. Think back Meems, you were the first one to hear everything, good and bad, because you were the most supportive and giving. You care the most."

Okay, foundation seriously rocking here. I thought I was the first one to hear the good news because they all wanted to show me how much more superior they were to me. And I have no recollection of any bad news. My three sisters were perfect.

Muffy continues, "When Lorenzo died, where did Renée go?"

"To Mom and Dad's."

"Don't be stupid, Meems, she came back to Pipsy because you were here. I was in California and Ginger was in England. She could have just as easily come to us, but she went home to you, because you're the one she needed. You were the one she could count on to help repair her heart."

I remember those months when Renée came home like they were yesterday. I also remember I saw her every single day and I spent hours listening to her talk about Lorenzo. I had no idea in this world my oldest sister was honoring me with her grief.

Muffy continues, "And when Ginger couldn't get pregnant? She told you after three months. Renée and I just found out when she announced they were signing up with adoption agencies."

What I can't help wondering is how I managed to only retain the memories that made me feel bad about myself. I wonder if it's true that my sisters may not be as perfect as I had always thought. If I had better health insurance I would seriously consider getting some therapy. But for now, I need to take care of Muffy. I ask her if she wants to stay with me for awhile and she tells me she has her bags in the car. When she goes to get them I promise myself at the ripe age of thirty-four, I am finally going to try to see my family as they really are and not as my insecurities would have me believe them to be.

Muffy settles her things into my guest room/office before coming downstairs for breakfast. I am making my diet French toast and offer to make some for her as well but she declares she'd rather lick the floor. While searching my fridge, she asks, "What's with all the diet crap in here?"

I answer, "Don't tell anyone, but I'm on Weight Watchers."

"What the heck for?"

"Um hello, because I need to lose weight?"

Muffy becomes indignant, "You do not. You look great!" Then she really looks at me and adds, "In fact you look gorgeous! I love you as a redhead!"

I thank her and explain the truth about my bunion. She calls Dr. Foster names like quack and misogynist pig and I feel remarkably better. She says that all I need to do if I want to lose weight is to work out more. I agree to let her train me, but I have no intention of quitting Weight Watchers. I need the structure it offers and God knows I need to keep being reminded what a serving size really looks like.

Muffy and I make an appointment to work out every evening at six. I ask if she minds if I have a friend join us and she declares, "The more the merrier." I vow that once I feel like talking to Kevin again, I'm going to invite him to exercise with us. I hope my sister runs his ass ragged too.

By three I'm feeling better and give Kevin a call. I tell him to be at my house at six and to be prepared to work out. He wants to reminisce about last night but I hang up on him. Although, not before telling him he can't discuss anything about my personal life tonight. He's confused as he doesn't know it won't be just the two of us. But that's okay, I'm plenty confused too and it's nice to have company.

Kevin arrives at five fifty-two looking like a bad stereotype from the eighties. He is wearing a sweat band and wrist bands and his sweatshirt, I swear, looks like it just walked off the

*Flashdance* set. Once I'm done laughing at him, I invite him in and introduce him to Muffy.

Muffy smiles and says, "Hi, Kevin. I'm glad you could join us."

Kevin replies, "Hphrg guhhh duuuh mmmm, ahhhhh."

I look at him to make sure that he's not stroking out on me and ask, "Kevin, what's wrong with you?"

He answers, "Flgkkkk shmuuuu guuuuuuh…"

Muffy looks alarmed and goes to the kitchen to get him a glass of water. As soon as she leaves the room, Kevin demands, "What is she doing here?"

"Kevin, you moron, that's my sister. She's here to help us train."

My friend's pallor takes on a rather grey tint and he confides, "Mimi, remember when I told you I had a crush on you in high school?" I roll my eyes and nod my head simultaneously. He continues, "I lied. I really had a crush on Muffy, a bad crush."

I smack him in the arm, "You bastard and here I thought I finally caused someone teenage angst!"

"Seriously, I think I'm going to throw up. I can't possibly work out with her." I ask why and he says, "Because I don't want her to know I'm fat."

"Well first off," I tell him, "You're cuddly, not fat. And secondly, she already saw you when you walked through the front door."

Kevin throws his hands up, "But I wasn't running or jiggling then. Please get me out of this!"

Too late, Muffy's back and she's carrying a whistle. She

hands Kevin a glass of water and as soon as he takes a sip she declares, "Okay then, let's take it outside." And then she blows her whistle for emphasis.

I tell my sister how thrilled I am she's going to train us but assure her that if she ever blows a whistle at me again, I'm going to kick her, completely involuntarily, but kick her nonetheless. Kevin doesn't say anything. He just meekly follows her out the door like a lamb to the slaughter.

# Chapter 15

I can't get out of bed to save my life. My body feels like it's been run through a pasta cutter and then beaten with a rolling pin. I have pain on top of pain on top of agony. Muffy did not start us out slow as she claims. She made us walk two miles at a brisk clip, then we stopped for jumping jacks, sit-ups and toe touches, then we jogged half a mile before walking home (barefoot in the snow carrying boulders on our shoulders).

Happily LeRon dropped off six new outfits for me last night so I can start my Jessica Rabbit campaign in earnest. I was too tired to really look through everything after Xena the Warrior Princess got done with me. But now, I can hardly wait to see what I've got to work with. If only I can drag my sorry carcass across the floor. Once I stand up I let out an involuntary groan of pure distress. There's no way I'm going to be able to try on clothes. I can't even lift my feet to walk. I shuffle my way to the bathroom and start the shower, then pop three Advil.

By the time I get out of the shower, my limbs are feeling a little more normal and I start to think that I may actually be able to go to work. Then I see the clothes I have to choose from and I let out a gasp of delight. My goodness, the boys have outdone themselves! Of course the designs are all Renée's but those two little worker bees have sewn everything to fit me like a second skin. The outfit I'm immediately drawn to is a cream colored linen skirt. It's a very slim cut and is mid-calf in length. The truly remarkable feature is the slit up the back that hits mid thigh. The top that goes with it is a pale pink silk sleeveless sweater with a low scooped front. It's worn with a small chain linked gold belt. The shoes I bought for Ginger's dinner party will go perfectly with it, if I can only manage to walk in them.

Edith Bunker is giving me seven kinds of hell for my footwear choices last week. I just wish there was some way to know if Elliot was going to be in the office or not, because truly I wouldn't mind schlepping around in loafers for a few days. But I don't have the luxury of slacking off now, especially after my announcement Saturday night. I have no idea what possessed me to blurt out that I liked him. Fortunately we were interrupted by the tango twins, so if he doesn't feel the same way, I can always claim that he misunderstood my declaration. You know like, "What I meant to say is, "I like you so much...as a brother, author, fellow human being, not as my knight in shining armor. Is that what you thought I meant? Hahahahahahahahahaa, oh Elliot, that's soooooo funny!" Don't worry, I don't buy it either so let's hope he's feeling the same uncontrollable lust that I am.

Muffy has already left for the country club by the time I come down for breakfast, a fact for which I am eternally grateful. It's enough she knows I'm on Weight Watchers and have changed my hair color, but she might really start to wonder what's going on when she sees the radical alteration to my wardrobe. I'm simply not up to explaining myself. My transformation is so profound to me that I'm not even sure how to act. But you know what's funny? I feel like I'm finally in the right skin. I feel like the librarian who lets her hair down, whips off her glasses, unbuttons her blouse and roars, "Come and get me, tiger!"

When I walk into the office, Elaine, Bob, and a few others look up from their cubicles and do a quadruple take. I feel powerful. I seem to have added a small hitch to my giddy-up as well. I'm positively channeling Jessica Rabbit with my sashay and it occurs to me to tone it down a bit before Bob sues for sexual harassment.

Not five minutes after settling into my office, Jonathan pops his head in, "Hey Meems, got a minute?"

"Sure, come on in."

He sits in a chair opposite me, without one comment about my makeover, and says, "We need a liaison with the New York office regarding Elliot's new book and I wanted to let you know you're my first choice."

I'm flattered by his faith in me as the liaison is responsible for coordinating all shared press duties and would involve my taking a couple trips to the Big Apple in order to arrange the particulars. Ever since *Sex and the City* came out while I was in college, I have positively loved New York. The truth is I have only been two other times and both occasions were in my childhood. I feel giddy at the prospect of going back as an adult. Jonathan explains that Elliot will be accompanying me as he needs to meet the key people in the Manhattan office. Plus, he declares, our mother ship has scheduled some book signings for him. Their feeling being he should autograph his old novels as a pre-marketing strategy for the new one.

I feel the uncharacteristic need to swoon come over me as I realize that Elliot and I will be traveling together, just him, me, Edith Bunker, Stan and Ollie. Oh crap! Of course my menagerie has to come along and for the first time thoughts of doom start to creep into the picture. I'm going to Carrie Bradshaw's shoe nirvana and flipping Edith Bunker is going to be yammering at me the whole time to buy some nice orthopedic old lady shoes.

By one o'clock there is still no sign of Elliot and I want to scream. My whole body feels like a raw, over-sexed nerve ending. If I don't see him right now, this very second, I'm going to spontaneously combust. I haven't actually had sex since Linden dumped me and if we're honest, I didn't have it for three months before that. If we're just going to bare our souls here and shoot for complete candor, ask yourself, how good do you think an overbred mama's boy could possibly be in the sack? Have I made my point? While I'm not some hot to trot floozy, I am human and I do have basic human needs. One of which is to have physical contact with a member of the opposite sex, with Elliot, Elliot, Elliot, Elliot, Elliot, Elliot, Elliot, Elliot, Elliot. I haven't been so worked up for a boy since Justin Johnson, senior year in high school.

Just as I'm about to start humping my desk, in walks the man of the hour. He's wearing dark trousers and a white dress shirt unbuttoned at the neck. He looks gorgeous and sexy and slightly rumpled. Elliot does not strike me as the rumpled type and I wonder why he looks that way today. He simply says, "Hello Mimi, how are you today?" the timber of his voice as soft as a caress.

I'm hornier than hell, you big hottie! What I actually say is, "I'm just fine, Elliot. How are you?"

He declares, "Fine, fine. I wanted to thank you for the restaurant recommendation Saturday night. Do you go there often?"

What I think he really wants to know is why I was having dinner there the same night I knew he was going too. As I have only been to La Petite Maison one other time, I answer, "I go all the time, which is why I recommended it." Then it occurs to me to add, "I'm sorry about Kevin. I'm sure you would have preferred to have a romantic dinner for two."

Elliot assures me, "I had a lovely time."

Stan and Ollie are up and they've had their coffee, so I ask, "And Beatrice? Did she have a nice time?"

Raising his eyebrow as though amused by my question, Elliot declares, "She very much likes your friend Kevin and is hoping to see him again before she leaves."

"Before she leaves? I thought she left today."

He replies, "No, it seems that she's decided to stay on for a few more days."

I demand, "Why?!"

Elliot responds, "She likes Hilldale more than she thought she would."

Then I add, "I'm sure she misses you as well."

With a shrug of the shoulder he mutters, "Perhaps."

Then we just stand there staring at each other with this intense energy darting between us. Neither of us says a word, nor do we take our eyes off of each other. All I can think is that there is no way I am the only one feeling this potent pull. But I refuse to make the first move. After all, he's the one with the girlfriend and I have already professed my feelings, therefore the ball is in his court.

Without taking his eyes from mine, he says, "I understand we're going to be traveling together."

I simply moan an affirmative sound to confirm I've heard the same thing. Then I manage, "I understand we leave on Friday. Will Beatrice still be in town?"

He answers, "I'm not sure."

I can't help myself so I ask, "So, she might be joining us?"

He declares, "She will not." No more explanation than that and I feel the heat rise in my cheeks. Elliot finally breaks our staring contest and makes a move to the door. Just as he's about to walk out, he turns around and says, "By the way, you look very nice today Mimi." Then he's gone.

I collapse in my chair and take ten deep breaths to keep myself from running after him and tackling him to the ground. Elliot stays at Parliament for the rest of the afternoon and every time he passes my office he peers in. I wonder if he knows how much I want him. A little voice inside my head answers, "Of course he does. Welcome to the mating dance."

# Chapter 16

On this our second day of working out, Muffy calls to cancel our session. She has lessons until sixty-thirty, but she commands us to carry on without her. Kevin gets to my house at five-forty-five looking a bit too suave for physical activity. His sweats look brand new, as do his shoes, his hair is slicked back with some kind of gel and he appears to either be wearing a girdle or he's just majorly sucking his gut in. I answer the door and simply burst out laughing.

He walks in with his eyes darting around for Muffy when he loudly declares, "Hey Mimi, ready to work out? I can't wait, I'm totally jazzed!!!"

So I let him off the hook, "She's not here, doofus."

He relaxes his posture and sighs, "Oh thank god! I didn't know how long I could keep that up." Then I tell him she can't make our workout tonight and he begs, "Let's not do it then. My body is so sore I thought I was dying when I got out of bed this morning."

I concur and by mutual consent we agree to skip the torture tonight. We convince ourselves if we exercise too much too soon, we might just overdo and wind up giving up on it. So for our long term fitness, we make the decision to take the night off. I ask Kevin, "How many points do you have left?" He has eight and I have nine so we can both have the extra cheese on our frozen dinners.

While Kevin is tossing the salad I tell him about Beatrice. I accuse, "I'm pretty sure you're the reason she's staying in town. I can't thank you enough."

But he just smiles and says, "Get her number for me. I'll be happy to keep her busy for you."

"You will, why?"

He laughs, "I know this sounds crazy but I really did have a nice time with her. In fact she's the only other person I've met in a long time who's as desperate for attention as I am."

I declare, "Kevin, you are not desperate for attention."

"Not from you or say from my mother; but from a viable member of the opposite sex? Let's face it, I'm desperate. My wife is having another man's baby and my self esteem is in the toilet."

I know exactly how he feels. There is no sensation so addicting as appreciation from a member of the opposite sex. I, myself, have gone without it for so long that I nearly forgot how amazing it feels. After all, if you're single for long enough, everyone around you starts to treat you like an aging relative. They're nice to you, they smile and pat you on the hand, but they totally forget you have needs. Kevin and I are just two sorry peas in a pod.

As we're eating our fudge pops, Muffy walks in declaring that her last lesson canceled. She looks at Kevin and me, with our feet propped up on the coffee table, amidst remnants of our dinner and declares, "You didn't work out!" Before either one of us can come to our senses and lie to her, she has us up and stretching. Before Kevin can even utter one unintelligible word, we are out walking. Muffy is carrying on the whole way telling us we'll be in more pain if we don't do some form of exercise every single day. I can't help but wonder what Kevin sees in her. But he just stares at her adoringly and works harder than I have ever seen, in hopes of impressing the dominatrix that is my sister.

I walk in silence tonight as I'm totally distracted by my messed up life. I am a thirty-four-year-old (yes, thirty-five is next!) single woman, with fifteen extra pounds and pathetic dating history. I have an inferiority complex where my family is concerned, I have a talking bunion named Edith Bunker, and everything coming out of my mouth is filtered through the pens of two not so funny comedy writers. I am also in heat (I would say love, but I don't really know him yet.) with a hugely successful British novelist who just so happens to be nearly engaged to another woman. It occurs to me my existence is so ridiculous that Stan and Ollie may well not be writing it on their own. There might be a whole roomful of failed comics having a whack at me.

I hear Muffy encouraging, "You're doing a great job, Kevin, keep it up!" And sure enough he picks up his pace in response. I'm really worried for my sister. She's never been one to easily express her emotions so I don't really know how to be there for her. I mean, I don't want to intrude on her heartache by asking too many questions and then again, I don't want to pretend that she isn't going through the hardest time of her life. I vow to try to be a little less self-involved and be receptive to any signals she sends for help.

Muffy and Kevin have started to talk about high school. He says, "I used to watch you at the tennis meets and you were always amazing." Wow, a full sentence without even one stutter or made up word. Progress!

Muffy answers, "That's right, your girlfriend was on the team, wasn't she?"

Kevin confirms, "She sure was, but she didn't have your natural gift."

In her typical self-deprecating style, Muffy responds, "I'm just lucky to have been born with ability. I see how hard some people work and I really admire their commitment." After a couple minutes of silence, she adds flirtatiously, "I remember how cute you were in high school."

Kevin responds by tripping over his shoe and falling into someone's lawn. But not before trying to right himself for an agonizing twenty steps. What could have been merely an embarrassing moment turns into an award-winning display of physical comedy. Poor Kevin. Muffy stops to help him up and he scolds her, "Don't do that."

"Don't do what?" she asks.

"Don't go telling me I was cute in high school. I used to have the biggest crush on you."

"Nuh uh," she says. "You had a girlfriend."

Kevin replies, "Who was certainly very nice, but she was no you." I'm having déjà vu.

Muffy eyes my friend like she too is enjoying the

appreciation of a member of the opposite sex. Even if it is just Kevin Beeman and not some buff, tri-athlete, thick-necked jock that has been her professed "type" since birth. But the truth is she doesn't look at him like he's *just* anything. She looks at him like he's still the high school boy she thought was cute. I can't help but think Muffy and Beatrice are going to do wonders for Kevin's self esteem. When we're done working out and Kevin leaves, I notice that there is a spring to his step I haven't seen before.

A horrible noise wakes me at three o'clock in the morning. It's as bad as nails on a chalk board or Styrofoam rubbing against itself. It's the sound of bone grinding against bone. It's my teeth. No wonder my mouth has been hurting so badly in the morning. I appear to be doing my best to pulverize my pearly whites whilst slumbering. I briefly think of the Asian beauty cream claiming to be made with pearl dust and wonder how a moisturizer made with my teeth dust would work. I'm guessing not real well.

I try to remember what I was dreaming about that caused me to gnash my jaw muscles together with such relish, but can't. My dentist can't see me for three more weeks as he and his wife are hiking the Grand Tetons with their kids for their summer vacation. And once he gets back there's a full week booked ahead of me. I figure I'll just have to go to the drug-store tomorrow and see if I can find a mouth guard or something to offer some sort of protection in the meantime.

Once I fall back to sleep, it's like I tune into the Elliot channel. I dream of him non-stop until I open my eyes in the morning. While I'm pretty sure that I've worked a molar loose,

I'm also deliriously happy and can't wait to see the object of my obsession at the office.

Muffy is still home when I come down-stairs and she announces she's ready to tell the family about Tom. I agree to let her use my house as long as she cleans it first and she agrees. She plans to hold the summit tomorrow night as I leave on Friday and she wants me there for support. She also wants me to call everyone so they don't ask why she's the one calling to invite them to my house. She emphasizes that under pain of death, I'm to make the invitation seem casual, so they don't know something big is coming. At the same time, I'm to insure they all know that they have to show up, no weaseling out. I envision it going something like this, "Mom? Dad? I'm having a little supper buffet at my house Thursday. What? No reason. Yes, Dad I know all your favorite programs are on Thursdays. Hmm, yes, well I can see how Friday would be better for you but I'm going to be out of town. Next Friday? No, I absolutely have to see you before then. Why? No reason."

But the bottom line is this is a small enough thing to do for my sister whose marriage is falling apart. After all, didn't I just yesterday say I would try to be the tiniest little bit less self-involved so I could help her through this time?

# Chapter 17

That fucking Edith Bunker is on my very last nerve today! "MeeeeeeMeeeeeeee, what about meeeeeeee?" Did you forget that you're supposed to wear the wedge? What about the loafers? MeeeeeeeeeMeeeeeeeeeee..."

So I gagged her. That's right, I take my right shoe off and tie a sock around her mouth to shut her up. The added bonus is that I've cut off the circulation in the top of my foot so I don't feel any pain at all. You could run over my toes with a truck and I wouldn't be any the wiser.

I start to think about tomorrow night and the Finnegan family council. Then I start to think about Friday when Elliot and I fly off to New York together. What will I serve (at the council), what will I wear (in New York)? What tortures are Stan and Ollie planning for me? Out of nowhere I get so hungry I have the urge to crawl under my desk to see if there are any spare nuts littering the vicinity from my South Beach days. Common sense tells me the janitor must have vacuumed in the last three weeks, so I opt to find a healthy snack for myself in the vending area.

Completely unconcerned that I may run into Elliot, I limp through the office, dragging Edith Bunker along to the break room where I purchase cheese and crackers. Then I put a few more coins in the slot and get some Fig Newtons. And as long as I'm in here alone, I decide to feed the machine once more and add a Three Musketeer's bar to the party. I rationalize my binge, by concluding cheese is good protein, figs are high in fiber and Three Musketeer's bars are so light they actually float in commercials.

Instead of hiding in my office to stuff my face, I sit right down at one of the little tables in the break room and start to munch my way into a less panicked state. Everyone in the family has promised to be at my house tomorrow night at seven. Ginger says she can't wait. Renée says she'll get a baby sitter for the kids so they can stay longer than an hour, and Dad never even mentions the Thursday line up. It's like they know something big is up because someone always has to reschedule something when we get together. Tomorrow night has to be the first time ever there's no conflict.

I have eaten all my snacks and realize if I don't go back to my office, I'm going to buy the peanut butter crackers next. I'm beginning to feel the need to unbutton my skirt and imagine what Marge would have to say if she saw me right now. As I go to walk out the door, Bob mysteriously shows up and blocks my path. I politely say, "Bob, will you excuse me? I'd like to leave."

He frantically declares, "Mimi, I'll leave my wife if that's what it'll take to have you! What do you think? Should I tell her about us so we're free to express our love?"

I answer, "Bob, what are you talking about? There is no us."

"There could be, if you'd only give me a chance. I could make you happy, Mimi. I know I could. I've been reading the Kama Sutra and I've gotten really good in bed. I know I could fulfill you if you'd just let me try."

I'm starting to really freak out here. I demand, "Bob, get out of my way before I scream!"

That's when he decides to try to physically persuade me of his prowess. Just as he is about to throw his arms around me, I hear, "Mimi, is there a problem here?"

I look up into the chilly eyes of Elliot Fielding. Elliot appears to be on the verge of beating Bob senseless and while I would very much like to see that happen, I answer, "I don't know, Elliot, let me find out." Then to my attacker, I ask, "Bob, is there a problem here?"

He mutters, "No."

Then I say, "Just to be clear, I am in no way interested in you. Do you understand?" He nods his head. "Nor will I become interested in you. Is this clear?" He nods again. To Elliot, I add, "I guess there's no problem then. But would you be so kind as to escort me back to my office? I would like to discuss some of the details of our trip with you."

Elliot leads the way and I'm seething as I follow behind. How dare Bob assault me like that? In all my years in the professional world I have never been treated in such an offensive manner. Ever. I'm still stomping my way behind Elliot when we get to my office. As soon as I follow him through the door, he shuts it behind me and then somehow manages to maneuver me up against it. Before I can say long live the queen, he leans in and clamps his mouth onto mine. Oh my sweet ever loving lord! Wow!!! His kiss is urgent and hot and all together, oh my! Where did this come from? But I can't think about that right now, I simply wrap my arms around his neck and reel him in like trophy fish. Elliot continues his passionate assault and I'm so dazed by it that I'm ready to peel his clothes off right there in my office. Apparently he has the same thought in mind, because the next thing I know my sweater has been lifted up over my head and I'm standing before him in my bra.

Elliot stops to look at what he's uncovered and gasps, "You're beautiful!" Then he's all over me again. Just as he gets my bra unclasped my intercom buzzes and I hear Jonathan say, "Meems, I'm on my way in. We need to discuss your itinerary for the trip." Then he adds, "I'll be in as soon as I find Elliot."

The intercom doesn't have any effect on us for several moments. Elliot comes to his senses before I do and slowly pulls himself together. As soon as we are no longer attached at the mouth, I also snap to and immediately lock the door so that my boss doesn't walk in on me half naked with our client, again. This saucy behavior seems to be becoming a habit with me.

As I struggle to redress before Jonathan arrives, Elliot regains his iron-clad British control and I don't like it one bit. The cold English prick is back, I can feel it. He clears his throat, and says, "Mimi, I'm terribly sorry. I didn't intend for anything like that to happen," as though he just stepped on my foot instead of ravishing me.

Well, now I'm just insulted. What? Did he slip on a banana peel and accidentally land on my face? Was I on fire and he had to whip off my top to keep the flames from consuming me? So I just stare daggers at him and ask, "What was it that you intended then, Elliot?"

He hems and haws and finally decides on, "I'm just so infuriated that Bob would dare to treat you so callously, as though your feelings weren't at all important."

"Yes, I see how what you did was so much more considerate. Thanks a bunch." The truth is I loved Elliot's kiss and if that damn intercom hadn't buzzed, I have no doubt I would currently be enjoying a lot more. But what really chaps my ass is he can act like it's all a mistake, like he didn't mean to do it. I want to shout, "Be accountable for your actions, you frosty dandy! Don't apologize you kissed me, apologize you didn't have time to finish it properly." Of course I don't say this to him, I merely finish tidying myself up and unlock the door so that Jonathan can get in. Then I plop down in my chair in a huff.

Elliot sits across from me and stares daggers right back at me. "Don't you get sarcastic with me. You liked what happened between us, in fact you loved it!"

I retort, "So did you and don't *you* forget it!"

Before either one of us can say anything else Jonathan walks in and declares, "I can't find him anywhere…" then he notices Elliot and says, "Mimi, why didn't you tell me he was already here?"

Elliot saves the day by announcing, "I was just walking by and Mimi called me in. She was just about to buzz you."

Jonathan says, "Well, then, let's get this meeting started, shall we?"

We spend the next fifteen minutes going over a list of our itinerary for our five days in New York. The trip will be full of parties, meetings, and book signings, but Jonathan declares that Monday night will be a free night so he has taken the liberty of securing us theater tickets so we can have a fun night out with no business obligations.

Elliot is the first to speak, "Thank you, Jonathan, but I might just need an evening alone after all the hob-nobbing."

As though I don't even hear him, I say, "That is so sweet, Jonathan. Elliot and I will be delighted to use the tickets."

Jonathan looks between us, finally catching on there are flaming spears flying across the room and stands up to excuse himself. As soon as he's gone I say, "Afraid to be alone with me, Elliot? Afraid you might not be able to keep your hands off of me?"

He glares back and replies, "Don't you worry. I can keep my hands to myself. The question is, can you?"

# Chapter 18

The family arrives in fifteen minutes and I swear I'm more nervous than Muffy, who isn't even here. It doesn't help that I hardly slept a wink last night. All I could think about were ways to execute revenge on Elliot. After all, how dare he regret our kiss? There is no way the frigid Beatrice ever kissed him with the wild abandon we shared and what does he do? He regrets it! I considered various forms of archaic torture, like tarring and feathering, before finally settling on old-fashioned death by seduction. Elliot is in for the time of his life in New York. I'd almost feel sorry for him if I weren't so furious at his stuck up English self.

After a miserable night's sleep, I couldn't wait to get out of bed this morning. I felt like the battling heroine in a Wagnerian opera. Yet unbeknownst to me, the powers that be decided that instead of an eight hour work day, today was going to run an atypical ninety-eight. It just dragged and dragged, and dragged, and dragged. And dragged…

Of course Elliot chickened out and didn't come into the office at all. Not that I expected him to. I'm sure he was spending his last moments in town with Beatrice trying to convince himself they are perfect for each other; which of course they are not. I have this new (ever since meeting Elliot) theory that Brits should never marry Brits because they just keep watering each other down. In another hundred years their whole society is going to be a bunch of righto, cheerio, pip-pip, polo playing, tea drinking, inbred, fops. Did I mention boring? Cause they'll be boring too and icy. God, they're an arctic lot.

I firmly believe the English need to shake up their gene pool. I'm thinking as a goodwill gesture we should ship a bunch of our wild American singles across the pond to bring some fire back to their civilization. Perhaps that will be my own personal PR project that I work on for my country. Private Finnegan reporting for duty! In grateful appreciation they can promise to quit looking down their noses at us.

Mom and Dad are the first to arrive and even though I told them not to bring anything, Mom is toting a tuna casserole, yum, and Dad is hauling a case of Guinness and Mom's purse. My dad has been carrying my mother's purse for as long as I can remember. It's one of the many sweet memories I have of him, Dad in a navy suit dressed for mass, carrying a black and white patent leather handbag, Dad in jeans and a sweater carrying a brown leather saddle purse with fringe, Dad in shorts and a t-shirt schlepping around a turquoise beaded pocket book. He never seems to mind either. It occurred to me long ago that my mom should start matching her purses to Dad's outfits instead of her own.

My mom kisses me on the cheek and greets, "Meems, your

hair is gorgeous, you're a natural redhead!"

Dad throws in, "You know your Grandma Sissy was a redhead and so was my Aunt Barb. Uncle Patty was a redhead, and then there was…" I start to tune him out as this litany could go on for hours. We are Irish, after all.

Renée and Laurent show up next, sans the wee ones. They both look a little frazzled as they just discovered Camille painted her closet with eight jars of raspberry jam from the pantry. Renée has finished a Guinness before I can even say hello to her. She compliments me on my hair and outfit and declares LeRon and Fernando will be devastated if I ever go elsewhere for my clothes again.

Ginger and Jonathan arrive next and they are not alone. They've brought Elliot and Beatrice with them. Why, you ask? Ginger tells me she thought it was just an informal family gathering and decided it would be nice for Beatrice to meet a group of Elliot's friends before going home.

Beatrice greets me with the warmth of a sleet storm. I'm about to offer her a laxative to correct her tight-assed disposition when Kevin shows up. I'm shocked by his appearance and ask, "What are you doing here? We're not working out tonight."

He hands me a bottle of wine and answers, "It's nice to see you too and Muffy invited me, so let me in. She said she could use all the moral support she can get."

Elliot is ignoring me to the point of pretending I'm not even in the room. Beatrice has latched onto Kevin, and Muffy is still nowhere in sight. So I decide to go ahead and put out the food on the table so people can at least eat dinner before the bomb is dropped. Yet I wonder if Muffy will still share her news now that Elliot and Beatrice, the beast, are here.

My sister finally shows up forty minutes later, still in her tennis clothes. She pops upstairs for a quick shower and change and once she's greeted everyone, she jumps right in with her news (even though there are foreigners in the room, one she hasn't even met before.) She says, "I asked Mimi to invite you all over because I have something to tell you …" Everyone waits with bated breath. She takes a fortifying gulp of air and continues, "Tom and I are getting divorced."

The room is dead quiet. Here's something you should know about Catholics. We, as a people, are against divorce to the point of absurdity. Old school Catholics like my parents will tell you that you've made your bed, so you've no choice but to lie in it. I've heard this pearl of wisdom my whole life. Every single time one of my friend's parents got divorced, they trotted it out. Alcoholic, wife-beater, transvestite, hop head, no matter the reason cited, they always declared that it was a bed of their own making.

So it is beyond shocking when my mother blurts out, "About fucking time!"

My dad adds a "Here, here!" And the gathering takes on an almost festive air.

My family as a whole rallies around my sister and declares Tom was never good enough for her anyway. Mom thinks he was shifty and Dad never trusted him because he drank micro-brews. Even Laurent jumps on board declaring that a man who won't eat cheese is no man at all. Beatrice is so enamored with Kevin that she doesn't even pay attention to the family drama and Elliot looks decidedly uncomfortable as the scene is simply too real for his delicate English sensibilities.

I take the opportunity to raise my glass and toast, "Here's to marriage. May none of us ever marry the wrong one!" I shift my gaze to Elliot and he is not toasting. Beatrice however, lifts her glass high right before snuggling back up to Kevin who seems to be enjoying the beast's attention. But you can tell his focus is on Muffy and Muffy alone.

Muffy reveals that Tom has been servicing the older ladies at the club and the Finnegans demand revenge! They start to visualize a river of his blood. It's all Dad can do not to go right down to that fancy pants country club and demand satisfaction for his offspring. But Muffy assures them they shouldn't worry about her. She's better off without the bastard.

More beer, more wine, and more food are passed and finally by ten o'clock I tell my family to hit the bricks. I have an early flight and I need my rest. Elliot disengages his intended from Kevin's side and is the first to say his farewells. Yet he says nothing to me. No "Thanks for the KFC," no "You have a lovely home," no "I'm leaving Beatrice because I ache for you," nothing.

My family disperses next and finally, finally, my marathon day is ending and I get to take a bubble bath. As I lay back in the scented foam, I realize that Edith Bunker has not said one word to me today and I couldn't be more grateful. I can barely retain consciousness long enough to crawl into bed and turn the light off. I feel more exhausted than ever before and yearn for the sweet bliss of a dreamless night's sleep.

That's when I hear it, "MeeeeeeeeeeMeeeeeeeeee...you

didn't wear your wedge again today. Why do you want to hurt me? What did I ever do to you? MeeeeeeeeeeeeMeeeeeeeeeeeee…"

Goddamned bunion! I shout, "Shut up, Edith Bunker, and go to sleep!"

But she doesn't stop. She keeps on with the, "Wear your loafers…British men like loafers…why won't you help me? You didn't even exercise for me today. And what about those Fig Newton's and candy bar yesterday? Why would you do that to me?" On and on she goes, nagging and stabbing at me all night long. It feels like I've just fallen asleep when the alarm rings and insists that I get out of bed before I miss my flight.

# Chapter 19

By the time I check my luggage and get to the gate, it's only thirty minutes before the flight is scheduled to leave. I'm in jeans so I can wear my blasted loafers and silicone insert. I do this to appease Edith Bunker. I'm desperate for sleep and it's my hope to catch a nap on the plane so I can be in good form by the time we get to New York. We have the first of three parties tonight and I would like not to look like a zombie.

Elliot is already seated on the plane by the time I board. He doesn't even look up from his paper when he says, "I thought perhaps you decided not to come."

I merely squeeze past him and plop down in the seat to his right. We are flying first class which is a total and complete luxury for me and I'm only sorry I don't plan on staying awake long enough to enjoy it. So he tries, "Lovely party last night," sarcasm dripping from his every syllable.

I don't have the energy to do battle with him this morning so I merely close my eyes and fall into a blissful slumber. I'm so far gone I don't have any recollection of the take-off. I'm just lost in the arms of the sandman and it's pure heaven.

As I begin to drift slowly back into consciousness I realize I slept as well as if I were in my own bed. The pillows are warm and soft. I snuggle my face deeper into one. Yet, as I burrow in I realize mine has a hard lump in it. I grind my face into it further trying to redistribute the feathers so that they are nice and soft again. But the more I try to fluff them the harder they get. That's when I hear the stewardess say, "Sir, your wife is going to have to sit up now, we're about to land."

His wife? Is that fricken Beatrice on board? Then I remember that Beatrice is going back to England today and she has mistaken me for Elliot's wife. Oh, how nice is that? But what does she mean, I have to sit up? Snuggling into my lumpy pillow again, it occurs to me that I'm laying down. Then it occurs to me that the arm rest between us must have been lifted because I am in fact lying on Elliot's lap and the hard pillow that I'm snuggling my face into isn't actually a pillow at all. And the reason it keeps getting harder is because... hello! Elliot Fielding is not as immune to me as he would like us both to believe. Before I sit up, I purposefully put my hands under my cheek and cop a brazen feel. Then I push up and stare into the eyes of the man who has allowed me to sleep on him for the past two hours.

Elliot looks like he's in pain, pure physical, glorious, aching agony! He groans, "Did you have a nice nap?"

Relishing my power, I answer, "It was delicious. I hope I wasn't a bother."

Groaning in response, he mumbles, "No, no bother at all."

"Oh, Elliot," I think, "you are about to have the most excruciating five days of your life. Do yourself a favor and break it off with Beatrice so we can get down to business."

Our cab ride from LaGuardia is another conversation-less trip but I don't care. I'm busy taking in the beauty of the Manhattan skyline and once we hit the Verrazano Bridge I nearly shake from excitement. Elliot, the seasoned traveler, merely reads his paper as though he drives into this fabulous city every day. His air of ennui makes me want to slap him and scream, "Get over yourself and look out the window! Have you ever seen anything like this before?"

He'd probably respond, "Yes, quite right, lovely and all that rot." So I don't say anything else to him.

When we arrive at The Plaza, I'm in jeopardy of fainting. It's everything I ever thought it would be and more. The movies have never done it justice because there is an energy humming through this place you simply have to experience in the flesh. Everyone is so sleek and stylish and it occurs to me how glad I am to be wearing my famous sister's designs. I look like I fit in with this crowd of sophisticates even though my insides are spastically performing a happy dance and I'm wearing loafers.

Once we check in, the bellhop loads our luggage onto his cart and takes us to our rooms, which are conveniently right next door to each other. They are also conveniently connected which is something Elliot doesn't know yet. I declare that I'm starving and tell him to be ready in an hour for lunch. He suggests perhaps he'll just order room service and I say, "Nonsense, we need to discuss our schedule." Then add, "We are here on a business trip after all."

He shoots me a look that says, "Keep telling yourself that."

Then he disappears into his room.

My room is not the palatial space that I had imagined, but it's lovely nonetheless. Drum roll please, I have a view of Central Park. If I look hard I'm sure I can see Carrie Bradshaw strolling through the trees with her girlfriends gossiping about the single scene in New York.

Here's the deal with me and *Sex and the City*. I went the whole six years it was on the air, never catching a single episode. I was convinced the entire serial was about a bunch of floozies just banging their way into spinsterhood. I was sure I had absolutely nothing in common with them. It wasn't until I came down with the flu that Muffy brought over her complete DVD collection and told me in no uncertain terms to watch them. My sisters had been fans all along. Perhaps this is one of the perverse reasons I didn't bother watching the show sooner. After all, if they related to it, how could I possibly hope to as well?

Anyway, I viewed the whole series in three days and I now cite the show as if it were a literary classic. You know how some people will quote Dickens and Shakespeare? I quote *Sex and the City*. "Carrie Bradshaw says...oh, now, Charlotte says never to do that...Miranda has a point about..." I have yet to quote Samantha because my sex life has been so polar opposite to hers I just haven't found the proper occasion to reference her, yet. I'm not giving up.

While daydreaming about *Sex and the City*, I wonder what Carrie would make of Elliot. Certainly he's no Mr. Big, as Big was the consummate bad boy and Elliot can't be bothered being bad. Although to give him his due it must be hard having a proverbial cob stuck up his ass. We Americans are not proper, uptight aristocrats by nature. So maybe I should cut him a bit of slack.

The bathroom is very nice but I can't help myself from scanning it for stray hairs. I'm a real stickler for cleanliness. Ever since I saw that *Dateline* special report, I search my lodgings for things like chewed gum, stray hairs and the more obvious stains that I choose not to think about for too long. My room simply won't feel like mine until I know that all visible traces of its last occupant have been obliterated. But no surprises here, The Plaza doesn't let me down. It's spic and span and ready for action.

I take a quick shower, reapply my make up, and change into a flirty summer dress before knocking on Elliot's door, exactly fifty-eight minutes later. He's on the phone when he answers, so I just walk in and sit down on his bed to wait for him. I hear him say, "Yes, well...but still...don't you think you should be getting back?" Pause to listen to the person on the other end. "I understand that you're having a nice time...yes, I'm glad for you...well then, if that's how you feel...alright, I'll see you when I get back then. Yes...bye."

Then he hangs up and I ask, "Your mechanic?"

He shoots me a look, "Beatrice."

Shocked, I ask, "She's not going back to England today?"

"She appears to be having such a nice time with your friend Kevin, she's decided to stay another week."

I just stare at him with my eyes bugged out and ask, "Kevin, what does Kevin have to do with anything?" Thinking, I'm gonna kill the bastard.

He answers, "Apparently he offered to take her to the miniature museum next week and Beatrice loves nothing as much as tiny little replicas of things." Obviously, she's not a big fan of napping on Elliot's lap then.

I manage to utter, "How fascinating." Stan and Ollie demand to know, "How did you and Beatrice meet?"

Elliot replies, "Doing research for a book. She works for a barrister I was interviewing for "Deadly Tortes.""

Relying on humor to break the tension, I say, "When I first saw that book on the newsstand, I thought it was an odd name for a cookbook."

He cracks the tiniest of smiles and declares, "Where shall we have lunch then?"

I don't know any restaurants in New York City and being we're going to be cooped up inside for the next several days, I suggest we grab a hot dog in the park.

Elliot replies, "I know just the place. Come on." He leads me through the hotel, out the door, and straight into Central Park. We pass about fifteen hot dog carts and I comment on each one, but he has another destination in mind. What surprises me the most about our walk is that Elliot and I actually have a lovely conversation with no combative undertones. I suppose even vinegar and oil can't always keep from mixing. After all, if you slowly drizzle vinegar into oil, beating it the whole time, it emulsifies beautifully.

During the next twenty minutes, I learn things about Elliot I would have never expected. For instance, every time one of his books comes out, he's convinced that it will bomb so badly people will demand their money back. I also learn that he's afraid of snails, due to a particularly nasty childhood prank. He loves espresso and considers Stephen King to be one of the great authors of our time. This last nugget being perhaps the most incongruous information I discover about him. One would think Elliot Fielding would have a taste for more obscure and cosmopolitan fare.

I confess more of myself to him as well. For instance, I tell him how I've always felt inferior to my sisters. He's an attentive audience so I go on to list all of their many accomplishments. I am deathly afraid of flying beetles. I spray canned whipped cream straight into my mouth while perusing my refrigerator for dinner and I feel that perhaps Sophie Kinsella is one of the great literary minds of our time.

He helps by adding, "And you have a talking bunion named Edith Bunker."

I agree, "Perhaps the worst thing about me."

He suggests, "But it makes you singularly individual, don't you think?"

"I'm afraid a criminal profiler might suggest that it makes me the obvious choice for a mass murderer."

He considers this and responds, "Is she telling you to kill people?"

With raised eyebrows, I answer, "Not yet, but I'll keep you posted." We have finally arrived at our destination. I have seen this place many times in the movies but somehow didn't really realize it truly existed outside of the silver screen. We are going to eat at the restaurant by the boating pond, smack in the middle of Central Park. Once we're seated, I look at Elliot and exclaim, "This restaurant has been in about a million movies. I can't believe we're actually eating here."

Elliot appears to be delighted by my enthusiasm and says, "You are a lot of fun to spend time with. Did you know that, Mimi Finnegan?"

The truth is I didn't know that. Certainly Linden never said so. But I never felt like I could be myself with him. And for some strange reason, I'm sitting with a man about a million times more impressive than Linden Fairbanks and I can't seem to help being myself. I mean, Elliot even knows about Edith Bunker and he's not running in the other direction. I don't feel any of the crazy sexual tension that's been lurking between us from day one either. What I feel is the beginning of another surprising emotion. I like Elliot Fielding and not just in the "want to get him horizontal" kind of way, I truly like him as a person. I realize I'm going to have to be very careful with my heart here. I could fall for this man in a big way and as long as he's involved with another woman, I had best try to keep my distance.

# Chapter 20

Elliot and I have a wonderful lunch and an invigorating walk back to the hotel. I try to watch my points as I'm missing a weigh-in tomorrow, but I'm not a fiend about it. After all, I'm sure I will get plenty of exercise this week, walking around this fabulous city.

Parliament's New York office is throwing a drinks party for Elliot tonight to introduce him to the key players on his PR team. We are due at the president of the firm's apartment at 6:30 and will be joining him and his wife for dinner afterwards. I am a little worried about the evening ahead as the PR game in Pipsy is a million time less cut-throat than the one in New York. I really want to make a good impression on everyone and first impressions being what they are, I feel a lot of pressure to be spectacular.

I wear one of the dresses Renée designed. Actually, the only clothes I brought with me are ones that she designed. The dress is a shortish black cocktail number with a whimsical fluttering hem that hits about three inches above the knee. It is sleeveless with a relatively low neckline. I accessorize with a simple strand of pearls and matching earrings. I am striving for understated elegance and am surprised when I look in the mirror as the reflection is one of a beautiful, curvaceous Amazon with fiery tresses. The not so impressive sister, with dirty blonde hair and fifteen more pounds to lose isn't anywhere to be seen.

I'm just spritzing myself with Eau de Adrienne when Elliot knocks. He looks like James Bond in his black suit and once again I'm hit with a blinding wave of lust. I want to jump him and ravish him, but first I want to go out with him and show him off to the world.

It turns out Marcus Goldman lives only a few blocks from The Plaza but we take a cab in deference to Edith Bunker, who is not at all pleased by tonight's choice in footwear. A liveried doorman opens the door to the Fifth Avenue apartment building and yet another one checks us off the guest list. We are shown to a small elevator that will take us directly to the Goldmans' penthouse. As Elliot and I (especially in heels) are well above average in size, we find ourselves standing very close together in the small space. By the twelfth floor I am leaning closer towards him, by the seventeenth, he's returning the favor, and by the twenty seventh, the blasted doors slide apart and we're there.

I feel like I'm in the movies again as the elevator opens directly into the Goldmans' foyer, not the hallway outside. Surely this is a luxury reserved for only the wealthiest of people and I find myself a bit awed. A maid offers us champagne and by the time we each have a drink a dapper older gentleman with silver hair and a brilliant smile descends upon us,

"Welcome, welcome, I'm Marcus Goldman." Marcus shakes Elliot's hand and declares, "We are beyond delighted to be handling your next book, Elliot." Then he turns to me and kisses my hand, "And you must be Mimi." His gaze travels appreciatively over my person, "Why are you being hidden away in Pipsy? You should be working in the New York office." A brief thrill runs through me at the thought of actually living in New York and working at Parliament here.

As Marcus leads the way to his palatial living room, Elliot leans in and accuses, "You let him kiss your hand. I thought for sure when he tried to put his lips on you, you would have punched him in the nose."

I pinch his arm, "Elliot, shoosh! Marcus Goldman is my boss's boss and he can kiss my hand anytime he wants."

Elliot gets a naughty look in his eye and retorts, "But only your hand." I know he's trying to be funny, but he is also jealous. I realize I can make this work for me. In fact the only time Elliot has ever tried to kiss me himself was when he saw another man, namely Bob, go after me. Well maybe that'll give him an idea of how I feel when I see him with Beatrice. And just like that, I'm mad again. How dare he be all possessive of me when he's nearly engaged to another woman? He may actually *be* engaged for all I know. Maybe he asked the beast to marry him before we came to New York. He might have done it anytime. Just because he didn't propose at La Petite Maison doesn't mean he didn't do it afterwards. I'm furious at the thought!

A foggy plan begins to take shape in my mind. I am going to trap Elliot Fielding by flirting my way through New York and showing him once and for all what he's missing. If that doesn't wake him up and make him realize he wants me too, I'm not sure anything will. With a smile on my face, I sidle up against Marcus and let him introduce us around.

Elliot and I are both bombarded by members of the opposite sex. It's like we're the chum and everyone at this party is a hungry pod of killer sharks. Elliot is swept away by a bevy of women from his "team" and as much as I try to keep an eye on him, I lose him as the men circle me. It's all very flattering actually, as I have never elicited this kind of response in the past. But still it's hard to enjoy myself when I can't see what Elliot is up to.

At eight o'clock the party disperses and Marcus leads Elliot and me out to his balcony where a gorgeous table for four has been laid. Marcus holds my chair for me and Elliot does the same for Mrs. Goldman, who interestingly enough is named Miriam as well, although she actually goes by Miriam and not the abbreviated Mimi.

During our soup course, Marcus outlines his plans for Elliot's book. He talks about the parties, the book signings, the movie premieres, all the things that go into keeping a famous author in the public eye. His book sales will climb in accord with his increasing public appearances.

By the entrée, Miriam starts to veer the conversation away from business. She asks me if there is a special someone in my life. With a brief glance at Elliot, I answer, "Not at the moment."

Then she announces to Elliot, "And I hear from Marcus you're newly engaged. How exciting! How did you do it?"

Elliot appears to be immensely uncomfortable and answers, "I don't know where you got your information, Miriam, but it's not accurate."

Marcus looks up, "Really? Jonathan told me last week you were on the verge of becoming shackled. Haven't asked her yet, huh?"

Desperate for a new topic, Elliot replies, "No, Marcus, and in all honesty I can't say we are headed for marriage."

Miriam casually comments, "Then why date her? I mean, after all, the only reason women bother dating is to get married. Don't you agree, Mimi?"

"Yes," I confirm. "There's no point in seeing someone for an extended time if you aren't planning a future with them."

Marcus interrupts, "You women leave Elliot alone. He's single, famous, and richer than all get out. Let him enjoy himself, why don't you."

Miriam responds, "I'm just saying it's not fair to the woman. When we reach a certain age, we start to think about husbands and babies. We don't have time to waste dating someone who isn't going to make an honest woman out of us."

Marcus replies, "Miriam, my dear. I'm not at all sure Elliot is used to our plain spoken American ways. I think perhaps we're making him uncomfortable."

Warming to the topic, I ask, "Are you uncomfortable, Elliot?"

With a grimace he answers, "A bit, yes."

I smile at him brilliantly, "Good." And with that one word, Elliot's and my eight-hour truce is over. I've declared war and he realizes he's not in Switzerland (or Kansas) anymore. No hope of standing on the sidelines in this battle.

Elliot and I leave the Goldmans' at eleven-thirty. The elevator ride on the way down to street level couldn't be more dissimilar to the ride up. Even though we are nearly standing shoulder to shoulder, we might as well be on opposite sides of a football field. My battle plan involves acting like nothing is wrong, so I ask, "Did you have a nice evening?"

He responds, "It was fine. It was work, so I wasn't actually intending on having fun."

"I had a great time," I tell him. "I met some of the most interesting people."

"Yes, I know you did, Mimi. Several men seemed to have made asses out of themselves trying to get your attention."

My face lights up. "Really? Which ones? I am single after all and have reached the age when thoughts of husbands and babies fill most of my waking hours."

Elliot curtly responds, "I'm sure you won't have any difficulty once you set your sights on someone."

Scrunching my face up in confusion, I answer, "You'd think. Yet I'm not finding it easy at all." That's it, gauntlet dropped. I have as good as declared myself.

My companion slams his mouth shut and cuts me off from all further conversation.

When the cabbie takes a hard right on Central Park South, I allow myself to slide into Elliot. I stay pressed up against him for the remaining half block and then gingerly glide my hand down his leg and push back to my own seat. I hear him let out a low growl as one of the many Plaza employees opens the car door for me. Elliot and I take the elevator up to our rooms together but there is still no talking. He bids me good night at my door but clearly his mind is on other things. So I lean into him and slowly kiss him on the cheek, "Thank you for a lovely day, Elliot."

As I pull away he stares at me long and hard and bends the tiniest bit closer to me. After an eternity, he closes the distance even more and gently presses his lips to mine, "I had a lovely time too." Then he pulls away, "Sleep well."

I walk into my room and think, "Sleep? I'm so beyond worked up, there's no way I'm going to be able to sleep." But once my makeup is off, and I've slipped into my nightie, I feel totally worn out. All the excitement from the day has finally caught up with me. I'm so exhausted I don't even eat the chocolate on my pillow, which I calculate is worth two points. I merely move it aside and crawl into the crisply ironed sheets. I'm sound asleep before my head even hits the pillow.

# Chapter 21

Edith Bunker starts ripping into me before I'm even fully awake. "MeeeeeeeMeeeeeeee, it's weigh-in day! Go find out how much you lost...cause it doesn't feel like much to me. MeeeeeeeMeeeeeeee..."

I tell her to shut up, that I have Marge's permission to skip my weigh-in this week because I'm out of town. She tries to guilt me into it by saying there are Weight Watchers branches in Manhattan, too. But I tell her I don't have my weight chart with me and they won't let me on a scale without it. This information shuts her up momentarily, but she's clearly not happy.

Once Edith Bunker quiets down, I open my eyes and the first conscious thought that hits me is, "I'm in New York. I jump out of bed, pull my curtains back and gaze lovingly at the street below. It's only seven o'clock but already the sidewalk is teeming with people. I briefly wonder where they're all going this early in the morning. Probably out for bagels and coffee. Suddenly, I'm ravenously hungry for an onion bagel.

I knock on Elliot's connecting door to see if he's up yet,

but there's no answer. I knock once more for good measure. Then I walk into my bathroom and start the shower running. But just as I'm about to strip off my nightie I see another reflection in the mirror and I let out a blood-curdling scream! Then I realize it's just Elliot and accuse, "How did you get in here?!"

"The connecting door. I heard a knock and when you didn't answer when I called out your name, I decided to come in and make sure that you were okay."

I respond, "Well I'm fine, except you've just taken three years off my life."

He apologizes and says, "Listen, I just got a call from Marcus and our ten o'clock appointment has been moved up to nine so I don't think we're going to have time to eat breakfast in a restaurant."

I tell him about my onion bagel craving and he offers to go out and get us a genuine New York City bagel with coffee while I get showered and dressed. He tells me to just pop through our connecting door when I'm ready and we can eat in his room.

As soon as Elliot leaves, I realize how really comfortable I am with him. I'm not in the least bit embarrassed he saw me without my hair and makeup done. I mean he's already seen me before my transformation, so it's not like he doesn't know what the real me looks like. While I'm shampooing my hair I realize how intimate it was talking to him in my bathroom. It felt very domestic and right, like we should always be able to do it, like we could if we were in a relationship together. I briefly wonder if he and Beatrice talk while one of them is in the shower and I nearly rub my scalp raw at the thought.

I dress in cream palazzo pants with a matching shell and a navy blazer. Staring at my reflection in the mirror, I think I look very East Coast yacht club. The good news for Edith Bunker is in this ensemble I can wear a conservative heel which allows room for her silicone pad. I accessorize in gold today which looks fabulous with my new red hair. And speaking of my new red hair, I blow it out straight and wear it long down my back. I feel like a Miss Breck girl of yore.

I grab my brief case and purse and open the connecting door to discover Elliot has set up breakfast on his little table overlooking the park. Staring out at the view, breathing in the fresh aroma of warm bagels, and sitting across from Elliot Fielding, I wonder if life could get any better. Then his cell phone rings and I remember it would be oh-so-much grander without Beatrice.

Elliot answers, "Good morning Beatrice. How are you today?" He listens to her talk for a very long time before adding, "Yes, I am. It's lovely here." Listen, listen, listen. "Yes, I'm aware you're not fond of it here but I am... Okay then, goodbye."

I look at him with my eyebrow raised in a question mark and he says, "My mechanic."

I decide to ignore his attempt at humor because all of a sudden I'm not feeling all warm and cheerful towards him. Leave it to Beatrice to pop my bubble. I'm going to have to call Kevin later and see if he wouldn't mind eloping with her while we're still in New York.

Our meeting this morning is with Elliot's New York agent,

Eliza Finch, and his editor from Dell, Maynard Stafford. They fill us in on the details of tonight's party which has been set up by his publisher. Parliament will contribute to the success of the event by bringing in press and celebrities. Elliot also has a book signing tomorrow morning at McJ Books and another one tomorrow afternoon in the Village. By the time our summit is over it's eleven-thirty. Marcus thanks everyone for coming and then invites Elliot to join him at his club for lunch. I'm not exactly sure what I'm supposed to do with myself, but clearly I have not been invited to join them. Elliot gives me a look as if to ask if I mind if he goes with Marcus, but how can I say no? So I just smile and declare, "I think I'm going to do a little shopping." I have no intention of doing any such thing, as I'm saving up for a new hot water heater, but I don't want to look pathetic and destination-less like I am. So I catch a cab back to the hotel and change into some casual pants and sneakers and decide to traipse around the city in comfort.

My first stop is a sidewalk café on Madison Avenue. The prices are shockingly steep, but I couldn't care less as I'm simply going to expense it. While I consider myself a very self-assured woman, the truth is I hate eating alone in public. I'm never sure what to look at. I don't want other diners' to feel like I'm staring at them and then if I just sit and read a book, what's the point of going out? Plus, I get really caught up in the conversations happening around me. To the point where I want to approach other diner's tables and add my two cents, "If I were you, I'd divorce the bastard. I mean it's bad enough he likes to wear women's underwear, but to stretch out your

LaPerla panties? That's just crossing the line." Plus when I eat alone, I feel like I wind up being seated near the kitchen door like a total loser.

But here in fabulous New York City, I'm seated right outside in the bright light of day with the world to look at as they walk by. There are the wealthy East Side ladies out for an afternoon of boutique shopping, the hardworking moms who are trying to catch up on all their errands, using their strollers as batting rams and then there are the bridge and tunnel people who have made the daily trek from New Jersey or Long Island.

As I scan the menu for something that can be translated into points, I settle on the Ahi Tuna Steak with the Miso Crème Fraiche (on the side please) and the steamed vegetables (no butter). I order a passion fruit ice tea and settle in to enjoy the best show on earth, not the circus, the New Yorkers.

I dive into my food when it arrives like I haven't eaten in a month. The truth is the half bagel I just had for breakfast wasn't that filling. Marge says a full bagel is enough to feed twelve starving African children for a week. But of course she's just trying to get us to see the reality of a true portion. The Ahi is divine and I nearly moan in pleasure. I close my eyes and savor every bite. I chew slowly and thoroughly so as not to miss any of the flavor sensation passing my lips. Even the vegetables are delicious, firm without being underdone and the most vibrant colors imaginable.

When my waiter clears my plate I order a fat-free, decaf, iced cappuccino for dessert. But before it arrives, something, or should I say someone else does. A very distinguished and good looking gentleman, in what I'm assuming is his mid-forties, is standing by my table carrying a ramekin of Crème Brûlée and a bowl filled with Peach Cobbler à la mode. He asks if he can join me. I have absolutely no idea how to respond, so I ask, "Excuse me?"

He answers, "I just wondered if I could join you for dessert." He smiles and indicates the plates he's holding, "I've brought my own so I really won't be any bother."

Normally I would have sent someone like this packing, but who am I kidding? Normally something like this would never happen to me. There's something about this man, so non-threatening and charming, I just gesture to the seat across from me and tilt my head to the side in invitation.

His name is Richard Bingham and he's an advertising executive at Bingham, Charles & Alexander. And yes, he is the Bingham in the title. He says, "I loved watching you eat your lunch. You really savored the flavors."

I am immediately mortified by his comment as I can only imagine what I must have looked like. I get an image in my head of a phone sex commercial for 1-800 Eat-This. I grimace and beg, "Please tell me you were not watching me eat."

But he just smiles, "I couldn't take my eyes off of you. That's why I brought the desserts over. I can die a happy man if you'll just take one bite of each of them for me."

I'm torn between jumping over the table and fleeing down the street and feeling down right flattered by Richard's unique approach. I opt for flattered and explain, "Richard, I would love more than anything to eat both desserts in their entirety, but I can't." Then shock of shocks, I tell him why, "I'm on

Weight Watchers and I'm sure even one bite of those will cause me to gain back the five pounds I've lost."

He looks surprised, "What are you doing on a diet? You're perfect the way you are. You're a gorgeous woman."

I can tell he means what he's saying and I offer a silent prayer of thanks that curves have not really gone out of fashion like Hollywood would have you believe. So I continue to bare my soul and I tell him about Edith Bunker. Then I mention, "She's bound and determined I lose this last fifteen pounds."

He seems amused and asks, "She talks to you, does she?"

I joke, "In French…"

This Richard Bingham seems to think I'm a delightful companion and I must confess to being a little charmed by him, as well. He asks me out to dinner tonight but I tell him I have a previous engagement. I also explain I am not from New York so while I think he's a very charming man, sadly, I'm only going to be around for three more days.

He replies, "I could go home with you on Wednesday and we could be married over the weekend. What do you think?"

I can't help laughing at his easy quips and confess the truth is I happen to be on the verge of being in love with another. Half way through my cappuccino and two bites of each dessert later, I tell him all about Elliot and Beatrice.

Richard listens thoughtfully and declares, "What you need to do is make him jealous."

I agree and tell him I had planned on doing just that. He suggests I invite him to this evening's party and he will work diligently to make Elliot green with envy. Although, he assures me he will be working for his own cause, first and foremost; to show me I really belong with him and not a man that isn't making himself available to me.

I only half joke when I tell Richard if he had only found me before I found Elliot, he could have been the one. I declare I've got my heart set on the Englishman, but if he really wants to help, he's more than welcome to come tonight. I pull an invitation out of my purse and hand it over to him.

He puts it in his breast pocket and assures me that he'll be there. When we say goodbye, he gives me a brief kiss on both cheeks and he's gone, leaving me to wonder if I dreamt the whole interlude.

# Chapter 22

Before going back to the hotel I window shop for a couple of hours. I go into an exclusive chocolate shop and buy several small boxes of fancy truffles for my family and then I stop at a newsstand and buy Kevin an "I heart New York" t-shirt. I know he'd prefer the chocolates but as his Weight Watchers buddy, I'm invested in working towards his ultimate goal. Speaking of Kevin Beeman, I start to wonder what's going on with him and the beast, so I call his cell phone.

He laughingly answers on the third ring, "Yellllloooooowww?"

I hear high-pitched giggles in the background and ask, "Kevin, what's going on? Who's laughing?"

He immediately sobers up and exclaims, "Mimi! How's New York?" So I tell him everything. Then I ask whose laughing and he mysteriously answers, "Just a friend."

I ask if the friend is Beatrice and he assures me it's not. Then I ask if he'd consider marrying her and moving off to Bangladesh before we get home on Wednesday. He laughs and declares Beatrice is a very nice person and if I weren't trying to steal her boyfriend, I would think so as well. I sense a little judgment on his part so I call him on it, "Kevin, are you saying I should back off and just let her have Elliot?"

He apologizes, "No, Meems, that's not it. It's just that she's really a tragic character, kind of like me and she's not a bad person. That's all I'm saying."

"Kevin Beeman, you are not tragic! I refuse to let you say things like that about yourself."

He declares, "Okay, how's this? I was tragic, but I'm not anymore."

I agree that sounds better and I promise to call him again before I come home. I also remind him to keep working out and he assures me he has been.

I don't get back to the hotel until five which gives me two hours to get ready. I call the concierge and ask if they can get me a last minute hair appointment. I'd like to wear my hair up tonight and the only updo I know how to execute involves a banana clip. Frederick confirms the salon will be expecting me in ten minutes.

When he's done with my hair, my stylist, Renaldo, suggests I let them do my makeup as well and in a caution to the wind moment, I agree. Why not? After all, I have to look my best if I'm going to have Elliot on his knees.

The dress I've chosen to wear is a floor-length red gown. I like to think of as the updated version of the dress Julia Roberts wore in *Pretty Woman*, and while I don't have diamonds hanging at my neck, I'm not sure I need them. I stand in the mirror and just stare at the vision before me. It's not only the change of hair color I'm seeing either. It's a change of attitude. It's a change of mannerisms, even. It's as though I'm a snake that has outgrown its skin, shedding the old for the new.

I knock on Elliot's door but he doesn't answer. So I call the front desk and ask if there are any messages for me. I'm told there's one from a Mr. Fielding. There's been a change of plan and he's going to meet me at the party, but a car will still pick me up at seven. To say that I'm disappointed would be an understatement. To say that I'm angry would be an understatement. I am full-blown enraged Elliot has something more important to do than escort me to his party. Even if I'm not his girlfriend I did travel all this way with him as his PR person. One would think common courtesy dictates that he treat me with a little more respect.

I take the elevator down to the lobby by myself and ask the concierge if my car has arrived. In a very *Sex and the City* moment, I'm led to a Lincoln Town Car, and then helped in. A formal Saturday night out in New York City has to be the most exciting thing that's ever happened to me. I feel like I'm floating on cloud nine. Edith Bunker hasn't complained once tonight which surprises me as I'm currently in three inch heels. I'm guessing she's been placated by a day of relative comfort. I even begin to wonder if Stan and Ollie missed the flight as there have been no signs of either of them.

The car pulls up to an art gallery in SoHo, which has been rented out for the evening, and I feel like Cinderella stepping out of her carriage. I walk into the party by myself and am immediately approached by two of the men I chatted with at last night's meet and greet. Both of whom happen to be much shorter than my current six-foot-two inch stature. I wonder what it is about short men that demands they approach the tallest woman in the room and try to romance her. I am not a height snob, but the truth is I feel like I'm being hit on by the neighbor boys I used to babysit. I peer effortlessly over both of their heads looking for any sign of Elliot but I don't see him anywhere. Who I do see is Richard and I can't help but smile. When he notices me, he makes a grab for his heart as though I've just stolen it.

He glides across the room towards me as if I am the Pussy Galore to his James Bond. The two men I am flanked by immediately sense they have been replaced by bigger game and disappear. Richard does not kiss my hand but rather pulls me into his embrace and whispers into my ear, "You look positively gorgeous tonight."

I whisper back, "Elliot isn't here yet so you can relax." The truth is, Richard looks pretty darn terrific too. He is dressed in a black tuxedo and wears it as comfortably as most wear jeans and a t-shirt. He is one of those elegant men who are perfectly comfortable at grand affairs and I find myself a little awed by him.

Richard kisses me on both cheeks and declares, "I told you making Elliot jealous was merely a byproduct of my true intentions. Which if you will remember, is to sweep you off your feet and marry you on Saturday."

I flirt back, "Richard Bingham, you would drop dead if I accepted your proposal and actually expected you to follow through with it."

Looking totally serious, he declares, "Oh yeah? Try me."

Just as I consider throwing all my eggs into Richard's basket, I see Elliot walk in. Or should I say limp in. The man has added a new accessory to his person in the form of crutches. I begin to move towards him when Richards stays my arm, "Let him come to you, darling. It's the cardinal rule of capturing a man."

In a haze, I look at Richard and say, "But he's been hurt. I need to make sure he's okay."

Richard assures me if Elliot were not okay, he would not be in attendance. Then he adds, "Come on, let's make him jealous." Then he leans very close to me and runs his hand up my back. "Now, I'm going to recite the Declaration of Independence in your ear and I want you to laugh like you're having the time of your life." I giggle at this and really do nearly bust a gut when I hear him murmur, "We the people, in order to form a more perfect union…"

Nearly doubling over in mirth, I reply, "Richard stop, you're too much!"

But he continues, "To establish justice, insure domestic tranquility, provide for the common defense…" Then he whispers, "Your target has spotted you and he's on his way over." I'm about to spin around and see when Richard body blocks me to keep me from looking like a lost puppy come home.

I can only imagine what kind of picture Richard and I make when I hear the singular sound of annoyance and I know Elliot has arrived, "Mimi, you look lovely this evening."

I turn around and pretend to be shocked anew by the sight of his crutches and declare, "My goodness, Elliot, what happened to you?"

He replies, "In a word, racquetball. Marcus convinced me to play him after lunch and I think it's safe to say, it's not my game." He doesn't say any of this while looking at me. He stands eye to eye with Richard and stares at him the whole time. He asks, "Mimi, who is your friend?"

Before I have a chance to speak, Richard puts out his hand and announces, "Richard Bingham, and you are?"

"Elliot Fielding." And then like a spoiled child he adds, "This party is being thrown in my honor."

"Oh yes." declares Richard. "Congratulations on your new book. I understand from Mimi it's much anticipated."

As the energy sparks between the two, I wonder which one of them would win in a Bridget Jones, knock-down-drag-out-street brawl. But before any such display can break out, Marcus arrives, "Mimi, you are easily the most beautiful woman here! Move to New York and come to work for me. I promise you won't be sorry."

Richard croons, "Darling, did you hear that? Now you have no reason not to marry me."

Marcus jumps on the bandwagon, "I didn't know you had a gentleman friend in New York, Mimi. I'm serious about my offer. If you're interested, just let me know and I'll send a moving truck straight to Pipsy."

Elliot intervenes with, "Mimi's family is in Pipsy. She'd never leave them."

I glare at him for making any such presumption and declare, "I will live anywhere I want, Elliot, especially if it means marriage."

WHITNEY DINEEN

With a naughty gleam in his eye, Richard contributes, "And babies, lots and lots of babies."

Elliot grabs a glass of champagne from a passing waiter and downs it in one gulp. He replaces his empty one for a full one and alerts the waiter not to go too far away. Then grabs my hand and asks, "May I see you alone for a moment?"

Marcus disappears to play host to the media and Richard declares, "I'll just go get us another drink, darling."

As soon as they are gone Elliot demands, "Who is that man?"

I answer, "Richard Bingham. You were just introduced to him."

Elliot explains, "What I mean is, who is he to you?"

Feeling my hackles rise, I answer, "He's a very successful advertising executive who also happens to be attracted to me in a romantic sense. As you can see he's even asked me to marry him."

Elliot declares, "You can't be serious, Mimi. There has to be something wrong with him."

Seconds away from throwing my champagne in his face, I demand, "Why, because he's interested in me? You know you're not the only one who gets to live happily ever after, Elliot. Just because you're getting married doesn't mean I can't too!"

He answers, "I told you I may not be marrying Beatrice."

Infuriated, I ask, "I see. How long do you suppose I should wait around to see what you decide to do?"

Elliot takes my hand and tries to explain, "It's complicated, Mimi."

I snap back, "Well Richard is not. So why don't you just take yourself off and leave me alone?"

Elliot looks hurt and mad and before he can respond to my demands, Richard is back, "Care to dance, darling?"

I take his arm gladly and storm away leaving Elliot to think about the choice he has to make. The rest of the night is a blur. While I truly have a wonderful time with Richard, I'm so mad at Elliot I want to scream. What could possibly be so complicated about breaking up with a woman he's not even engaged to? I understand it wouldn't be a pleasant scene but it's not as though he would be asking for a divorce. People break up all the time.

At the end of the evening Richard asks if he can escort me back to The Plaza and I gladly agree. Without so much as looking at Elliot, Richard and I leave the gallery arm in arm.

# Chapter 23

Richard helps me out of the Town Car and leads the way towards the hotel entrance. I tell him I had a lovely evening and there is truly no need for him to see me inside, but he insists, "If I'm right, your Mr. Fielding will be arriving shortly to make sure you go to your room alone."

And just as we approach the elevator, I see Elliot hobble through the front door. I smile and declare, "Methinks this is a game you have played before, Richard. Elliot has just walked in." With an intimate smile, I ask, "Would you care to come up?"

Richard graciously agrees, but first he draws me into his arms and gifts me with a truly-toe curling kiss. I swear, if I didn't have this crazy, infuriating lust for Elliot, I'd run off with Richard tonight. This is the moment I realize Stan and Ollie didn't miss the flight after all. There is no way I, Mimi Finnegan, would have attracted the attention of Richard Bingham without them. Richard and I get on the elevator and just as we hit the button for the fourteenth floor, I hear Elliot call out, "Hold the elevator." But of course, we don't.

As soon as we arrive at my floor, Richard bids me goodnight and says, "Hurry into your room so he doesn't know whether or not I'm in there with you."

Surprised, I ask, "You're not coming in?"

"My dear, Miss Finnegan, when I go into a hotel room with you, there will be more than conversation happening. Remember that should you invite me up again."

I thank Richard for a wonderful evening and sprint away as fast as my three-inch heels will carry me. I briefly feel like I'm taking advantage of his kind disposition but I remember I leveled with him from the start. And who knows? The way things are looking with Elliot, Richard might be the man to sweep me off my feet after all. I realize I would be very lucky to have him even though he isn't my first choice.

Once I get into my room, I turn on the clock radio to a classical station so Elliot will hear music should he press his ear to the door, as I expect him to do. I hear him go into his room moments later and smile because he's cursing, "Bloody this, bloody that...bollocks of a night, etc. He's making an inordinate amount of noise and it occurs to me he's trying to interrupt whatever is happening in my room.

Smiling to myself, I change into my new pink silk nightgown, compliments of LeRon and Fernando and pull my bed covers back. The banging next door has increased so I knock on the connecting door and ask Elliot to please keep it down. Instead of doing as I ask, he pulls his door open and demands, "Why, am I interrupting something?" then he charges into my room like a stampeding bull, all the while hopping on one foot. He is obviously in search of Richard.

The whole scene is rather comical especially as he starts to lose his balance and has to throw himself onto the bed in hopes of a soft landing.

Elliot lays spread eagle on my duvet and grumbles, "Racquetball is the stupidest bloody sport."

I walk over and try to help him up, but he refuses to move. Instead he rolls over and demands, "Is your bloody boyfriend in the loo, then?"

I grab Elliot's arms and try to haul him up saying, "Come on, Elliot, time for you to go to bed."

He yanks back and agrees, "That's right, Mimi, time for bed." And he pulls me down on top of him. Before I know what's happening, Elliot has rolled over and pinning me beneath him. He groans, "You're mine, Mimi Finnegan, and don't you forget it." Then his mouth is on mine and he's kissing me with all the passion of a sex-starved cowboy. Elliot leans up long enough to slide the strap down on my nightgown. Once his mission is complete, he runs his hand up my bare leg, dragging the hem with it. At this moment I'm not sure I have the willpower to hold him off until he is officially broken up with Beatrice. I'm not sure that I even want to. I'm just so lost in the pure physical heat the two of us seem to generate I can't even think straight.

Elliot props himself up on his elbows and uses his knee to open my legs. He devours me with his eyes and repeats, "You are mine, Mimi Finnegan, do you understand?" Then he collapses right on top of me in an unconscious heap. What in the hell? This is simply not like love scenes in the movies. Why does something always happen to keep Elliot from fully declaring his true feelings? I'm so irritated I could spit.

I push him off of me and sit up wondering what I should do with him. I decide to roll him over and remove his tuxedo jacket in an attempt to make him more comfortable (as if he'd even know in his passed out state.) I eventually get it off, and as I do, a bottle falls out of the pocket. It's a prescription for Percocet and it clearly broadcasts an alcohol warning. "Drinking may increase drowsiness." Well that's for sure. So I take his shoes and tie off as well and settle him in bed next to me. As I crawl under the covers I briefly wish that Stan, Ollie, and Edith had gotten their own room. I would have happily paid for it.

I wake up the next morning wrapped around Elliot. I am nearly on top of him and my arms and legs are encircling him like he's a tree trunk I'm attempting to climb. I realize this is an apt description as I do indeed feel some wood between us. It takes me a moment to remember how exactly we came to be in bed together. Then it takes me another moment to realize nothing really happened.

The tricky part was going to be disengaging myself without waking him in the process. Slowly, I try to roll off of him but he merely slides his hands up my silky nightgown and settles them on my bottom. Now what? I gently push his hands away but he replaces them more firmly. Elliot is obviously a morning person as the next thing I know, he's flipped me onto my back and begins nibbling my earlobes. I try to get his attention by saying, "Elliot, could you please let me up?"

He doesn't respond right away, but when he does he claims, "Oh Mimi, this is better than any of the other dreams

I've had about you."

He dreams about me? This is good news but I still feel I should tell him this is in fact real and not a dream at all. I don't want him under false pretenses. So I say, "Elliot, this is no dream. We're in my bedroom at The Plaza in New York, remember?"

I can tell instantly when he comes to his senses, as I can feel the return of the frosty Brit.

Elliot slowly moves off of me and asks, "How did I get here?"

I remind him about last night and inform him about the alcohol warning on his pain medication. He asks where Richard is and I say, "He's obviously not here, Elliot. It's not like we had a threesome or anything."

Looking worried, he asks, "Did we have a twosome then?"

I'm so fed up with his passive aggressive behavior I shout at him to get the hell out of my room. He gradually staggers to his door and I throw his prescription bottle after him.

Elliot doesn't close the connecting door, so once I hear him in the shower, I write him a note and drop his itinerary on his bed. I'm effectively telling him to have a nice day as I have no intention of joining him at his signings. Of course it's my job to be there, but there are going to be enough folks around from the New York Parliament office. I can't imagine I'll be missed.

As I walk back into my room, the hotel phone rings. I wonder who's calling me on that line instead of my cell phone. So I demand, "Hello?" in a way that suggests that this better be worth my time.

It's Richard. He says, "I'm just guessing here but it doesn't sound like you slept well."

I immediately soften my tone, "Good morning, Richard. I slept fine. I'm just irritated with the Englishman, again."

Richard suggests, "Then why don't you spend the day with me? I'll show you the sights only a true New Yorker knows about."

I'm sold. Not that I need any real enticement to spend time with him. Richard has so far been the high point of my trip and if things work out for Elliot and me, I'm seriously considering introducing him to Muffy. Of course I won't be doing that until I'm safely married. After all, he is my fallback guy. Richard tells me to meet him in the lobby in forty-five minutes and to dress comfortably. I assure him Edith Bunker will be delighted.

I wear a long A-line denim skirt with an orange t-shirt (which looks surprisingly good with my hair), a big brown and gold gypsy belt and ballet flats (with Edith Bunker's pad). I smile when I see Richard. He's wearing jeans and a light weight summer sweater. He looks years younger than his James Bond persona when he dresses like this. I accept an easy kiss on the cheek from him and we're off to enjoy a day of play.

At breakfast I fall off the wagon with tremendous abandon. We eat at a cheery restaurant on $92^{nd}$ and Madison called Sarabeth's Kitchen and we share a sticky bun, a pumpkin muffin, and a raisin scone served with a trio of homemade jams. I complain to Richard and tell him that Edith Bunker is going to give me seven kinds of hell for this. He tells me not to worry about it. If she so much as breathes a word of complaint, he will personally write her a check for any exorbitant sum she demands.

Our first stop after breakfast is The Metropolitan Museum of Art where we don't take time to actually tour the museum; instead we go to the gift shop and buy a coffee table book on Ireland for my mother. I try to tell Richard that I've already bought my family souvenirs but he doesn't think chocolates are very New York. The next stop is The Frick where we buy Ginger a t-shirt that says, "My sister went to New York and all I got was this "Frick"en t-shirt. He assures me, as an art person, she will love it.

Before hopping into a cab across town to The Museum of Natural History, where we buy Finn a large plastic dinosaur, we stop off at FAO Schwartz to get another baby doll for Camille. On our way downtown, we stop at the hotel and ask the front desk to take my bags to my room. I try to insist I'll just run them up but Richard claims we are on a very tight schedule so he slips the bellman a twenty to take care of it.

Next stop, The Village, where there's cart after cart of people selling the coolest things right on the street. I buy Kevin another t-shirt that says, "My other wife is a model." And I buy my dad a Guinness wardrobe, complete with t-shirt, hat, and beer mug that hangs on a chain so he can wear it around his neck. On impulse, I drag Richard into a racy lingerie store where I purchase a pair of five-inch hooker heels, for Renée, as a joke replacement for her five hundred dollar Giuseppe Zannotis.

As we hike through Chinatown to get to our Little Italy lunch destination, I buy Muffy a Chinese paper umbrella and pick up tire tread sandals for Jonathan and Laurent. Then in Little Italy I purchase wife beaters for LaRon and Fernando. One of them asks, "What size do you wear in a cement loafer?" The other one boasts, "There's No Salami Like an Italian Salami."

I'm exhausted by the time we sit down and order a meal that will have me confessing my sins in church before repeating the fun to Marge. But I don't care; I'm having the best day. Plus we've walked more in the last six hours than I think I've walked in the last six weeks. I learn all kinds of things about Richard too. For example, he was married when he was in his twenties and was divorced by the time he was thirty, no kids. He's had several girlfriends but no one has moved him to thoughts of marriage. He claims he knew he could marry me on sight, as a woman who enjoys her food as much as I do must have her priorities straight. And even though his business is thriving, he has decided there is more to life than constant work. Richard is ready to have a family and enjoy all the fruits of his labors.

I'm quiet when he announces this and he says, "I'm just telling you where I am in my life, Mimi, I'm not trying to pressure you." Then he jokes, "Although, if you don't marry me, I may be heartbroken and have to move to Romania to take up with a tribe of gypsy women for consolation." I tease him back and tell him to send me a postcard.

It's three o'clock by the time we finish lunch and I inform Richard I should really stop by Elliot's second book signing. He claims we can walk it faster than we can cab it and I'm delighted for the chance to burn off some of my lunch. By three-thirty we are standing outside of Book Stew where a long line has formed down the street. I ask Richard if he wants to come in and he says, "You couldn't keep me away. I want to see the look on His Highness's face when he realizes the reason you weren't with him today is because you spent the day with me."

I admonish, "Richard that is very childish."

He smiles, "Yes, darling, but you should know I'm a child at heart."

When we walk into the bookstore I immediately see Marcus scurrying around lining up stacks of books. He waves when he spots us and asks me to run in back and get Elliot a cup of black coffee. Of course I do it, as it is my professional duty to be as helpful to our client as possible. The non-professional part raises its ugly head when I almost spit in his cup. At the last second I manage to refrain.

Elliot is surprised to see me. He icily thanks me for the coffee and asks where I've been all day. Enter Richard. "Darling, are you ready to go?"

I answer, "In a minute Richard," at the same time Elliot announces, "She's not going anywhere. She's staying right here where she's needed."

Richard claims "No one needs her as much as I do."

Elliot smirks and counters, "Yes, but I'm paying her."

Richard lunges towards Elliot and announces, "You bastard…" and Elliot stands up as if to roll up his shirt sleeves for a fight.

Believe me when I tell you that no one appreciates this potential scene as much as I do. I've been hankering for years to be the reason two grown men beat the shit out of each other but the bottom line is I think way too much of both of them to risk either of them getting hurt at my expense. So I stand up and demand, "Stop it! Richard, I'll call you later and thank you for a truly wonderful day, and Elliot, sit down before I kick your good leg out from under you."

Richard leans down and captures my mouth in a tender kiss and promises we'll do something extraordinary before I leave. Elliot nearly shouts, "Get your lips off of her!"

I say goodbye to Richard and then lean into the Brit and demand, "What in the hell is your problem? As far as I'm concerned Richard can kiss me anytime he wants and until you are in a position to reasonably object, you are to keep your mouth shut, do you understand me?"

He responds with a curt nod and I look up and realize that Marcus has witnessed the whole scene. He asks for a moment of my time and I follow him into the back room in sheer dread. I'm convinced he's going to fire me but Marcus just grins and declares, "Every PR firm needs a good dominatrix! I'm prepared to offer you double your current salary if you'll move to New York and become ours."

I thank him for the kind offer and promise to think about it. Then I return to Elliot's side and help in any way I can. I can't stop wondering why I can't just let myself fall for Richard. After all, he's the perfect man, right down to the fact he's not almost engaged to another woman. But then I look at Elliot and my heart skips a beat in the yearning I feel for him. I say a silent prayer for Stan and Ollie to get taken off their current assignment. I need some honest to goodness romance writers to take their place as I can't bear the thought I might yet wind up alone.

# Chapter 24

The rest of the afternoon is excruciatingly long. It's amazing how many people come out to get autographs and tell Elliot how fabulous they think he is. One lady even says he is her hero. I can't quite figure why she says this as how can a novelist she's never met before be her hero? But I think it's awfully sweet. Elliot signs all her books and asks for her address. He promises to send her a signed copy of his new novel when it comes out. I'm not sure why he does this, but the turban wearing young woman is beyond thrilled and before she leaves, she tearfully announces, "I wish there were more men like you in this world."

It's past six by the time we finish the book signing and get back to the hotel. Elliot trails behind me as I stride to the elevator. He's off his crutches and seems to be doing pretty well for himself. When we get off on our floor, I walk to my room and open the door without saying one word to him.

He on the other hand states, "I'll be over in fifteen minutes to pick you up for dinner."

My reply is delivered with arctic chill, "Sorry, I think I'm going to order in tonight."

He demands, "Fifteen minutes, be ready."

That arrogant son of bitch. Who does he think he is? Just because weird women in turbans think he's the end-all-to-die-for, doesn't mean it's true. I'll show him. But the whole time I'm ranting in my head, I'm putting on more make-up and brushing my hair. By the time I'm changing into a frilly summer dress, I realize I must have decided to eat with him.

When Elliot knocks, I open the door without saying a word and merely follow him down the hall to the elevator. The summer evening is so beautiful I stop and breathe it in as soon as we're outside. There's a slight breeze and the sun hasn't quite set. It is the most magical moment of my life. I feel as though I've been lifted out of my normal humdrum existence and have been given a glimpse of heaven. I become so overcome with emotion that I don't realize I am crying until twin tears slide down my cheeks. Elliot doesn't ruin the moment by saying anything; he just takes my hand in his as we walk to our destination. I let him do this, I reason, as it is part of my definition of heaven.

Elliot and I walk up the park several blocks before he turns right and leads me into it. That's when I realize he's taking me to Tavern on the Green. Of course I've never been here, but like the restaurant at the boating pond, I recognize it from the movies. The maître d' greets Elliot and gushes, "Mr. Fielding, we are so happy you are joining us this evening. If you'll follow me?" He leads us to a beautifully set table right by the window and offers us menus. Mine curiously doesn't have any prices on it.

Finally I utter, "You planned this, didn't you?"

Elliot smiles at me across the table and acknowledges, "Yes. I made the reservations the other day after our lunch at the pond. You seemed so delighted the restaurant there was real and not just in the movies I thought you would appreciate this institution as well."

I don't know what to make of Elliot Fielding. He is so thoughtful and considerate and lovely, all at the same time he is a stuck up, tight-assed, English prig. I wonder, not for the first time or even the fifteenth, why the combination is so appealing to me. I simply stare at him and reply, "Thank you."

Elliot reaches for my hand across the table and asks, "Mimi, is there anyway you and I can enjoy our evening tonight, just the two of us? No Richard, no Beatrice, just us?"

I don't answer right away as I'm not sure that's possible. Both of the people he mentions are sitting here with us whether we acknowledge them or not. The question is, can I make it through the night without listening to what they have to say? So I answer, "We can try, Elliot. But you have to know that just because we pretend they don't exist, doesn't make it so."

"I know," he acknowledges, "Believe me, I know. But please, let's just try, okay?"

I agree and we spend the next two hours getting to know each other even better. The more I learn about Elliot, the more I realize that my heart recognized him as my mate the moment we met. I fought it because it terrified me. But now I know the instant I laid eyes on him, I had come home. I pulled my hand away from his by the pool that day because I was panicked if I let him take it I would never be the same again. And guess what? I will never be the same again.

After dinner we walk through the park hand-in-hand and I am full of such melancholy I feel like my heart is breaking. Why won't Elliot just leave Beatrice? He can't possibly feel for her the things he claims to feel for me. I want to ask him about it so badly, but I've promised not to bring her or Richard up in conversation tonight. It's just so hard not to mention them when they are walking right behind us.

Elliot and I stroll over to Strawberry Fields at seventy-second street and sit down on a park bench together. We sit quietly for several minutes when an older gentleman comes and joins us. He asks us if we mind sharing our bench.

Elliot answers, "Certainly not. It's such a beautiful night. We'd be delighted to share."

The man introduces himself and says, "My name is Joseph Collins, and tonight is my sixtieth wedding anniversary." My eyes immediately fill with tears as it's obvious that Joseph is sitting on the bench alone, without his wife.

I manage to keep the emotion out of my voice and say, "Congratulations Joseph, that's a marvelous accomplishment."

Joseph tells us that he and his wife, Elizabeth, were married across the street at The Majestic when it was still a hotel. He reminisces it was the most magical night of both of their lives. So much so that years later, when the building broke up into apartments, he and Elizabeth, sold their place on the East Side and bought one in The Majestic. He says, "The West Side wasn't at all fashionable then, but to us, it was like coming home."

My heart is positively breaking for this wonderful man and I ask, "Do you still live there, Joseph?"

"No," he answers, his voice fraught with emotion. "After Elizabeth died, I couldn't manage living in the city on my own." He takes a moment to compose himself and says, "I live in Westchester now with our son, Joe Jr., and his wife." He points to a parked car on Central Park West to show us Joe Jr. is waiting for him. "But I come into the city every year for our anniversary and I pay tribute to the woman who gave me the best gift of my life. Elizabeth made me whole." Elliot and I are both crying at this point and he squeezes my hand to offer me some small degree of comfort. Then Joseph continues, "We used to bring our babies right here and let them play in the grass." He looks at the ground as though he can still see them and gentle tears stream down his face. Then Joseph pushes himself up and announces, "I wish you kids the love Elizabeth and I shared," then he smiles and adds, "I hope you'll bring your babies here too." As he walks away, he thanks us for sharing the bench and queries, "Maybe I'll see you here next year, okay?"

We wish Joseph a goodnight and then we sit in silence, both lost in our own thoughts, both of us wondering if it's possible we might just meet him back here next year after all.

# Chapter 25

I will remember that evening for as long as I live. It almost feels like Joseph Collins has become our mascot; someone else cheering our way to a happy ending. After all, Kevin is on my side, but he also really likes Beatrice so I don't quite feel like I have his undivided loyalty anymore. My family doesn't even know how I feel about Elliot and while Richard wants me to be happy, he sure doesn't want it to be with his competition. I finally feel like there's someone else on this earth pulling for Elliot and me and it feels really nice.

After we walk back from the park, Elliot sees me up to my room. I invite him in, not sure what I'm expecting to happen. What does happen is I change into my nightgown and Elliot holds me until I fall asleep. We hardly speak as our bargain forbids us from talking about the one thing at the forefront in both of our minds.

I only remember one of my dreams this morning and it's a doozy. I dreamt that I was walking down the aisle in a packed church, all decked out in my wedding dress and veil. I recall having no idea who my groom was and as I walked and walked and walked down what felt like the mile long walkway. I finally reached the altar to find both Elliot and Richard waiting for me. The minister recited the wedding vows as though they were one man and asked, "Do you Elliot Richard take this woman to be your lawfully wedded wife? To love honor and cherish until death you do part?"

The Richard part of the equation says, "I do" at the same time that Elliot answers, "It's just so complicated." As I relive my dream, the realization hits me that I'm going to keep seeing Richard. I know I've just met him and no sane person would consider marrying a man they had only set eyes on for the first time, days earlier. But I'm not saying I'm going to marry him. I'm saying I'm going to keep seeing him. And if love should grow between us before Elliot comes to his senses and declares himself? Then I will marry Richard. After all, he's no Linden Fairbanks and in no way would I be settling with him. If Richard and I wind up together, I will always know I did very well for myself.

As soon as I get out of bed, I knock on the connecting door. When Elliot opens it, he's already showered and dressed for the day. He bestows a sad smile on me and asks me in. Things between us have changed since last night. I no longer feel the need to scream at him or wring his neck or even call him names. My energy has shifted to a place of acceptance. Whatever will be, will be.

Elliot looks like he hasn't slept at all. In fact, he looks like he's battling an inner war and neither side is showing signs of surrender. I inform him I've made a decision and he looks at me both nervously and expectantly. I confess, "Elliot, I've decided I have to choose once and for all whom I want to make happy." Again with the puppy dog look. I continue, "So I choose me. I've spent the better part of my adult life without a companion and even when I've had one, I've been lonely. I don't want that for myself. Therefore, I simply choose me. I'm not going to settle for a man who doesn't love me and I'm not going to settle for one who won't put me first. So you've got some thinking to do and some choices to make."

He inquires, "You're going to keep seeing Richard then?"

I ask, "Are you going to keep seeing Beatrice?" He is clearly upset by my decision and I continue, "Elliot, it's not the Middle Ages. A woman can get married if she wants. She doesn't have to settle for being a man's mistress if she wants more for herself. I'm not going to continue to see Richard to make you jealous. I'm going to continue to see him because I deserve to have a wonderful man love me and me alone."

Staring out the window, Elliot says, "I want that for you too, Mimi. It's just that it's so complicated."

Again with the complicated! So I ask, "Why? Why is it so complicated? Tell me about it and maybe the two of us can figure it out together."

He turns to me with a pained expression and says, "I can't tell you. I gave someone my word." Then with a pleading look, he continues, "But you could find out if you wanted to."

Ah, the familiar anger is coming back, "I'm not going to turn detective to try to unearth your secrets, Elliot. If you want to share them with me, then share them with me. If not, I'm going to move on. Let me know if you decide to open up and maybe I'll still be around. But just so you know, maybe I won't."

I get up to leave and Elliot blocks my exit. He opens his arms to me and I gladly walk into them for what could be the last time I feel them around me. In a very bold moment, I declare, "Just so you know, Elliot Fielding, I love you."

He groans and replies, "I love you too, Mimi Finnegan. I really do."

It occurs to me that the schmaltzy romantic endings in chick books are not the way life works out. But then again, last month there was no one beating down my door and now, I have two extraordinary men vying for the role of "man in my life." I am not going to go against my Grandma Sissy's advice and look a gift horse in the mouth. No siree, Bob. I am going to thank my lucky stars I have a gift horse at all. Then I briefly wonder what the hell a gift horse is anyway.

As I go back into my room, I feel a renewed sense of well-being. I could have easily told Elliot I would wait for him always, but then I would most likely spend my life waiting and that's not what I want. I want to actually live. Too many years have passed me by and at the grand old age of thirty-four, it's time to quit watching from the sidelines. This is my play (Ollie's and Stan's really, but I'm starring in it) and I'm ready to kick my understudy off the stage and take over. I'm not sure if you've noticed, but we Irish love nothing as much as a mixed metaphor. Well, perhaps a mixed metaphor with a Guinness on the side, but you get my meaning.

Elliot and I meet Marcus and his crew at ten a.m. for a breakfast meeting. I cringe to think how much I'm going to weigh when I step on the scale Saturday, so I order half a grapefruit and two pieces of dry whole wheat toast. No, it's not in the least bit satisfying but hopefully it will keep Edith Bunker quiet. Edith Bunker, by the way, has been remarkably tight lipped for the last twenty-four hours and I try to encourage her silence by wearing sensible shoes today. You see, I am a team player, regardless of what she would have you believe.

After breakfast, Elliot goes off with Marcus to speak at a book convention, and I spend a couple of hours in Marcus's office at Parliament hammering out the details for tomorrow night's party at Daniel, yet another New York institution. While sitting behind his big desk staring out at the Manhattan skyline, I wonder if I'll take Marcus up on his offer to move to New York. I mean I love being so close to my family in Pipsy, but New York would be an adventure. I could be the heroine of my very own *Sex and the City*. The thought makes me a little giddy. So I pick up the phone and call Richard.

He answers on the third ring, "Hello?"

"Good afternoon, kind sir. How are you today?"

I hear the happiness in his voice as he jokes, "Well, Mimi Finnegan, as I live and breathe. What are you doing right now?"

I groan, "I'm starving is what I'm doing. My breakfast stopped working hours ago."

"Where are you?" I tell him that I'm at Parliament and he says that he'll pick me up out front in twelve minutes for lunch."

I laugh, "Twelve minutes, huh? That's a pretty exact science."

He laughs, "Well, eight to sixteen really."

I quip, "So I might actually have to wait for you?"

He responds, "Or I might have to wait for you." His words carry a double meaning that mine don't. I tell him to hurry up and get here, I'm famished.

Richard picks me up in a Town Car and we drive over to the docks. We stop at a small café and pick up an order he has already called in and he suggests we eat by the water. As we walk down one of the piers, eyeing the gorgeous boats, or should I say yachts, I declare, "This is lovely but I'm ravenous. Let's find a park bench and eat."

Instead of going back towards the benches, Richard grabs my hand and speeds up. He stops in front of a pristine white vessel named "The Soapy Sails" and gestures for me to climb up. I'm horrified, "Richard, I'm not going to eat on somebody's boat. What if we get caught?"

Just then a man in white pants and navy jacket, with a very official looking captain's hat peeks over the side. I immediately apologize, "I'm so sorry. We were just fooling around."

But he ignores me and says to Richard, "Mr. Bingham, we're all gassed up and ready to go."

I look at Richard in shock, "This is your boat?"

He smiles, "It sure is. I hope you don't get seasick."

I'm so excited I'm about to pop out of my skin, "We're going out on the water on your very own boat?"

He confirms, "As long as you don't get seasick."

I have no idea if I got seasick or not because let's be honest, I've only been boating on a lake, as Pipsy is not exactly ocean adjacent. Without actually lying, I tell Richard I've never been seasick and I happily climb up on deck ready for my next adventure.

I simply cannot believe this is really happening to me. Richard's yacht is easily big enough to host a party of two hundred. The deck is a beautiful polished teak and the fittings are blindingly, shiny brass. I lay back on a deck chair and look up at the sails and exclaim, "I can't believe you are taking me out on the ocean!"

He is enjoying my enthusiasm and says, "This is why I love being with you so much. All of the women I've gone out with in the last several years, take this sort of experience for granted, but you? You're really excited and you don't mind showing it."

"Really excited?" I demand, "Really excited? How could I not be really excited? This is amazing!"

Just as I finish my declaration, Richard leans towards me and kisses me. Not the kind of kiss we shared to make Elliot jealous either, but a real live honest to goodness, hot-blooded, full throttle lip-lock. And I let him. In fact, I do more than that, I kiss him back.

When he finally pulls away, he says, "I should apologize as I know your affections lie elsewhere, but I'm not going to because I'm not at all sorry."

With a shy smile, I reply, "Neither am I."

Richard inquires hopefully, "So there still might be a chance for me?"

Remembering that I choose my happiness above all others, I answer, "Yes, Richard, there's still a chance for you."

I don't even mind that our lunch consists of greasy burgers and fries. I eat every last bite, points be damned, and tell

Richard if Edith Bunker starts complaining, I'm going to give her his number. He sits up with a funny look on his face and declares, "I think it's time I meet this Edith Bunker, don't you?"

With a look of horror on my face, I declare, "I do not. Good lord, Richard, I am not going to introduce you to my bunion!"

But before I realize his intent, he grabs my right foot and runs his hand up my calf. He pulls my leg towards him until my bunion and I have scooted right up against him. I beg, "No Richard, please, please leave Edith Bunker alone."

But he pulls my shoe off anyway and gradually runs his fingers over my foot. When he gets to the bump beneath my baby toe, he starts to rub it with deep kneading strokes and I let out a groan of sheer pleasure. I hear him say, "Edith Bunker, I'm Richard Bingham and I'm delighted to meet you." He continues to rub my foot and asks, "What is she saying?"

I smile and answer, "She's saying, don't stop." And he doesn't. Moments later, I add, "She likes you. She just said that you have amazing hands."

Richard grins; "Tell her to pass the word to her friends." Then he naughtily adds, "My specialty isn't actually bunions."

I want to know what his specialty is but I don't ask. However, I do feel a wicked thrill run through me as I speculate. We spend the better part of four hours out on the water. We cruise around the statue of liberty and then around the East Side of Manhattan before finally pulling back into Richard's slip. The last two hours have been spent sitting side by side with his arm around my shoulders. By the time we're back in the harbor, I think Elliot had better hurry up and make up his mind because given a little more time, I could fall for Richard Bingham in a big way.

# Chapter 26

Tonight Elliot and I are going to the theater to see *The Book of Mormon*. I'm looking forward to spending another evening with him with no ulterior motives other than just enjoying our time together. After all, he knows I'm going to continue to see Richard and if he wants to keep me from winding up with the competition, he had better get a move on.

I pick out another new dress tonight. This one is white chiffon with rhinestone encrusted straps. It's as simple and elegant as it gets and with my new red hair, it's also quite stunning. I strap on a pair of silver sandals that are going to make Edith Bunker scream, and grab a matching evening bag. I'm ready to go when Elliot knocks on our adjoining door at six-thirty.

He looks as wonderful as ever and I just stare at him for a moment before I brightly ask, "Are you ready to go?"

Smiling, he asks, "Would you lend me an arm for a little extra support."

Concerned, I inquire, "Do you want to bring your crutches?"

He affirms, "I don't think I'll need them. They were more for precaution than anything else." So I offer Elliot my arm, and he in turn wraps his around my shoulder in a very proprietary manner; a way that doesn't seem to offer him any support at all, but makes me smile.

We have seven o'clock reservations at Gramercy Tavern and I make a great effort to eat reasonably, roasted chicken breast and steamed veggies, no bread, no butter, no dessert. I'm trying to atone for my afternoon of debauchery. Marge would have been very disappointed that I ate the whole bun with my burger (there was no onion though so it wasn't technically a bunion, much to Edith Bunker's relief) right along with a whole order of French fries.

"The Book of Mormon" is hysterically funny and Elliot and I have a fabulous time. When it's over, I'm ready to hit the hay. It's been a long day. Yet I discover that Elliot has made different arrangements. Once we get back to The Plaza, he leads me across Central Park South to a handsome cab that is waiting. Inside is a bucket with chilled champagne and long stemmed red roses. He hops in first so he can help me up and I am thoroughly touched he has planned all of this for me.

After he pours me a glass of champagne, we sit back and enjoy our ride through the park. Elliot tells me about his day and offers that the conference went well. Then he asks me what I did. I've already decided I'm not going to go out of my way to tell him about Richard but I'm not going to lie to him either. So I relay that I spent the afternoon on Richard's boat. Elliot is not pleased, and he takes my champagne glass from me and puts it in the bucket along with his. Then he pulls me next to him and asks, "Did he kiss you?"

I reply, "Elliot, why do you want to know that?"

"Because I do. Did he kiss you?" I tell him yes and he asks, "Did you enjoy it?"

I'm starting to get mad and answer, "Yes, he kissed me and yes, I enjoyed it. Is that what you want you hear?"

Before I know what's happening, Elliot has pulled me into his arms and is devouring me with his mouth. This is more than a kiss, it's a branding, a show of ownership. His breath tastes sweet like champagne and his hands are rough and insistent as they slide up the back of my dress into my hair. There is an urgency to his assault that leaves me feeling like I'm free falling from an airplane. It's all I can do not to jump into his lap. Elliot is apparently reading my mind because before I know it that's exactly where I am. I cannot seem to get enough of him, this stuck up, uptight, hoity-toity perfectly wonderful Englishman has taken over my brain. Elliot becomes frenzied as he pulls the straps of my dress down as the cab slows. He calls out for the driver to keep going and before I can come to my senses, he's kissing me again. His hot tongue is running up my neck and into my ear. He whispers, "Mimi, I want you so much," as his hands cover every inch of my body. I feel like a switch has been turned on and I light up like a Christmas tree. I have never been this out of control in my life. Elliot groans, "I want to make love to you, Mimi. I need to make love to you." He has moved so he's on top of me and I'm lying on the bench beneath him. He inches my skirt up all the while kissing my neck and sliding the top of my dress down. The cool air feels decadent as the motion of the carriage seems to rock us like we're in a cradle.

Elliot forces himself to slow down and manages to say, "Mimi, I want you more than I've wanted anyone in my life. But you had better tell me now if you don't feel the same way." I don't say a word, I can't. I know I should tell him to stop, but what if this is the only time I get to be with him in this way. Could I live with myself knowing that I passed up this opportunity? So I just stare at him and keep my mouth closed. Elliot falls on me and nearly devours me whole when he realizes that I'm not going to call a halt to his desire. He reaches to unbutton his pants and before I know it, he's inside me rocking to the motion of the carriage. My body splinters apart like a detonating bottle rocket and I feel the tears streaming down my face.

Elliot whispers, "I love you more than anything, Mimi Finnegan. I'm going to find a way for us to be together, I promise."

But I don't want to hear his promises. I'm afraid to believe him. So I just hold on tightly and savor the intimacy of this very fragile moment. When our ride is over, it occurs to me I should be full of shame for acting so brazenly. I'm really not that easy to get into bed as my very few lovers would attest. But it's so different with Elliot. I feel like I belong with him. He is the other half that makes me whole.

We walk back to the hotel hand-in-hand and while I want to invite him in to spend the night, I don't. I merely kiss him at my door and thank him for the most wonderful night of my life. Elliot tells me once more he loves me and that I need to trust him. I whisper good night and close my door, hoping I haven't just chosen Elliot's happiness over my own.

As soon as I crawl into bed, Edith Bunker starts in on me. "I like Richard better. He gave me the most wonderful massage! Why don't you marry Richard?"

I shoot back, "I am not taking relationship advice from my bunion. Leave me alone."

"But MeeeeeeMeeeeeeee, I like Richard...why not Richard?"

So I retaliate, "Edith Bunker, Richard is always feeding me which is going to keep you around forever. I thought you wanted me to lose weight so you can go away?"

She responds, "But did you feel the way he rubbed me? I like Richard."

I decide to just ignore her and try to go to sleep. I have kissed two different men today, making love to one of them in a horse-drawn carriage while riding through Central Park and I am totally and thoroughly confused about what happens next. I honestly don't feel it would be fair to keep Richard on a string any longer. Even if Elliot refuses to leave Beatrice, I like Richard too much to toy with him. I care about him enough to have a future with him (if Elliot lets me down that is.) But I also think enough of him to want him to be with somebody who considers him her first choice.

I say my prayers and ask God to please demote Ollie and Stan and send me a nice pair of romance writers. Jude Vixen, an American like me, and Hermione Meriwether, a Brit that will help me understand Elliot. I fall asleep feeling like my head is the epicenter of the Mideast peace talks right before they declare war.

# Chapter 27

Today is my last day in New York and I am both sad and relieved. I'm truly looking forward to going back to Pipsy and getting on with my normal routine. This trip, while totally thrilling, has also been exhausting. Elliot has a meeting this afternoon with his editor, Maynard, and I have decided to see if Richard is free for the day. I've invited him to the party tonight, which I'm sure I would not have done had I known I was going to make love with Elliot last night. The two men in my life are already like oil and water. Now, I imagine they'll be more like gasoline and a flame thrower.

I'm pretty sure I'm going to tell Richard my relationship with Elliot has progressed to the next level. I don't want to hurt him, but I do want to play fair. My head is throbbing, and what's more my teeth are killing me again. I really have to get a sleeping guard when I get home. I'm starting to worry I'll wake up one morning with a mouth full of gravel-like nubs in my mouth, in place of teeth.

Elliot knocks on our adjoining door before he leaves for his meeting. He looks very dapper in a cream colored linen suit and once again I nearly melt at his feet when I lay eyes on him, especially after last night. He kisses me good morning and asks, "How did you sleep?"

I tell him, "I slept very well, and you?"

He answers tenderly, "It would have been better if you were in my arms."

I have a vague inkling my prayers have been answered and Jude and Hermione are on the case. Elliot informs me his day is pretty much booked with appointments with his publisher. His last meeting is with their marketing department and I have been invited along although my presence isn't mandatory as Marcus will be there with his New York contingent. I tell Elliot I'll try to make it, but if I don't, I'll meet him back here by six-thirty so we can go to tonight's event together. With a sweet kiss he's gone and I start the process of getting ready for my day.

I decide to go casual and slip on jeans and a pink t-shirt. I pull my hair back in a pony tail and apply the sheerest layer of war paint my thirty-four year old face will allow. Then I pick up the phone and call Richard. His secretary answers his cell and explains he is in meetings all day, but she was supposed to tell me he'll meet me at my hotel at six-thirty, to escort me to tonight's party. In a full tilt boogie panic, I demand, "Please tell Richard not to pick me up at my hotel! Tell him to meet me at the restaurant." Then with more force than necessary, I ask, "Okay?!"

She assures me she'll pass on my message and I take a moment to imagine what would have happened if Richard and Elliot both showed up to accompany me to Daniel. Especially now that I won't be able to warn Richard about what happened last night. There's no telling what kind of scene might have ensued. Again, I realize how strange it is that something like this could be happening to me, Miriam May Finnegan.

The last time I incited a near riot between two members of the opposite sex was in the second grade when I promised both Ricky James and Tommy Stark the extra Twinkie in my lunch box. Now, almost twenty-five years later, I've graduated and have become the Twinkie myself. I wish there was some way I could tell all the single women out there to never give up hope. I mean heck, if something this ridiculous can happen to the ugly duckling sister of four, with a bunion, and fifteen pounds to lose, I'm pretty sure it can happen to anyone.

I decide to spend the morning simply walking the streets of New York. Marcus's job offer has intrigued me and I plan on trying to get a feel for the city to see if I might actually be able to call it home. I start by going to the zoo in the park where I pick up a couple more little trinkets for Finn and Camille. I spend the most time with the monkeys, laughing at their antics, until one fresh fellow starts to get a little familiar with himself. So I leave to give him some privacy.

My next stop is Sheep's Meadow. I know from *Sex and the City* this place is packed on the weekends but it turns out to be pretty deserted on a Tuesday morning. In the center of the field, I decide to lie down in the grass. I close my eyes and concentrate on shutting up all the yammering voices in my head. I think I may have actually dozed off when something wet and slimy drips onto my face. I'm afraid to open my eyes to see what it is when I hear a man's voice admonish, "Titan, that's no way to treat a lady."

Opening one eye at a time, I realize that I am looking up at a man that must have walked out of the pages of a *GQ*. He is positively stunning! I wipe what turns out to be dog drool off my mouth and say, "That's telling him."

He laughs, "Actually, I purposefully send him off to track beautiful ladies for me."

That's when I realize this Adonis, who I'm sure is no older than twenty-six or twenty-seven, is flirting with me! I welcome Jude and Hermione to the team. Then suggest, "You should walk around with handy wipes to offer Titan's victims."

He sits down next to me and pulls a paper napkin out of his pocket, "How's this?"

As I clean the offending slime off my face, I answer, "Not as good as a wet wipe but better than dog spit."

My new friend introduces himself as Jeremy Sterns. I learn he's a stockbroker, twenty-eight, single, born and raised in New York, and he apparently has a thing for older redheads on the curvy side of the spectrum. I assure him that while I am flattered to the ends of the earth by his interest, I am in the midst of a relationship conundrum that has taken me right out of the dating scene.

He asks if he can help me figure out my dilemma and I promise him that a group of tactical warfare specialists at the NSA couldn't help. We spend the next few minutes chatting before I decide I should bid my new friend adieu. No sense in adding another man to the stew that has become my life.

I spend the next three hours walking around the upper

West Side and realize if I moved to New York, this is where I would want to live. It's funkier and livelier than the East Side and about a million times more conservative than downtown. Plus Jerry Seinfeld lives on the Upper West Side, so I feel like I already know it. I eat lunch at Ray's and am now officially terrified to go back to Weight Watchers on Saturday. I'm just hoping that I'm balancing out all the cheating with the copious amounts of walking I've been doing.

By four o'clock, I stroll back to The Plaza and try to take a little nap before I get ready for the night ahead. "Try" is the optimal word here as there seems to be no way to calm myself enough to actually sleep. I'm very worried about tonight and while I'm pretty sure I can keep Richard and Elliot apart, I still have to tell Richard his competition is more than inching ahead. By four-thirty, I realize I am not going to get any rest so I begin the two hour process of transforming myself from mild-mannered PR person into a sex-pot super hero.

I'm going to wear the turquoise dress that I wore to La Petite Maison and I'm going to blow my hair straight and then put it in Velcro curlers for an hour for extra volume. Big hair makes me feel fierce and gives me courage. I briefly toy with the idea of a six-inch beehive.

I'm ready by six-fifteen and decide to kill the next few minutes drinking a glass of wine from the mini bar. I'm pretty sure the Merlot will cost Parliament around fifty bucks, but I'm using it for medicinal purposes so that shouldn't be a problem. Elliot knocks on our connecting door at sixty-thirty sharp. As I let him in, there's another knock, but this time at the front door. The Brit looks at me raising that irritating eyebrow of his and opens the other door, only to have Richard walk in. Oh shit! What's he doing here? I told his secretary I would meet him at the restaurant.

In his most self-righteous Lord of the Manor, condescending way, Elliot demands, "What are you doing here?"

Confused, Richard answers, "I'm here to take Mimi to the party."

Realizing this is in fact happening and not a vividly realistic nightmare, I ask, "Richard, didn't you get my message?"

He answers, "No."

"I told your secretary I would meet you at the party."

He responds, "I haven't checked in with her today."

Like a spoiled brat, Elliot declares, "This is my party and I didn't invite you."

I turn on Elliot and retaliate, "Don't be a baby. Richard is my guest and you have nothing to say about it."

Elliot demands, "How can you still want to see him after what happened last night?"

Richard, not being a complete moron, easily guesses what happened last night and asks his rival, "Have you broken up with your girlfriend, Elliot?"

Elliot retaliates, "That is none of your business!"

Richard inquires, "Really? It would seem to be very much my business. I don't think Mimi is the type to play second fiddle. So if you still plan on seeing this other woman, I still plan on seeing Mimi."

I want to throw my arms around Richard in gratitude for being so loyal to me, while I have certainly not returned the favor. I mean, here he is being treated to more information than I'm sure he wants, but he's standing his ground in his desire for me. I don't deserve this kind of devotion. I turn to Elliot and declare, "He's right. As long as Beatrice is in the picture, Richard will be as well. And I won't wait forever Elliot. Because I really like Richard and I'm not going to string him along for much longer."

Elliot looks torn between punching the wall and Richard, before declaring, "I told you to trust me, Mimi. I told you it would all work out."

Dripping sarcasm, Richard contributes, "That's original, Elliot. No man has ever told a woman to trust him before and then went right on to screw her over. You're a real prince, aren't you?"

I want to do something to stop this scene, but I also want to hear what Elliot has to say. While I do love him and want to trust him, Richard makes a very good point. Stan and Ollie must be back because Richard then asks me, "What does Edith Bunker have to say about this situation?"

Shocked, Elliot asks, "He knows about Edith Bunker?"

Richard retaliates, "Know about her? We've met and she loves me."

Elliot turns to me and demands, "He's met Edith Bunker?"

Richard intervenes, "Met her? I've rubbed her."

My head feels like it's about to blow apart into a million pieces and I scream, "Both of you, shut up! Just. Stop. Talking. None of this is going to get settled tonight and we have to get to the party." Then I ask, "How pray tell, do you both propose we do that?"

Elliot suggests that Richard go by himself and that he and I go together. Interestingly enough, Richard has the same idea about Elliot. So I intervene, "I am going by myself and I don't give a fig how the two of you get there." Then I grab my purse and storm out the door on my own. Lest you think I'm allowed a beautiful exit scene, both men are beside me in seconds and we all wind up going to Daniel together.

By all reports, the party looks like its going to be a major success. The marketing department at Dell has encouraged a good number of journalists to show. Everyone from the *New York Times* to *People* magazine is here and Parliament has enticed most of the stars from Elliot's books-turned-movies, who are based in New York, to appear. Although, getting stars to come out isn't that difficult as they are in constant pursuit of the next opportunity to stay in the public eye. Not to mention all of them would give their eyeteeth to be in another one of the films based on Elliot's work.

Elliot is immediately engulfed by the crowd of his admirers, so Richard and I slip away to the bar together. Once we're granted a moment of privacy, I apologize, "Richard, I'm very sorry about what Elliot told you at the hotel." As though he needs clarity, I add, "You know, about last night."

Richard takes my arm and replies, "You're a grown woman, Mimi, and you're allowed to sleep with whomever you wish. I knew from the start you and Elliot have something going on, although for the life of me I can't figure out why you're interested in him." Then he adds, "At the risk of sounding like one of the neutered men in a Lifetime movie, I really like you. So as long as you're willing to keep me in the picture, I'm willing to be there."

Clearly Jude and Hermione are back in charge. I kiss Richard on the cheek and say, "You know you're too good for me, don't you?"

"Never," he responds. Then he pulls me into his arms for a tender embrace.

The rest of the night is a whirlwind of introductions and schmoozing. I don't spend very much time with either Elliot or Richard. But I'm relieved to see that they seem to be keeping as far away from each other as humanly possible, keeping the *Bridget Jones* scene at bay for awhile longer.

Marcus and Miriam are both here tonight and Miriam spends a good amount of time introducing me to people from the New York social scene. She asserts, "If you're going to live here, you'll need to make conquests of all of these people." She adds helpful information, like, "Don't worry about Fern Childers, she's the biggest hanger-on in the whole room. She'll try to make you think she's a mover and shaker, but the truth is my cat has more power in this town." I tease Miriam and suggest a meeting with Fluffy as soon as he has an opening in his schedule.

Marcus introduces me to the likes of Barbara Walters and Kathy Lee Gifford and I'm hard-pressed to believe I'm actually at a party with people like this. I meet more movie stars than I ever realized existed, and the good news is, the party is so loud that I can't even hear Edith Bunker giving me shit over the shoes I'm wearing.

# Chapter 28

I feel like Dorothy from *The Wizard of Oz*, as her signature line loops through my head, "There's no place like home, there's no place like home." Pipsy may be small and boring, but after five fun-filled days in The Big Apple, I'm looking forward to a little of the same old, same old. When Richard and I say goodnight after the party he promises to call me twice a week to continue our courtship over the phone. I assure him I'll be back in New York within a month or two for the next wave of Elliot's book promotion. While he's delighted I am coming back, he rolls his eyes at the news Elliot will be there as well.

He cajoles, "Let's make a deal. If Elliot still hasn't lost the girlfriend by your next trip, how bout you bump me up to first string and let him warm the proverbial bench for awhile." I agree to consider his proposal as it has a lot of merit. Then I wonder how much I'm really going to see of Elliot, in the social sense, now that we are back home where we are obliged to be on our best behavior.

The first thing I notice after walking through my front

door is the odor. It smells like something has died in my house and I gag at the noxious stench. After dropping my bags in the entry, I follow my nose into the kitchen where I discover the plug for the refrigerator has been pulled out of the socket. Although the Mr. Coffee machine is still plugged in and turned on. Muffy must have pulled the cord on the fridge accidentally. By the aroma in the house, it's my guess that was days ago. I say a silent prayer of thanks the house didn't burn down and wonder where she's been staying.

I open all the windows and turn on the fans. I feel like a stranger in my own home. While everything looks just like it did when I left it, I realize *I* am not the same person I was before New York. Five days ago, I had a school girl crush on Elliot Fielding. But now, I'm full blown in love with him. Not to mention, my interest in Richard and the job offer I've received. Marcus informed me again last night he was serious about me coming to work for him. These are the things I always dreamed would happen to me, but I'm afraid they've caught me completely by surprise. I don't feel at all prepared. I know what you're thinking. You're thinking, Mimi Finnegan, you're thirty-four years old. How much time do you need to prepare for life? And while I would agree with you, I'm still freaking out.

Jonathan told me not to come into the office today as our plane didn't land until two-thirty. But here it is the middle of the afternoon and I'm home and I don't know what to do with myself. I decide to unpack and take a shower. Maybe a little steam will help clean the cobwebs out of my head.

My brain is so full of thoughts of Elliot and Richard and

New York and my future that I have no idea where to begin processing everything. What I really have to decide is how much time I'm going to give Elliot to call things off with Beatrice before I recognize he isn't going to. Again, I wonder why he doesn't just tell her it's not working out and make a nice clean break.

As I'm washing my hair, I toy with the idea of calling Kevin, but I'm not really in the mood to hear nice things about the beast. I consider ringing various members of my family, but I don't think I have the energy for that either. That's when it hits me who I really want to talk to. I want to talk to Marge. I want to confess how much I've cheated while I was away and I want her to tell me everything is going to be okay. Although she'll think she's just comforting me about my weight, but I'll take it as so much more. Marge is a solid, no-nonsense, practical kind of woman and I truly need her calming presence.

When I get out of the shower, I dry my hair as wet hair weighs a lot more than dry. I also put on the lightest weight clothes and shoes I own to try to negate some of the damage. I know I'm in trouble when I consider clipping my fingernails in hopes of losing a millionth of an ounce that way.

My car takes me right to Weight Watchers without stopping anywhere else first and I'm so excited I nearly run inside. I spot Marge through the glass door before I even walk in and already I feel the comfort of her aura. She greets me, "Hey there stranger. How was your trip?"

I confess, "I've been bad, Marge. Almost three whole days went by when I didn't even calculate my points."

"But you sure do look good! I love your hair." I thank her for the compliment and ask if she has time to weigh me in. She answers, "You betcha. Just let me get Mildred to cover the front."

As soon as Mildred emerges from the back, Marge asks for my chart and leads me to the weigh-in area. I feel like a semi driving up to the big scales off the freeway, hoping against hope that I haven't crossed the legal limit. I flip my shoes off and climb aboard, keeping my eyes closed the whole time.

Marge says, "Well let's see here, you were one hundred and sixty-seven on your last weigh-in and today you're one hundred and sixty- five point seven. Congratulations! That's another one point three pounds down."

I'm shocked by this news. I say, "How is that possible? I've been really bad."

Marge asks, "Exercising?"

"Like crazy," I tell her.

"That explains it, honey. I told you before, the more you exercise the more you can eat." Then she says the words I've been longing to hear, "You've done a great job. Everything is working out just fine."

Marge has no idea she's my spiritual leader and I am her grasshopper, but it's almost more mystical that way, don't you think? It's like my weight has become the barometer for my whole life. If Marge had told me my weight was up and I was going to have to try harder, I would have interpreted that to mean I'm slacking off on a spiritual level. I briefly think there's a book here, "The Tao of Marge." Okay, maybe the title isn't quite right, but the book has potential.

I drive home feeling a lot better about everything. When I pull up to my house there's a huge vase of flowers waiting for me at the front door. I immediately think of Elliot and wonder why I ever doubted him. I hold the card close to my heart before I open it, just savoring the moment. Then I flip open the envelope and read: "Dear Mimi, Come to New York, we NEED you!!! Love, Marcus." Marcus? How full of myself was I, thinking I was being romanced? But hey, there's no down side here. The flowers are beautiful and I'm wanted in New York. It's still a great feeling.

I flop onto the couch and wonder what my family would think if I up and moved to Manhattan. Certainly they would miss me, but they all had each other. Then I wonder if at thirty-four, I really have what it takes to start all over in a big city. I really am a small town girl and I'm not sure I have the inner strength to survive a move of this magnitude. I wonder what Marge would say. I briefly consider I am giving this woman too much power over my life, but then I think, "No, this is Marge, my counselor, my inspiration."

Kevin will be here any minute to work out as per our standing six o'clock arrangement. So I drag myself off the couch and change into shorts and a t-shirt. I can't help but think that even though I'm still a size twelve, my legs are looking gorgeous. I'm actually noticing the muscle tone for the first time and am more than a little impressed with myself.

Kevin and Muffy show up at the same time and appear to be having a grand old time. They're laughing and carrying on like a couple of kids and I'm delighted. They've both been going through difficult times in their lives. I'm glad they are becoming friends. It's got to be nice to share your burdens with someone who's been where you are. Kind of like me with Weight Watchers. Luckily they've brought groceries with them as they didn't yet know that the contents of my refrigerator and freezer are fit only for a landfill.

Upon seeing me, Kevin exclaims, "There she is!"

And Muffy announces, "Welcome home!" and I realize how nice it is to be missed. Muff feels awful when she discovers she unplugged the refrigerator. I ask her where she'd been staying and she cryptically answers, "With a friend."

Our workout is invigorating as my sister has decided we need to start adding sprints to our routine. We walk three blocks, then sprint one, then walk two blocks, then sprint one, and repeat. My heart is kabooming in my chest like mad but I love the way it feels. It's the perfect means of release for my angst over Elliot. The silver lining is that even if he never leaves Beatrice, I'll still get a rockin' ass out of the deal.

While Kevin and Muffy microwave our Weight Watchers dinners and throw a salad together, I run over to Rite Aid to buy a mouth guard. As dental isn't part of my health plan, I realize I had better start taking care of my grinding problem before it become an astronomical out-of-pocket expense. I find a guard for twenty bucks and buy two just incase I pulverize the first one in a week.

After a very pleasant dinner of vegetable lasagna, a salad, and a double fudge bar, I leave Kevin and Muffy to their own devices while I boil my mouth guard and form it to my teeth. I feel like Rocky Balboa once it's in and I bounce into the living room, spreading my hands open in a full bouquet, shouting,

"Yo, Adrian!" What I bounce into nearly causes me to swallow my new rubber insert. Muffy is snuggled up to Kevin on the couch with one leg wrapped over his lap and her mouth cemented to his. My first instinct is that Kevin has choked on his fudge bar and Muffy is giving him CPR. But when they pull apart as they hear my Rocky impersonation, I realize this was in fact a kiss and not a life saving medical procedure.

My sister and friend are both a little uncomfortable that I just caught them mid-tryst and I inquire, "Well, well, well, when did this happen?"

Kevin smiles first and says, "The day you left for New York."

Muffy injects, "Do you mind?"

Do I mind? Why would I mind? So I tell her just that. After all they are two people I care the world about and I'm delighted they have found each other. I'm a little jealous that they're the first ones to make out on my couch, but I'm still jazzed for them. I decide to leave the new lovebirds alone and take my mouth guard upstairs for its maiden voyage. With all the travel and exercising, I realize I'm exhausted and can't wait to hit the hay.

I dream I'm stuffing my face at the Mall of America food court. The smells are out of this world, the food looks amazing, but why is it all so rubbery? I'm chewing and chewing but I'm not getting any closer to actually consuming anything. That's when I realize that my mouth doesn't hurt because I'm a tooth grinder. My mouth hurts because I'm a sleep eater. In my semi-conscious state I realize this is something I can't even confess to Marge. It's simply too humiliating.

# Chapter 29

Going back to work on Wednesday morning is painful. I can't seem to get back into the groove to save my life. I'm supposed to be working on a promotional tour for a local band, but my heart just isn't in it. So I recommend Think Tank's music to three different venues by declaring 1. They could be worse 2. Their music's okay if you like that sort of thing, and 3. They're not my cup of tea, but what do I know, I'm old. None of the clubs booked them. It's like I had been hired by their competition.

In the office Elliot is back to treating me like he did before we went to New York, with arm's length indifference. He doesn't try to engage me in conversation once and he barely even speaks to me at our debriefing with Jonathan. He spends the day pacing around taking notes for his book, then retreats to a spare room set up as his office where he writes for hours on end. I try to convince myself that I'm being paranoid, but it isn't working. It feels like he is trying to detach from me. By five o'clock, I have a splitting headache and I walk out the door without saying goodbye to anyone.

Thursday is a blur. Friday is no better except for the fact Richard calls. We have a wonderful conversation and I recognize how lucky I am he still wants to be in my life. After hanging up, I start to realize I do not deserve to be treated the way Elliot is treating me. There is another man out there who full-blown adores me and my bunion and he is not otherwise committed to another woman. I start thinking perhaps it is time to try to refocus my energies on him.

Today is Saturday and the family is gathering over at Ginger and Jonathan's. They have an announcement they want to make. We're all pretty sure they are going to tell us they have been matched up with an adoptive child. That's what we're guessing anyway, as they're keeping quiet until we're all together.

I am really looking forward to being with my family. It hasn't been very long since we've all been together, but I feel so vulnerable right now I crave the company of a group of people who love me. It occurs to me this party would be perfect if only I could invite Marge. Then my whole support team would be assembled in one place. Of course today is officially about Ginger and Jonathan, but still, a girl can dream.

I am the last one to arrive at my sister's because I have to turn around when I realize I forgot Camille's baby doll. I figure today is the best time to distribute all of my booty from New York as I'm sure it's going to be a day of celebration.

Muffy opens the door for me and Kevin is at her side. I'm surprised to see him and say, "You again! Are you coming to all our family gatherings now?"

He gives me a cocky look, and answers, "Maybe."

Muffy interrupts sounding like she's had about fifty-eight cups of coffee and rattles off, "I wanted to let the family know Kevin and I are dating. I mean, I know it's totally fast after breaking up with Tom. But let's be honest, my ex has been servicing all the old broads at the club, not his wife. So it hasn't been much of a marriage for a long time. You know?"

I give her a look confirming that I think it's a wonderful idea and then push my way in. My family makes me feel like a movie star as they cluster around asking questions about my trip. It occurs to me my sisters have all gone to exotic locations throughout their adult lives, but this is the first time I've gone outside a three state radius since my senior year in high school when my class took a trip to Washington D.C. My family is treating my adventure with the proper level of enthusiasm.

I tell them all about The Plaza and the wonderful restaurants and parties and I even tell them about Richard. They are so excited for me that I feel like I'm living the fun all over again. Of course I don't breathe a word about Elliot because I'm really starting to wonder what's going to happen with him. It breaks my heart to think it, but the way he's treating me is not the way a man treats the woman he loves.

I pass out the gifts and everyone is very appreciative. Renée prances around in the drag queen shoes like they're flats, Dad has already filled his Guinness stein, the kids are going nuts for their toys, and Ginger can't stop laughing at her "Frick"en t-shirt (I'll have to remember to tell Richard it's a big hit.) I tell Kevin what his t-shirts say as I didn't know he would be here, so they are still at home under my bed.

The doorbell rings again and I look around wondering who

has yet to arrive. The only person missing is Tom, and let's be honest, he'd have to have a death wish to show up at a gathering of the Finnegans' right now. Ginger answers the door and she leads Elliot and Beatrice into the living room. Elliot looks surprised to see us all and I am certainly surprised to see them, and Beatrice is surprised to see Kevin. Are you getting a feel for the scene here?

Jonathan starts passing around mimosas and once everyone has a glass he raises his in a toast, "Now that we are all together, Ginger and I want you to know we are going to have a baby!"

And the crowd goes wild. We were expecting as much, but actually hearing the news is positively thrilling. Mom asks, "Now what kind of baby are we getting? Chinese, Romanian, American?"

Ginger smiles and replies, "We are getting a half-Irish, quarter-German and quarter English-baby."

Dad interjects, "What are the chances you're going to adopt a baby with the exact same heritage as you and Jonathan? That's just amazing!"

Dad's question sort of hits everyone at once. What *are* the chances they are going to get a baby sharing their identical heritage?

Smiling more brilliantly than I have ever seen, Ginger announces, "The chances are pretty good when we're the ones who are making the baby."

Mom bursts into tears at the same time that Renée yells, "Oh my god, oh my god!" It's total and complete pandemonium. The family gathers around Ginger and

Jonathan in a ring of celebration.

Jonathan explains that he and Ginger decided to try in vitro fertilization. They didn't tell us about it ahead of time because they weren't sure it would work and they didn't want to disappoint us if it didn't.

Muffy asks, "This means there could be more than one baby in there, right?"

Ginger answers, "A pretty good chance actually."

This is such wonderful news that the Finnegans are beside themselves with happiness. Jonathan has to shout over the noise to get everyone to calm down and he raises his glass again, "Now I would like you all to help me toast Elliot and Beatrice." I feel like my blood has been replaced with ice water when he announces, "Congratulations on your engagement!"

Holy fucking what? Their what? What, what, what, what, what?! Elliot catches my eye and appears to want to crawl under the couch to hide. I just stare at him completely oblivious to the fact my family is toasting their marriage and offering their good wishes for a long and happy life. I of course don't join them as I'm pretty sure my heart stopped beating as soon as I heard Jonathan's words. I feel like a dead woman standing. I'm as still as a statue as the energy of the rooms hums around me desperately trying to resuscitate me. But it's not working. I'm just waiting for my body to realize I've died and to fall over in its final act here on earth. But I don't fall, I just stand and stare, and wonder what the fuck?

Muffy gets all caught up in the celebration and raises her glass and announces, "I would like you all to toast Kevin Beeman!" My family looks very confused until she explains,

"My new boyfriend!"

And the Finnegans go crazy again. They are all cheering when Beatrice shouts out in indignation, "But Kevin can't be your boyfriend. He's gay!"

That gives my family a moment for pause. It also makes Muffy laugh out loud, "I don't know where you got your information Beatrice, but I can assure you that Kevin is not gay."

She vehemently replies, "Yes he is. He's gay with the black bartender from La Petite Maison. I saw them."

Muffy treats Beatrice like she's got a screw loose and the rest of the family takes their cue from her. After all if she claims to know first hand that Kevin isn't gay, that's good enough for them. They don't need the particulars.

But Beatrice isn't done, "Kevin, didn't you say you were gay?"

Kevin turns beet red and looks like he wants to join Elliot under the couch. He answers, "That was just my American sense of humor, Beatrice. I'm sorry if it confused you."

Beatrice responds, "But you were kissing Mimi to make your boyfriend jealous, you said so." That has to get my family wondering what's what so I save the day by nearly shouting, "I'd like you all to toast me now!" Everyone looks surprised as I declare, "I'm moving to New York to be with Richard! I've already been offered a job there with Parliament and I'll be moving as soon as I can pack."

My mom cries out, "Oh Meems, I don't want you to leave home! I mean now that we're all together..."

She's really getting choked up, so my dad takes over, "But

if that's where your young man is, we are thrilled for you. We only want you to be happy, dear."

Well they're shit out of luck because happy is the farthest thing away from what I feel. I feel miserable and betrayed and mistreated and madder than hell, but I do not feel happy. I want to stay home and be here for Ginger. I don't want to leave my parents or any of the rest of them. But how can I stay now? How can I keep seeing Elliot knowing what a good for nothing rat skunk bastard he is? I just can't. I deserve to be happy. I deserve to have a life of my own. And it would seem the only person willing to cast his lot with me is in New York.

Once everyone breaks off into smaller groups, Elliot tries to get my alone but I tell him to go to hell. He pleads there are mitigating circumstances and I declare, "If you don't get the fuck away from me right this fucking minute, I'm going to scream." He seems to believe me, because he walks off to join Jonathan.

Meanwhile Beatrice is hanging all over Kevin demanding an explanation. Kevin hems and haws until Muffy comes to his rescue.

I go off by myself and try to figure out how my life has turned into such a total and complete shambles. The man I love is marrying someone else, I'm moving to New York and have just realized I don't want to. I'm desperately sad to leave my family and if that isn't enough, Edith Bunker hasn't spoken to me in days and I kind of miss her. My eyes start to leak and before I know it, I'm sitting out in my sister's gazebo clutching my stomach and doubling over at the staggering amount of grief coursing through my body.

# Chapter 30

Somehow I manage to get through the rest of the afternoon at Ginger's but I'm not sure how. It doesn't help that Elliot and Beatrice stay until the bitter end either. Elliot keeps trying to get his bride-to-be to leave but she is bound and determined to stay. She wants answers from Kevin and isn't going to give up until she gets them. Kevin on the other hand stays very close to Muffy for protection.

When I get home, I go straight to bed even though it is only six-thirty. I don't even take my clothes off first. I just lay under the covers and cry until I nearly dehydrate myself, which takes some doing as I drank about twenty-seven mimosas this afternoon. Sometime before falling asleep Edith Bunker actually speaks her first words to me in days. She said, "Yay, we're going back to Richard! I told you he was the one for you."

So much for missing her. I grumble, "Go to bed, Edith Bunker. I don't care what you think." While I know I will enjoy being around Richard, there was simply no other part of me looking forward to living in New York. All of a sudden, it doesn't feel like some grand *Sex and the City* adventure, it feels desolate and bleak and lonely. My family won't be there and Kevin won't be there and Marge won't be there and Elliot "fucking" Fielding won't be there. Why oh why oh why oh why oh why am I going to miss him so much? What's wrong with me?

But I know what's wrong with me. I'm in love with the jackal. That's what has really set me over the edge, "There are mitigating circumstances, Mimi." What mitigating circumstances? What could possibly have compelled Elliot to propose to Beatrice? I suddenly think of the one thing that would force his hand. What if Beatrice is pregnant? Oh no, could that possibly be the reason? What if she got pregnant before Elliot and I realized we were in love with each other? It dawns on me that Stan and Ollie have kicked Jude and Hermione to the curb. My romance writers would have never let something this horrific happen to me, but Stan and Ollie would rejoice at their comic genius. Those cruel hearted bastards!

I am in such a state of despair I simply can't get out of bed. So I go back to sleep and don't wake up until two the next afternoon when the phone rings. It's Renée calling to tell me I should move into the apartment she and Laurent keep in Manhattan. She says something like, "Try it out and see what you think. That way if you decide you don't like it there, you're not committed to a lease."

I think I thanked her and agreed it was a good idea, but I may have just hung up on her too. I don't really remember. By five-thirty the phone rings again but I don't have the energy to pick it up and I just go back to sleep. The next thing I know, it's two-thirty in the morning and I have to pee like a race horse. On my way to the toilet, I briefly look in the mirror and am stopped short by what I see. There is a wild-eyed harridan in my house and I have no idea who she is. All I know is she looks demented and she's scaring me so I go back to bed.

I crawl under the covers and don't wake up until ten o'clock the next morning. I wouldn't even bother getting up now except that it's been over forty hours since I've last eaten any food and my stomach is growling. I briefly realize it's Monday and I'm supposed to be at work but the gnawing in my stomach supersedes any other thoughts. That's why I make myself seventeen pieces of Weight Watchers French toast. I put them on my turkey platter because it's the largest serving dish I own. Once I pour half a bottle of syrup over the whole shebang I dig in. Sadly, I'm full after only a few pieces, so I save the rest for later and curl up on the couch. I don't wake up again until five-forty-five when I hear Kevin and Muffy come through the front door.

From what I'm able to gather, they are horrified by how I look. Muffy wants to know what's wrong and Kevin declares he's left me eight messages in the last day-and-a-half. He says he even came by but no one answered the door, so he thought I was out. Again Muffy asks what's wrong and without my permission Kevin tells her all about Elliot. Muffy is totally heartsick for me and I think she is about to leave and go murder him when Kevin whispers something else to her. Her expression is one of such horror I can only assume I was right and Beatrice is pregnant after all.

I stare up at the two of them but all of a sudden I can't understand what they're saying. It's like they're the grown-ups in a *Peanuts* cartoon and all I can decipher is wwhhhhaa whhaa whhaaa wwwwha... Thank God the blissful arms of sleep capture me again and I don't stir until morning.

The first sensation I feel is a warm wash cloth on my face. It's heavenly and wonderful and soothing, but then it's gone and I'm cold. It's the cold that catapults me into consciousness. Muffy smiles at me and asks, "How are you Meems?"

I can actually hear her, so I answer, "I want to die. Could you please just leave so I can die?"

"No." My sister declares, "No dying on my watch." Then she proceeds to inform me that Kevin told her all about Elliot. She says she knows that my heart is breaking but the best thing I can do is to pick myself up and move on.

I mumble something like, "Can't" so she merely pulls the covers off of me and runs a bath. While she's dragging me into the bathroom and trying to take off my stinky clothes from Saturday, she tells me she's informed the family that I have the flu which is why I haven't returned any of their calls. She also explains she called work and told them I'm sick and that she will update them every day so they might get an idea when I'll be back.

Muffy washes my hair for me and even shaves my legs as I don't seem to be capable of lifting my arms. My appendages feel like they weigh five hundred pounds each. Once she gets me out of the tub and dried off she asks, "Who's Marge, Meems?"

I'm confused and wonder how my sister knows about Marge but I don't have the energy to ask, so I just answer, "She's my Weight Watchers leader."

Muff tucks me back into bed and the next thing I know, I'm waking up again and staring into the eyes of my spiritual leader. Marge is standing right here in my bedroom. It briefly occurs to me that I've died and Marge is my angel meeting me on the other side. I reach my hand out to hers and ask, "Did you die too, Marge?"

She takes my hand in hers and says, "No one died, honey. Not me, not you. We're both still kicking."

I believe her, but I'm confused, "What are you doing here then?"

She answers, "Your sister said you've had quite a shock and you've been calling out my name in your sleep. She called me and asked if I could stop by." Then she asks, "What can I do for you, honey?"

I stare up at her as tears stream down my face and I ask, "Is it all going to be okay, Marge? I just want to know it's all going to be okay."

She squeezes my hand and bestows a beautiful comforting smile on me and says, "You're doing just fine, Mimi. You're doing just fine and it's all going to be okay."

As I close my eyes again and fall back asleep, I remember actually believing her.

I stay home for the rest of the week, but by Thursday I start to return my family's phone calls. Muffy has done a good job convincing them not to bother me, but they were really starting to get worried. I assure my mom that I am well enough to keep her homemade chicken soup down and I have a nice long conversation with Renée regarding my plans to move to New York.

You'd think I would have decided not to move but I'm afraid that if I stay here in Pipsy, I'll never be able to get out of bed again. That's why I call Marcus on Friday and accept his job offer on a three month trial basis. If either one of us doesn't think it's going to work by the end of the time period, we can call it quits with no worries, no hurt feelings, no legal action. Plus, this way I won't have to sell my house and move all of my earthly possessions right away, as I will be staying at Renée and Laurent's furnished apartment. I tell him I can be in New York as soon as Monday.

My next call is to Jonathan to explain why I'm not giving two weeks notice. He assures me he understands the pull of love and wishes me and Richard well. He says if Ginger were over a thousand miles away from him, he couldn't bear it either.

My mom and dad are throwing me a going away party on Saturday and my flight leaves at ten o'clock Sunday morning. None of my family, with the exception of Muffy and Kevin, can understand why I am departing so abruptly, but they wisely don't ask a lot of questions.

When I finally hang up the phone after all of my calls, I begin the process of deciding what to pack. I promise myself I will only take three suitcases so it doesn't feel like I'm really moving. After all, I've just ripped the scab off an open wound and now I have to find some way to staunch the flow of blood.

# Chapter 31

I wake up this morning and have a hard time believing it's already Friday. Only two days until I start my new life. I finished most of my packing yesterday and today I'm going to pay my bills and relax. Muffy is going to stay in the house so I don't have to worry about closing it up. But as a precaution, we moved the Mr. Coffee pot away from the refrigerator so she doesn't get confused over the outlets again.

Kevin is taking me to dinner tonight, just the two of us, which I'm really looking forward to. On the way, I'm going to stop in for my final Pipsy weigh-in and say goodbye to Marge. I know I've lost weight this week, but not in any healthy way as I've hardly eaten anything and I haven't worked out once. Unless of course you consider crawling out of bed to go to the bathroom a workout, which it most certainly felt like.

I never fully realized how miserable depression could be. When I'd see the TV commercials with the sad little cloud bouncing along in the rain, I'd just think it was clever advertising. Never in my wildest dreams did I realize the overwhelming physical as well as emotional toll the disorder takes.

Once I'm clean, I dab on a little makeup. The thought being to not scare myself should I pass any more mirrors. The doorbell rings while I'm pouring my raisin bran and I assume it's one of my family come for a last minute visit before I leave. This is why I simply open the door without asking who it is.

Elliot Fielding is standing on my stoop. While I'm not happy to see him, I am delighted to see that he looks absolutely miserable. If this was his idea of a going away gift I'm all for it, although I truly did not want to set eyes on him at all. He takes a step towards the threshold and says, "Mimi, we have to talk."

I don't have the energy to slam the door in his face or to even get angry. I'm totally and thoroughly drained, so I just answer, "No, Elliot, we don't need to talk. You've made the decision who you want to be with and now, so have I. So please just leave."

He begs, "Please listen to me, Mimi. I really want to explain."

But I interrupt, "Will explaining make you any less engaged to Beatrice?"

He says it won't so I simply say, "Goodbye, Elliot," and I close the door in his face.

Why did he have to come over? Some men just can't stand having a woman mad at them. But there is nothing that he can say to make this all right for me. Sure, he could tell me Beatrice is pregnant, and I would understand getting married is the right thing to do. But it would not make it any easier for me to hear the words.

I've lost my appetite again. Just so you know I've been through small depressions in the past which have always resulted in weight gain. I'm an "eat for all emotions" kind of gal. But this time, I can't even think of food. I don't want to look at it, smell it or even taste it, nothing. I'm grieving and the thought of eating trivializes my heartache. I just want to go back to bed. But I'm afraid if I do, I may never get up.

I decide to go see Marge and weigh in early. When I get there, she's in the middle of a meeting so I just sit and wait for her. Marge is telling everyone to buy pre-washed spinach leaves and to put two cups of them onto their frozen entrees at night. The spinach will help bulk up their meals at the same time adding fiber, vitamin D and iron. I take a mental note to remember this should I ever decide to eat again.

When she's done with the meeting, Marge comes right over and asks how I'm feeling. Before I can stop myself, I tell her everything. I tell her all about Elliot and Richard and my move to New York. She listens with the patience of the Dalai Lama and says, "Let's weigh you in." Marge steers me towards the scale and once I get on she announces, "Mimi, this is the first time I've ever said this to one of my girls, but you've lost too much weight." She tells me I am down five pounds and considering I didn't have a lot to lose, in addition to my emotional upset, she is not at all pleased. She advises me to go out with Kevin tonight and to order at least three courses paying no attention to points at all. She says she'd rather I have a gain next week than another loss.

Before I leave, Marge gives me the address of the Weight Watchers meeting closest to Renée's apartment and encourages me to call her to let her know how I'm doing. She even gives me her home number in case I need her after business hours. It's harder to say goodbye to her than I thought. I can't imagine my new leader in the Big Apple is going to care about me this much.

I haven't heard from Edith Bunker since she cheered over the move to New York. I have therefore decided perhaps I should drive to Burger City and order a bunion for lunch. After all, as long as mine is no longer nagging me, I might as well see if I can eat them again. This is the first time I have to force my car to take me there. Normally I'm all shocked and surprised to find myself in the drive-thru line, but today I feel like I'm behind a manual steering wheel. I have to actually fight with it to get it to make the turn.

The tantalizing aroma of bunions hits me as soon as I pull in and I immediately inhale the heavenly scent. I wait for Edith Bunker to stop me but she doesn't say a word, so I order a single cheeseburger with a small order of fries and a large diet coke.

As soon as I pay for my food, I drive around the corner and park under a shade tree and eat. I start slowly at first, just a small bite that I chew about twenty times before swallowing. Then I take a bite of a French fry. It's beyond delicious. After a couple more bites, I start to munch with gusto and by the time I'm done I realize I'm going to be okay. After all, I'm pretty sure the high school crush I had on Eric Dilman caused me as much angst as this, although that was drawn out over an agonizing four years instead of just a few weeks. Plus, it's not like there isn't a wonderful man waiting for me in New York. I feel like the little engine again, but instead of just thinking I can, I actually know I can and I will.

Kevin takes me to Bumble Bee's for dinner. It's a chain restaurant that is known nationwide for its comfort food. I tell him what Marge said about me trying to gain weight this week and Kevin is delighted. So when we sit down I order potato skins with bacon, cheddar cheese and sour cream as an appetizer. Kevin orders a salad with dressing on the side. For my main course I have meatloaf with caramelized onions and macaroni and cheese. Kevin has the broiled chicken breast with grilled vegetables. And for dessert I have the triple layer frozen mocha mud pie extravaganza. Kevin has a bowl of fresh berries.

I cannot believe he's being so good with such a wealth of temptations in front of him. But he just says, "I can't either. But you know what? I'm happy for the first time since Megan left me and I realize I don't even want the junk anymore. I just want to be my old self again."

I'm thrilled for my friend. I know his newfound happiness is a result of his relationship with Muffy and while I don't know what their future holds, I do know they are the perfect support for one another right now.

Over dinner, Kevin and I have an unspoken pact not to talk about Elliot and Beatrice. Instead, he asks me all about Marcus and the new people I'll be working with. I tell him as much as I know and he declares it sounds very exciting. He also promises he and Muffy will come out and visit me next month to make sure that I'm doing okay. That is the best bit of news I've had all week and I promise to show them all over the city.

When Kevin drops me off at my house, he gives me a kiss on the cheek and says, "I'm so happy we stumbled back into each other's lives again."

I laugh and reply, "Of course you are. I'm the reason you reunited with your high school dream girl."

Kevin laughs, "There is that. But seriously, Meems, I love you like you're a member of my family and please know there's nothing I wouldn't do for you."

Before I can start boohooing all over again, I tell Kevin I'll see him at the party tomorrow and warn him to keep upbeat. Saying goodbye to my family is going to be hard enough as it is.

# Chapter 32

The captain has cleared us for take off before I've decided whether I'm going to stay on the plane or not. Of course once we actually start accelerating down the runway, I'm committed to go. I'm moving to New York. Somewhere over Ohio I start to get my first twinge of excitement. Not so much excitement of leaving home as anticipation of being hundreds of miles away from Elliot. I figure with that kind of distance, the pull he has over me will have to dissipate somewhat.

Marcus is flying me out first-class which is one of the perks he promises I will always have working for him and before I know it, I'm eating a delicious omelet with fresh fruit and bacon. I imagine the poor folks back in cattle are begging for a second bag of peanuts. If I could, I'd smuggle some bacon to them as I have only ever known coach before my last two flights and I know how stingy they can be with their snacks. I may have to keep working in New York for the flying privileges alone. As Marge has advised, I'm letting myself enjoy food this week. Yesterday at my going away party I even ate fried chicken and coleslaw, two of my most favorite foods.

Saying goodbye to my family was difficult, but not as hard as I expected as they were all going out of their way to be cheerful and bubbly. Plus, in addition to Kevin and Muffy promising a visit, everyone else said they would come as well. Ginger wants to get a bigger size in her "Frick"en t-shirt so she can wear it into her pregnancy, Jonathan wants to meet with Marcus regarding Elliot's PR campaign (now that I'm not there to be the liaison between the offices), Mom and Dad want to visit some authentic Irish pubs, and Renée and Laurent are desperate to get away from the kids for a few days. All in all, it looks like the Finnegans aren't going to let me get too lonely for them.

My flight lands at three-thirty and by the time we hit the tarmac, my pulse starts to pound double time in anticipation. I've never actually been to Renée and Laurent's apartment and I'm anxious to see where I'm going to be living for the next three months. Renée assures me it's not grand but it's head and shoulders above the accommodations of the average New Yorker. She claims a five hundred square foot apartment easily runs over twenty-five hundred a month in rent. I'm shocked when I hear this, but then she adds a lot of those only have windows facing brick walls of other buildings. Apparently television shows are very misleading.

As I exit the terminal, I see a man holding up a sign that says "Mimi Finnegan." I briefly wonder if there could possibly be another Mimi Finnegan at LaGuardia this afternoon. I decide to ask him just in case. Joey, the man holding the sign, informs me he is looking for the Mimi Finnegan that is friends with Richard Bingham. I smile brightly and assure him he is looking for me then. Leave it to Richard to make sure I arrive in style. Joey collects my luggage from baggage claim and then leads me out front to a shiny black stretch limousine. Inside are flowers and a note from Richard saying he's sorry he wasn't able to meet me himself. He wishes me a wonderful first night in the city and promises to take me out to dinner tomorrow night to celebrate. I'm starting to feel the tiniest wee little bit like Carrie Bradshaw. I wonder if Richard is going to be my Mr. Big after all.

Joey drops me off at Renée's apartment on Eighty-Sixth Street and Central Park West. The building is a lovely red brick structure dating from the turn of the century. It positively takes my breath away. Joey hands my luggage over to the doorman, Julio, who in turn helps me lug it to the elevator. Another uniformed man pushes the button for the eighth floor and helps me schlep my belongings to my new home, apartment 8B. I briefly wonder how much this is all costing my sister but I know the actual number might give me a coronary so I force myself not to think about it.

Renée is right. By Pipsy standards this is not a big place to live, but what it lacks for in size it more than makes up for in charm. And, drum roll please, there is a terrific view of Central Park! That alone makes it feel three times as big. All total there are four rooms plus a bath, living room, small dining room, teeny kitchen, and bedroom. For me, it's love at first sight.

The first thing I do after settling in is to check the kitchen and make a list for the grocery store. The refrigerator is stocked with the non-perishable essentials of any model turned designer; Perrier and Champagne, but nothing else. The freezer houses coffee and shriveled ice cubes, and the cabinets, my friend, are totally bare. Renée has already told me which grocery store to go to for the basics and happily, she explains, it is located right down the block from Zabar's where I simply must go for my gourmet treats. I wonder if they carry Cheetos.

Once I pay for my provisions at D'Agastino's, they promise to have them delivered within a half hour so I don't have to worry about lugging four heavy bags home. I walk down the block to Zabar's and am immediately shocked by the number of people packed into this establishment. The cheese counter alone is enough to make me an agoraphobic. While one lady shouts for eight ounces of the Exploratore, another man angrily demands the *Extra-Sharp* Cheddar, and an old lady rams her elbow into my ribs so hard I swear I hear a crack. I expect her to apologize, but instead she demands, "No cuts. Get a number like everyone else." I want to tell her old ladies are supposed to be nice and sweet, not bullies. But it occurs to me she might beat me over the head with her baguette so I opt to walk away.

I force my way out of Zabar's and try to remember to call Renée to find out a less crowded time to shop there. I also make a note to ask her what exactly I should buy. I have the feeling it's the kind of place where you're expected to move through the aisles at a brisk pace and not take up valuable space by browsing. After all, if an old lady will attempt an ass-kicking by what she perceives as a cut, imagine what a young, healthy person would do to you if you diddled around in front of the olives for too long.

Once my foodstuffs have been delivered to the apartment, I

choose a take-out menu from the stack Renée has by the phone and pick which one I'm going to call for dinner. I decide on Empire Szechwan and immediately start hankering for the Cashew Chicken with Snow Peas and the Egg Drop Soup. Once my order is placed, I set about unpacking my belongings.

As I'm hanging up all of my lovely new clothes, the phone rings and nearly scares the life out of me. I am greeted by Richard's enthusiastic, "Welcome to the Big Apple!"

I thank him very much and ask if he wants to join me for Chinese, but unfortunately, he says, he is still in the Hamptons visiting his mother. I feel very cosmopolitan when I ask if he took the Jitney. This is more lingo I've picked up from watching *Sex and the City* and while I'm sure Richard, did not in fact take public transportation, I still feel really cool using the word Jitney. Before hanging up, he promises to pick me up tomorrow night at seven for dinner and I ask if we can't make it six-thirty. I confess that I'm not used to eating so late. Once the words are out of my mouth I realize that I sound like a total hick, but it's not like I've ever pretended to be someone I'm not with Richard, so why start now?

After the most delicious Chinese food I've ever eaten, a sumptuous bubble bath, and a very comfortable night's sleep, I'm up at six to get ready for my first day at New York's Parliament office. I am terrified to be going in. It's one thing to pop in from the sister company for a few days. It's quite another to actually be a part of the daily whirl of activity.

I decide to bluff them by wearing my sleekest summer suit, which happens to be an off-white linen blend, and boldly pairing it with citron green shoes and matching shell. Then I throw my hair in hot rollers for the necessary amount of time to achieve the confidence boosting "bigness" I'm after. I look in the mirror to garner the full effect and am once again hit by how stunning I look. I still don't recognize my reflection as the insecure Mimi Finnegan who rules my brain but I live in hope that my two identities will merge sooner rather than later.

Marcus introduces me around the office and assigns a co-worker by the name of Trish to show me the ropes. Clearly Trish has more important things to do as she treats me like I'm a hundred and sixty pound bowling ball chained to her ankle. More often than not, she acts like I'm not even there and simply carries on with her normal routine. The day is saved when Jim Burger, Trish's immediate boss, tells her he wants me to work on the Shimmer account with him. Trish shoots me a look like I just stepped on her injured cat before showing me to Jim's office.

Jim Burger is a very nice, forty-something, short, chubby Jewish man. I like him on sight. He jokingly explains that spending the morning with Trish is their office's version of trial by fire. More than one person has apparently quit within two hours of tagging along with her. Being I've lasted a whole four, he assures me I have what it takes to make it at Parliament, New York. Jim hands me the folder for the Shimmer account, which is a well-known Los Angeles based cosmetics company. He explains they are adding a new line called "Pink" and half of the proceeds will be donated to finding a cure for breast cancer. We are responsible for promoting the line in as many magazines as we can get to cover it.

I'm immediately excited about the project and realize my new assignment is a far cry from pimping bad rock music to small suburban night-clubs. Jim takes me along to his team's meeting and introduces me to Helena, captain of our crew, Jocina, party planner, and Imelda, all around workhorse. I don't know if it's my excitement for the project itself, but I immediately like all of the women. Helena announces I will initially be working with Jocina on party planning as we have three rather large events we need to put together for the launch.

By the end of the day, not only am I delighted with my new job, but all of a sudden I feel like I'm doing something worthwhile for society. It's a nice boost for my sagging ego.

I get back to the apartment by six-fifteen and decide to wear my work clothes to dinner as I don't have time to agonize over which dress to change into. I fluff my hair, darken my makeup and reapply my perfume just as the doorman calls up to announce my guest.

Richard looks good and when I answer the door, I immediately realize how much I've missed him. I happily give him a quick kiss and we're off to dinner. Tonight we're eating at a very elegant restaurant off of Madison and Seventy-Ninth called Ravine. In case you're wondering, this is where Edith Bunker makes her first attempt at conversation in several days. She wants me to tell Richard how thrilled she is to see him and wonders if he might be interested in rubbing her after dinner. I of course refuse to pass along her request and she pays me back with punishing jabs all night.

Richard orders us a lovely bottle of Viogne and then we get down to the business of catching up. He shocks me by demanding, "Tell me about Elliot."

Before I begin the saga, I lament, "Richard, you won't believe it when you hear it." Then I fill him in on all the gory details.

He asks, "What reasons did he give you for proposing to her?"

"Reasons?" I demand. "What reasons? I didn't let him explain why he did it because the bottom line is that he did. He's engaged to Beatrice."

My nice sweet suitor takes my hand and very genuinely asks, "How are you doing?"

And just what any man wants when he takes a woman out for an expensive meal, I burst into tears and bemoan the fact another has broken my heart. It's like every bad dating cliché that's ever been told except Richard consoles me and tells me that it will eventually get better. Then he assures me when it does, he will be there for me.

He tries to elevate my mood by declaring for the waitress' benefit, "I don't care how much you cry, I will not have sex with you in a public bathroom."

Our server stares at Richard and then at me in total shock. I mean, I'm sure she's heard her fair share of juicy comments whilst waiting tables in this city but this one seems to particularly capture her attention. So I play along and reply, "I understand why you won't do it under the table, but if you don't let me have my way with you in the bathroom by the time the night is over, we're through!"

Trista, our waitress, apparently shares our conversation with everyone else on the staff because the rest of the night involves a string of restaurant employees slowly walking by our table giving us the once-over. When I get up to use the bathroom, no less than three staff members join me, probably to make sure my date and I don't get into trouble. Richard worked magic by taking the focus off of Elliot and giving us an inside joke to enjoy. Of course when we leave I say, "It's too bad we can never eat here again." He agrees.

# Chapter 33

The next day, Jocina and I discover we work very well together. She thrives on planning these affairs and when she describes some of the other parties she's been responsible for throwing, I'm duly impressed. The first of our events is a lunch for the Susan G. Komen Foundation. We are currently working on a list of celebrity guests to invite as speakers. Jocina mentions a few high profile movie stars known for their philanthropic work and then surprise, surprise, she mentions a name I am very familiar with; Elliot Fielding.

Trying to look nonplussed, I ask, "Why would Elliot Fielding be a good match for breast cancer? It seems like a strange fit to me."

Jocina looks shocked and says, "But you've been working with him on his book launch, surely you know."

"Know what?" I demand a little too sharply.

Jocina answers, "Know about his girlfriend."

With a sense of dread I ask, "What about Beatrice?"

Jocina explains that shortly after becoming involved with Elliot, Beatrice was diagnosed with breast cancer. Elliot, unlike the majority of men in his situation, actually stayed with her and helped her through it, a fact that would make him an excellent candidate to speak at our lunch.

I feel like I've been punched in the stomach. I have no idea what to say so I simply nod my head in agreement. He would be a good choice. Jocina requests I do the honors of asking him being that he and I have a prior working history. Of course I agree as I'm sure it wouldn't be very professional to explain I can't because I had sex with him in a carriage right before he proposed to his girlfriend, the one that once had breast cancer.

As soon as I get a few minutes to myself, I run into my office and call Kevin. He answers but before he can say more than, "hello," I bombard him with questions. "Did you know about Beatrice's breast cancer? Why didn't you tell me? Is that what you meant when you said she was a tragic figure? What is going on Kevin?!"

Kevin asks how I found out and I answer that apparently it isn't a secret as I heard it from a co-worker at Parliament.

He slowly starts to explain, "I didn't tell you because Beatrice asked me not to. She doesn't like meeting people and then having them automatically feel sorry for her because she's a cancer survivor. Of course that was before she went to the specialist in Hilldale last week and found out that the cancer is back."

I interrupt, "The cancer is what?!"

Kevin answers, "It's back."

Oh god, I want to vomit. "I don't know what to say."

He responds, "Oh Meems, that's why Elliot asked her to

marry him. Beatrice says their relationship has never been a grand passion but he has been her rock. She doesn't know how she would have gotten through her first two bouts of chemo without him."

"Two bouts?" I'm shocked.

Sadly, Kevin answers, "This is her second recurrence and her third battle. She's already had one mastectomy and one partial."

I remember the turban wearing young woman at Elliot's book signing, the one who declared he was her hero and I feel tears start to fill in my eyes. She must have been dealing with cancer herself and my guess is her significant other was not up to the task of seeing her through it, hence her declaration she wished more men were like Elliot.

I thank Kevin for the information and hang up. Beatrice isn't pregnant after all, because in all likelihood she's dying. What are the chances she will fight cancer three times in three years and live to a ripe old age? My heart breaks for her and I wonder if I have it in me to begrudge her marriage to the man who has stood by her side through it all, even if he is the man I love with all of my heart. Those fucking bastards Stan and Ollie simply don't know when to leave well enough alone, do they?

I'm not sure how I get through the rest of the day. But between you, me, and the devil, I fantasize all afternoon about Beatrice dying. Isn't that the singularly most horrific thing you've ever heard? I mean what kind of self-centered, heartless, cruel bitch would do something like that? The truth is I would have never conceived of her death on my own but now that it's out there and she has cancer anyway, what harm would it do if she dies before she marries Elliot? I have to force myself to stop thinking these thoughts as they become a cancer in and of themselves. Plus only me, and say, a serial killer, would ever ponder such a horrendous outcome. I begin to think I should go to confession but I'm afraid of shocking the priest on duty.

I realize as much as I try to prevent it, I fall more in love with Elliot than ever before. Not only do I love him, but I also love his unselfishness that makes him do this heroic thing. This is obviously a finer attribute than I possess as I am secretly harboring thoughts of premature death for the woman he is so valiantly supporting. I realize if Beatrice doesn't die first, Elliot should marry her. There is no way that he can abandon her now after being her rock through all of her years of struggle.

I, Mimi Finnegan, who has gone on a diet, changed her hair color, joined Weight Watchers, move to New York, and has finally begun wearing stylish clothes, am apparently not through with my reinvention. I must also cut ties with Elliot Fielding and find a new love. It's the right thing to do, for him and me. His life shouldn't be made any harder by knowing I am pining away for him. Therefore I choose to embrace a romance with Richard Bingham. When I see Elliot next, as I'm sure to do, I will treat him like a supportive friend but nothing else. No more pining, no more whining, I will be lovely to him and let him know I encourage and respect his decision. I will be a beneficial member to his PR team and on a personal level, I will take him off the hook and let him know he has my support in marrying Beatrice. The brand new Mimi Finnegan is now the brand new and improved Mimi Finnegan.

# Chapter 34

Renée says the best time to shop at Zabar's is from ten to eleven-thirty and two to four-fifteen Monday through Wednesday. To which I say, "Renée, I have a job, I can't shop then."

She responds, "So does everyone else in New York which is why those are the best times to go." I briefly wonder if the store could possibly be worth all the drama of going back, but my sister assures me it is. I plan to see if Richard will escort me this weekend. Maybe he can be my body guard against old ladies wielding long loaves of crusty bread.

It is already Friday evening and I can't believe I've been at my new job for an entire week. In some ways it feels like I've worked there for years. There's such a hum of activity and excitement about the place I can't imagine I ever enjoyed my career without it.

Richard has a business meeting tonight, so we're not going to see each other until tomorrow, when we are planning to spend the whole day together. He is a champ when I tell him about Elliot and Beatrice and how I decide to let go of any hope that Elliot might be the one for me. He actually asks if I am sure this is what I want. I am shocked that he would question a decision that is so obviously slanted in his favor, but he declares he cares about me enough to want me to have my heart's desire. "Of course," he amends, "I hope I'll be your heart's desire, but if I'm not, I'll always support the choices that make you happy." Once again I realize that Richard Bingham is too good for me.

Tonight I am going to go out with Jocina and Helena for drinks. We are meeting up at a hip new club called Slaughter. It's so now and right this very minute that they don't even have a door that faces the street. They don't even have an address. When I ask how I am supposed to find it, my co-workers instruct me to meet them in front of the Pink Palace Wig and Weave on Avenue B. They'll lead the way from there.

I'm wearing a gorgeous new black dress (sent to me by LeRon and Fernando as a welcome to New York gift) with a hot pink belt and a new pair of hot pink and red stiletto sandals. I have not yet figured out how I am going to be able to stand wearing these shoes all night but they are so gorgeous I imagine any amount of pain will be worth it. Speaking of pain, Edith Bunker is once again my new best friend. She isn't even giving me shit about my choice in footwear. While my bunion still occasionally hurts like the dickens, she is no longer chastising me. Her most frequent line is, "Do you think that Richard will rub me tonight? Ask him to rub me." Of course I haven't done that yet, but promise that tomorrow night she might get lucky.

The cab drops me in the heart of alphabet city and as far as

I can tell there is no club within blocks of where I'm standing. Luckily, Jocina and Helena show up within minutes of me, releasing the fear I am in the wrong place. Jocina leads the way to Slaughter by taking a left into a tiny obscure alleyway that leads to a fire escape. We climb the rickety steps to the second floor where we proceed to wait in front of a large window. At this point it occurs to me I have only known my co-workers for five days. I wonder if perhaps they are really taking me to a drop point for a white slavery ring. This is like no other club I have ever seen.

The window eventually opens and a burly bouncer type asks us what the password is. I'm thinking, you have got to be kidding me? I'm too old to go through these kinds of machinations for a night out with the girls. Jocina surreptitiously speaks the words as though she's imparting the secrets of the universe, "Spinet piano, marmalade pie" and boom, we're in. That's of course after we pay a twenty-five dollar cover charge, each. For that kind of money there had better be a masseuse on staff that's willing to spend the next hour making Edith Bunker happy.

The inside of Slaughter is nothing like the name would indicate. I half expect to see dead cows hanging from the ceiling, yet there are no farm animals anywhere in sight. Instead it's a very sleek and cosmopolitan looking venue, with lots of chrome and polished black surfaces. I try to get a mental image of all of these fashionable people crawling through the window to get in, but simply cannot. Helena later explains that there are alternative entrances to the building. So I ask, "Why didn't we use one of them?"

She shrugs her shoulders, "We don't know where they are." Apparently this is part of the mystique of Slaughter. People keep coming back in hopes of learning where the other entrances are located. It's at this moment I long to be on the relatively normal Upper West Side, in my robe, watching Friday night television. I have never been a cool person so this level of trendiness is totally wasted on me.

After an hour, we are able to secure a perch for ourselves and our drinks in the form of a tiny cocktail table with even tinier stools. Rear ends like mine were simply not meant for these contraptions so I take turns leaning my butt cheeks against the minuscule seat. I'm afraid to sit on it like a normal person for fear that it will impale me and do serious internal damage to my intestines.

Jocina and Helena are having a fabulous time and have each gone off several times to dance with different men. While I have been asked to dance as well, I choose to stay put and guard our table and drinks. I saw that *Dateline* special on Rohypnal and I'm not about to take the chance that one of our twenty-three dollar cocktails will be tampered with. As much as I'm not invested in the party scene, I am enjoying watching all the people. I feel like I've landed smack in the middle of a *Sex and the City* episode. This is just the kind of place that Carrie and the girls would frequent; so "in" that you're lucky to find your way in. I realize if I decide to stay in this city after my three month probation period, I'm going to need more than my previous salary doubled in order to survive.

I have no idea how idea how singles in New York can afford to live. I imagine most of them have roommates and eat only ramen noodles during the week in hopes of having the funds for any kind of social life on the weekends. The average date night in this city has to cost in excess of two hundred dollars. No wonder men feel entitled to sex within the first couple of outings. I would too.

That gets me to thinking about Richard. I know he doesn't expect me to sleep with him yet, but I wonder how much longer it will be before that becomes the protocol for our evenings. Then I wonder what I think of that. Richard is very funny, handsome, sexy, and rich. He's also single and attracted to me and what's the problem? The problem is that after making love to Elliot, I recognize that I won't be able to sleep with anyone else unless I am in love with them. All of a sudden I feel the beginnings of a headache coming on and I want to go home. When Helena comes back to the table I let her know that I'm leaving. She's surprised I want to go so early (as it's only one a.m.) but understands when I tell her about my headache.

After grabbing my purse, I retrace my steps to the big window on the second floor, but the bouncer won't let me out. Apparently, the window is only an entrance, not an exit. When I ask him where I can find an exit, he assures me that there are three on the first floor. I can't help but fantasize about calling the fire department should I ever find my way out of this place. As I roam around the dance floor looking for bright red EXIT signs, I start to think this club is like The Hotel California. You can check out anytime you like, but you can never leave.

I eventually spot a couple gathering their belongings and in hopes they are vacating the premises I follow them through a long hall, past the kitchen, and bathrooms. The passage is pitch black and I am on the verge of panic when I hear a door open and see the street lights come flooding in. Hurray!!! I'm actually going to get out of here. I make a promise to never put myself through this experience again and flag down a cab to take me home.

# Chapter 35

Richard spends a good part of Saturday giving me lessons on shopping in New York City. Apparently you have to treat it like an aggressive contact sport. "This is not golf," he says seriously. There's an offensive and defensive strategy you must be conversant with in order to walk out of the store with all intended purchases and no bodily damage done to your person. I laugh as he explains this. I picture him in a black nylon jacket with the word "COACH" emblazoned on the back and a whistle hanging from his neck. In my head, he's writing on a dry-erase board and marking off sections that read: cheese, dairy, wine.

Richard asks why I'm laughing, so I tell him. Then in all seriousness he says, "When you shop in this city on a Saturday, you had better be on your guard." I'm beginning to think I don't want to go when he winks and I realize he's just joking.

Richard uses tactics on the women in Zabar's that I am not equipped to employ. He shamelessly flirts with them and they treat him like he's the emperor of Rome, to the point where he is even offered a cut in the coveted cheese line. I ask him what's going on and he enlightens me that men without wedding bands on their fingers are a premium in this city. "They treat us like the fatted calf until it's time for dinner."

Rolling my eyes, I comment, "But the lady from the cheese line had a huge rock on her finger."

Richard pulls a scrap of paper out of his pocket with the name Rachael on it, next to a phone number, and replies, "But apparently her friend Rachael doesn't."

I am totally and completely aghast at this, "She slipped you her friend's phone number while you were here with me? That is unbelievable!"

"All's fair in love and war, darling. And the single scene in New York makes the Middle East look like Club Med."

I am appalled and realize more than ever how fortunate I am to have this wonderful man's interest. I ask, "How often does this happen to you?"

With a shake of his head, Richard replies, "If you only knew the number of trees murdered for the cause."

After Zabar's, Richard wants to know which store I want to go to next, so I drag him to The Silver Palate and then to a specialty shop down the street known worldwide for its marinades. All in all I have an absolutely wonderful time but have no idea how I will ever reenact this on my own. I share my concerns with my shopping partner and he suggests I simply use the curves that God gave me. I raise my eyebrows in confusion and he explains, "I don't know who all these women are feeding, but it is not themselves. Have you noticed how emaciated they are?"

I confirm I have noticed. In fact the girls in my office seem to only partake in coffee and cigarettes for lunch and I have it on the best authority their dinners primarily involve martinis. The only potentially nutritious nibble being the gin-soaked olives they imbibe.

So Richard explains while the women before us are mean and aggressive and skinny, I am delightful and sweet and womanly. I smile as he shrugs his eyebrow like Groucho Marks. "Therefore," he declares, "If one of these city gals tries to bully you, I suggest you pop them with one of your gorgeous hips." Then he pantomimes the "pop" he envisions and I can't help but burst out laughing at his suggestion.

I respond, "Richard, I could knock them into the next century if I execute a move like that on them." And then I get the most absurd image of a pile of formally shopping skeletons heaped in the corner of Zabar's while I have the whole store to myself. It's at that moment I discover I want to try the maneuver. So I drag Richard back into Zabar's to walk me through it.

In the cracker aisle he points out a particularly vicious looking customer and whispers, "She looks like the type who wouldn't let you within three feet of her." Then conspiratorially suggests, "Go try to pick up a box of crackers in front of her."

Invigorated by the potential conflict, I stroll right up to her and reach for a box of water biscuits located directly in front of her. She rotates to the left with her shopping basket to block my action but I circle around to her other side. Before she has a chance for another body block, I wind my hip and give her a bump which actually sends her stumbling for a good three steps. I can feel the power and I love it! Once the snippy woman rights herself, she declares, "Well I never!" That's when Richard saunters up next to me and wraps his arm around my waist. He looks at her and suggests, "That might be the problem." I try to but fail to contain my laughter and realize I may be able to make it in this city after all.

After dropping my various purchases off at Renée's apartment, Richard and I cross the street to Central Park and walk through to the toy boating pond on the Fifth Avenue side. I am astounded by all of the grown men playing with their boats. These are not toys either. They are full blown baby yachts. One man is actually dressed in white pants with a navy blazer and captain's hat. I look at Richard and try to contain my mirth. I comment, "They're pretty serious about this, huh?"

He replies, "You don't know the half of it. Actual fights have been known to break out when one captain doesn't respect another's boundaries."

I'm convinced Richard is pulling my leg when I hear a man shout, "Ahoy there, captain of the Royal Princess. You're about to clip my bow side. Give me my space."

The other "captain" yells back, "This is public domain! If you feel crowded, then you should move!" Before the whole confrontation can come to blows, a third captain breaks up the argument by engaging one of the men in conversation.

I whisper to Richard, "I feel like I'm on a grade school playground."

He smiles, "Boys and their toys."

I ask, "Are actual children allowed to use this pond for their toys as well?"

Richard looks at me in mock horror and declares, "Good god, no!"

We spend the rest of the afternoon wandering around the city on foot, occasionally stopping for a coffee or a bite to eat. We don't get back to my apartment until six and Richard announces we have an eight o'clock dinner reservation so he had better get back to his apartment to change. But I've had such a nice relaxed day I don't feel like getting all dolled up so I suggest, "Why don't we order in Chinese and a movie?"

Richard likes my plan, so he picks a movie while I open up a bottle of wine. I ask him what we're going to see but he won't tell me. Once we order our dinner, he plops on the couch and asks, "So how's my good friend Edith Bunker doing these days?"

Edith Bunker, meanwhile, is screaming, "Tell him I want a rub! Tell him I love him!"

I smile at my friend and flirtatiously declare, "She misses you."

"Really?" he wants to know. "Why don't you bring her over here so we can get reacquainted?" I'm next to him on the couch, with Edith Bunker in his lap before you can can say Kung Pao Shrimp and he starts to work his magic.

Richard comments, "Edith looks like a shadow of her former self, what's going on?"

I explain that her silicone insert and my ten pound weight loss have actually helped to shrink her inflammation. Richard comments "Don't get too thin on me. I like you and Edith just the way you are."

"That's very sweet," I tell him, "But Edith is a royal pain in my ass and I'm looking forward to sending her packing."

Richard leans towards me and brushes the hair from my face and says, "No one likes a bone but a dog."

I have never heard that saying and I love it. "Don't worry," I tell him. "I'm only aspiring to lose ten more pounds which will probably make me a size ten. No single digits for me."

Richard pulls my legs until I am nearly sitting on top of him and then he very gently and very sweetly kisses me on the lips. He murmurs, "I want to know what man started the rumor that men as a species like skinny women. If I ever meet him, I'm going to kick his ass." Then he kisses me again with a good deal more passion. Before things have a chance to get too involved, Julio rings up to announce that our food has arrived. I jump off the couch and ask, "What movie are we watching?"

"*The Karate Kid.*"

I demand, "You had better not have chosen *The Karate Kid.*"

So he counters, "*Apocalypse Now.*"

I start to laugh, "Richard Bingham, if you didn't pick a wonderful chick flick, you had better leave right now." The doorbell rings and Richard hands over a wad of bills in exchange for our dinner. Then he proudly declares, "I think I've made the perfect selection." He grabs the remote and turns on *An Affair to Remember* with Cary Grant and Deborah Kerr.

I cry, "This is only my favorite movie of all time! How did you know?"

He smiles, "You're not totally unique in that arena, darling. I thought it was a safe bet."

We snuggle up on the couch with dinner and settle in for a cozy night of vintage romance. The only problem is while I'm watching the film, I can't stop myself from thinking about Elliot's and my ill-fated love affair. So by the time Deborah Kerr gets hit by the cab and becomes a house bound invalid, I am sobbing my eyes out. By the end of the movie when Cary Grant finds out her secret and re-declares his undying love for her, I have snot and tears running down my face and I'm gasping for breath. Richard turns the lights on and looks at me with a horrified expression on his face, "Good lord, Mimi, do you always cry so hard during this film?"

I shake my head miserably and he pats the cushion closer to him inviting me to snuggle in. When I do so, He wraps his arms around me and asks, "Is it Elliot?"

I nod my head as a new wave of grief overwhelms me and my friend simply holds me and lets me cry my heart out.

# Chapter 36

Elliot returns my call this morning at the office. I rang him on Friday night, on my way out the door, hoping I would get his voice mail. When I did, I thought I would have a whole weekend free of thoughts of him, as I knew he'd wait until Monday to return my call. Of course we all know how well my Elliot-free weekend went. That road to hell and those good intentions, huh?

On Saturday morning, it occurred to me Jude and Hermione were back in charge of writing my life's script but by Saturday night I was toying with the idea my romance writers had begun working in tandem with Stan and Ollie as there is no way my current situation would make a decent romance novel or even made-for-TV movie.

When my phone rings this morning, I simply pick it up without wondering who might be on the line. So when I hear the love of my life say, "Mimi, its Elliot Fielding returning your call," I almost panic and hang up on him.

Yet somewhere deep down, I realize I am an adult and not a freshman in high school because I answer, "Elliot, thank you for calling me back."

He asks, all business-like, "What can I do for you?"

I explain about our Shimmer campaign and how they are launching a line to aid research and the cure for breast cancer. I tell him we were hoping to secure him as one of our celebrity speakers as he has such a close tie to the disease. Then I just jabber. I'm not quite sure what words come out of mouth, but I'm positive that they are total nonsense.

Elliot finally interrupts me as it doesn't appear I'm going to come up for air anytime soon and asks, "How did you find out?"

There's a long pause before I find the words, "I heard it from the people on my team." Then add for good measure, "Apparently it's not a big secret."

Elliot answers, "It's not. It's just that Beatrice has asked me not to tell people who don't already know. She likes the feeling of pretending she doesn't have a history with the disease."

"Yes, well…" I stammer, "Is there any way we can count on you to speak? There will of course be press at the event so I'm thinking it will help to promote your new book as well, even though I'm sure it won't have any bearing on your decision."

Without even asking the date first, Elliot declares he will come. I offer, "Of course you will have two tickets in case Beatrice would like to join you."

Elliot says that he will ask her but that she is not a huge fan of New York. Then he quietly asks, "Mimi, do you understand now?"

I'm at risk of bursting into tears for the four-hundred-millionth time in the last forty-eight hours, I take a sip of water to see if I can dislodge the lump in my throat and answer, "Yes, Elliot, I understand." Sounding a little wobbly, I add, "And I want you to know you have my support. Beatrice is lucky to have you."

Elliot is quiet for about thirty seconds too long when he adds, "I still love you."

Damn lot of good that's going to do me, so striving for a business-like pitch, I state, "Thank you. But I'm sure it's the best thing for both of us to simply move on and pretend nothing ever happened between us."

Elliot responds angrily, "Is that what you really want, to pretend that nothing happened?"

"What I really want, Elliot, apparently has no chance of happening so I think it's best if we forget we ever meant anything to one another and get on with our lives."

He heatedly inquires, "So you've already moved on have you?"

I know he's hurt and I know in my heart I haven't moved on, but for the sake of my thready sanity, I answer, "Yes, Elliot. I have."

He demands, "With Richard?"

I'm getting mad at his proprietary tone and ask, "Why does it matter who I've moved on with? You're engaged to another woman. Therefore, I can be involved with anyone I like."

Elliot declares, "I'll be in New York by Wednesday. I'll call you when I get there."

Surprised by the change in topic, I say, "But Elliot the luncheon isn't until next week. You certainly don't need to arrive that soon."

He exclaims, "I'll be there Wednesday," and then he hangs up on me.

That conversation went well. I'm not sure what I expected, but I certainly didn't expect him to be mad at *me*. I mean if anyone has a right to anger, it's me, right? It briefly occurs to me that it's no wonder nuns live longer than other women. There are no men in their lives to make them crazy.

The rest of the day is spent going over the RSVP list for the luncheon and beginning the long process of hammering out a seating chart. There was an incident at a recent fund-raiser where the first wife of a local real-estate mogul was seated at the same table with the second wife, the very one who destroyed her twenty-year marriage. It didn't help matters that the second wife was recently dumped and a third wife was in the works. Helena was seated at a table next to them and claims they spent the whole meal shooting barbs at each other, until wife number one got so angry she replaced her barb with a buttered roll. Wife two retaliated with a chicken breast and before you knew it was a full-fledged food fight. I started to laugh when I heard the tale but it also reinforced how tricky these seating charts can be. The New York society scene is totally beyond me. I mean, the worst thing that could happen in Pipsy would be two ladies at the same table wearing the same dress and chances are they would simply laugh off the coincidence or congratulate each other on their good taste.

Jocina caught up with me at lunch to relay how her Friday night at Slaughter ended. She brought home a gorgeous man who claimed to be an account executive at Morgan Stanley, but when she Googled him this morning, she discovered he was, in fact, a school teacher from New Jersey. She was incensed by his duplicity and asked if I could believe the nerve of him. I asked if it mattered that much what he did for a living and she happily said no. The problem was that he lived in NEW JERSEY. She said it in capital letters too, indicating that he in fact lived in THE GUTTER. I said I had heard that New Jersey was a lovely place to live and asked if I had been given incorrect information.

Jocina is so irritated with my Elly May, c-e-m-e-n-t pond, knowledge of life in the big city that she simply claims, "You don't know yet. But just you wait, in another couple of months you'll know exactly what I'm talking about."

I smile and nod all the while thinking, who cares where the guy is from as long as he's not hiding a wife and three kids there. It occurs to me there should be some sort of handbook written for new singles who move to this city so we can at least speak the same language as the natives. For instance NEW JERSEY equals outside the realm of possibility and the phrase, "I'd love to, call me," equals "I gave you the phone number for the pizza place down the block."

I'm once again relieved I have Richard in my life. He was so sweet with me on Saturday night when I broke down over the movie I can't help but wonder how much longer he's going to be able to put up with my sadness over Elliot. After Richard let me cry my eyes out, he packed himself off to his own apartment across town. I wish I could tell him an exact date when I would be ready to put Elliot in my past. At least then he'd know there's a light at the end of the tunnel. And now Elliot is coming back to New York, so I won't be able to bury him quite yet. Although I do vow to only see him in conjunction with work. That ought to keep some of my angst at bay.

I didn't weigh-in at Weight Watchers over the weekend so I'm going to go now, over my lunch hour. I discover a center not even two blocks from work. When I walk in, I'm immediately struck by how very similar this location is to the one in Pipsy and while my leader does not have Marge's Zen-like Buddha nature, she's still pretty cool. Her name is Babette, which makes me feel like I've walked into a French film, yet she is as American as they come. Babs, as she prefers to be called, lost forty pounds on Weight Watchers after the birth of her fourth child and with the help of the program, has kept it off for ten years. She's all gung ho about the plan and I find her enthusiasm very inspiring. She doesn't even cringe when she announces I'm up a pound and a half from last week. She just looks at my chart and says that sometimes happens after a week of big loss. I stare at her and wonder how she knows about my big loss, as I assume she's talking about Elliot. But then it occurs to me she might be simply talking about my last weight loss, or is she? I start to think maybe Weight Watchers is run by a group of weight conscious psychics.

On my way back to the office, I realize it's once again time to reel myself in and start counting points. I'm actually looking forward to it as counting points makes me feel like I have some power over a life spiraling out of control. Yes, I know I'm being a wee bit dramatic, but I can't seem to help myself. My emotions have been all over the board this week; from deliriously happy one second, to inconsolably miserable the next. It's like reliving my teen years.

I'm running a few minutes late for a "Pink" meeting when I get back to the office so I hurry straight into Helena's office before even dropping my purse on my desk. I learn that while I did a pretty good job with the seating chart, I did make one terrible mistake. I inadvertently put a mother and daughter at the same table who have not spoken in three years. The mother, a famous author, refused to let her daughter use the same last name of her nom de plume and the daughter cut ties immediately. She felt it was her mother's duty to afford her every step up possible. "The thing is," Helena explains, "the mother is a serious novelist and the daughter writes erotic women's fiction." The mother didn't want her fans to pick up her daughter's book and in anyway assume she was responsible for spawning a child that wrote sentences like, "He speared her velvet sheath with his throbbing hard man sword." I had to vote with the mother on this one. I know if my mom were to ever accidentally buy such a book there would be masses said and forgiveness begged with a Hail Mary here and an Our Father there. It would be the Catholic version of "Old MacDonald Had a Farm."

Once the seating arrangements are finished, I announce my good news (this is a relative statement of course.) Helena and Jocina are delighted Elliot will be one of the speakers as having a man at these events always seems to bring out additional press. Why, they aren't sure, but this has always been the way. Somehow men give cachet to women's diseases. Jocina claims she's surprised that more of them don't publicly support breast cancer as she explains, "Our boobs are just as important to them as they are to us."

With the exception of having to see Elliot, I'm really looking forward to the event. Shimmer is setting up booths to give free makeovers and the gift for buying a seat at the luncheon is a big pink gym bag full of goodies from the new "Pink" line. We have six confirmed celebrity speakers and another twenty-three confirmed celebrity guests. I can't help but think, Mimi, you're not in Pipsy anymore.

# Chapter 37

It's been a few days since I've talked to Kevin as he and Muffy are enjoying the honeymoon phase of their relationship. I haven't wanted to bother him with constant "poor me" phone calls. But now I feel like I should fill him in on what's going on with Elliot. So when I get home from work, I call. He picks up on the second ring and I demand, "Are you ever going to get a job?"

"Heya, Meems!" He's excited to hear from me even though I've just slandered his work ethic. Kevin is such a happy-go-lucky kind of guy that I want to kick his ex-wife all over again for putting him through so much. He declares, "I have decided to open my own business and I'll tell you all about it when I see you next week."

"When you see me next week?" This is the first I've heard about him and Muff setting a date to visit New York. I'm thrilled to hear it as Elliot will be here then and I can use every buffer I can get.

Kevin replies, "We were going to call you today and let you know we'll be arriving on Tuesday and we'll be there until

Sunday."

Genuinely excited, I declare, "I can't wait to see you both! I'll have to check and make sure Renée's couch is a roll out, but if it's not, you guys can take my room and I'll sleep on the cushions on the floor."

"We're not staying with you, Meems." Kevin seems shocked I had thought so.

So I ask, "Why not? Hotels are expensive in this city." Then just to give him a hard time, I add, "Especially when you're not working."

"Oh, ha ha ha. Just because I've taken a couple months off to get my act together does not mean I don't still have a great savings. Plus, we got a terrific rate on Expedia and this way we won't be tripping all over each other."

I'm a little disappointed that I won't get to have a slumber party with my little sister and friend, but I soldier on, "Have you heard that Elliot is going to speak at the luncheon that I'm helping to organize?"

Kevin asks, "The breast cancer thing? As a matter of fact I have heard and I'm hoping that Muff and I can get tickets to come."

I'm shocked by this and answer, "I'll see what I can do, but why do you guys want to attend?"

He answers, "To support Beatrice. I know she'll be happy to have some friends there."

"Beatrice is coming?"

My friend replies, "You didn't know? I thought she was invited."

I stammer, "Well of course she's invited but Elliot said she didn't like New York. So I just assumed she'd bow out."

"She'll be there. There's a doctor at Sloan Kettering she's going to meet with and her appointment is next week. So she figured she might as well attend the luncheon while she's in town."

This makes sense as Sloan Kettering is one of, if not *the* premier cancer facilities in the country. So I ask, "Will she be arriving with Elliot on Wednesday?"

Kevin didn't think so, but inquires, "Elliot's going this Wednesday? Why so early?"

I don't know what to tell him, so I simply reply, "I think he's mad at me. I'm under the impression that he's coming early to simply be nasty to me for a few days."

"Why's he mad at you?"

I reply, "Because I told him I've moved on with Richard."

Kevin inquires, "Yeah, so? He's engaged."

See, I'm not the only one who thinks Elliot has no reason to be put out with me. So I agree, "I know! I told him the same thing. But apparently in the mind of Elliot Fielding I'm supposed to stand back and watch while he marries another woman, all the while staying single and pining for him like a tragic gothic figure."

Kevin is quiet for a moment then asks, "Did Elliot tell you that he loves you again?"

I answer, "Yes. But so what? It's not like he plans to do anything about it."

"Oh Mimi, your life is like watching bad television."

I know this is true but to hear it said outside of my head is actually quite painful. I snap, "Thanks, Kev. It's nice to know the critiques are in."

He apologizes, "I didn't mean it like that. It's just so sad to see two people who love each other not be able to be together. Then there's Beatrice. I feel awful for her too."

And while Beatrice's story is a million times more tragic than mine, I still can't help but feel sorrier for myself. So I say nothing. After discussing my new job, new city, and new Weight Watchers branch, Kevin and I sign off until next week.

I feel drained when I hang up the phone and all I want to do is crawl into bed and sleep for another week. Of course with my recent history of depression, I don't do this. Instead I check the freezer for anything with the names Ben and Jerry written on it. Sadly, as I am the one who stocked the freezer, I come up dry. I settle for three Weight Watchers fudge bars. Marge has previously warned me that just because they are only worth one point each doesn't mean that the calories don't still add up, but I don't care. I need comfort and this is as close as I'm going to get given my recent grocery list.

As I plow my way through the fudge bars, I realize I feel very alone. Of course my family is always there for me, but they're home in Pipsy with their own lives. Kevin is there for me, but same story as my family, plus he's friends with Beatrice. Richard is there for me, but I simply can't bring myself to pick up the phone and complain to him about Elliot again. Certainly I owe it to him to do *some* grieving on my own. There are a couple of friends I could call back home, but let's face it, my current situation would not exactly make the average small town girl pull out her violin and play me a dirge. I hear a phantom conversation in my head.

"Joan, this is Mimi Finnegan, how are you?"

A beleaguered Joan replies, "Both kids have the chicken pox and Bob is always away on business, the sump pump stopped working, and the gophers are back. How are you?"

"Oh Joan, I'm so glad you asked. I'm terrible! I've lost almost ten pounds, dyed my hair a gorgeous shade of red, got a whole new wardrobe, and I've moved to an amazing apartment in New York City. My life couldn't be any worse! The hardest part is two extraordinarily wealthy and attractive men are both head over heels in love with me. What am I going to do?"

Joan obviously hangs up around the "I've lost ten pounds." mark. No matter how you cut it, people are going to have a hard time feeling sorry for me in light of all of my recent good fortune, even though this good fortune is very, very recent. Remember up until a month ago I was just an average, mousy brown-haired frump. I was okay in their eyes then, but only because I hadn't dared to set myself apart. The minute I started to make positive changes, I got cut from the herd. While I am certainly nowhere near as gorgeous as Renée, I have a brief moment of empathy for her. She has probably garnered very little sympathy and understanding in her life. After all, who pities a supermodel?

I still long to call someone. I need to hear the comforting voice of someone who will tell me that it's all going to be okay. That's when I realize there is only one person in my life that fits the bill and yes, that person is Marge. I dig through my purse and unearth the business card she gave me with her home number on it. As I punch in the area code, I wonder if I should really intrude on her. Yet, who am I kidding? I need her. I have to intrude. A kindly sounding man answers the phone and I ask if Marge is available.

She picks up the phone a moment later and trills, "Yelloooowwww! This is Marge."

I stammer, "Marge I'm not sure if you remember me, but this is Mimi Finnegan. I belong to Weight Watchers..."

Marge cuts me off, "Of course I remember you, dear. How's that big shiny apple?"

I inform Marge the move went well. I love my job and apartment. Then she asks how I did on my weigh-in. I confess I gained a pound and a half and she declares, "Excellent! I was hoping you'd have a gain this week." Then she proceeds to utter the magic words, "Everything is moving along right on track."

I ask, "Are you sure Marge?"

She answers, "I'm sure, honey. You took off too much weight with your little depression. This gain is actually a good thing. Now next week, I say go ahead and go for another loss, but only a small one." Then she adds, "Everything is going to be just fine."

What she doesn't say, but what I hear is, "This is path you've chosen, Grasshopper. It is all meant to be."

# Chapter 38

I spent all of yesterday in a pre-Elliot fog. The first thing I thought of when I woke up was, "Elliot is coming tomorrow." The first thing I thought of before I went to bed was, "Elliot is coming tomorrow." My thoughts during breakfast, lunch, and dinner were all pretty similar. Then I open my eyes this morning and it's, "Holy crap, Elliot is coming today!" I have no idea what time he'll be arriving and I have no idea if I'll even see him, but just knowing that he'll be here in the same city is pretty much toying with my sanity in a major way.

For reasons I choose not to ponder, I take extra pains with my appearance this morning. I wake up an hour early so I can do both a blow-dry and Velcro rollers. I even stopped by Saks yesterday and bought a new outfit, which wasn't on sale. If that isn't a clear giveaway that I've lost my mind, I don't know what is. The only other time that I've ever shopped at Saks Fifth Avenue was to buy mascara and that was somewhat of an emergency.

I have been getting appreciative glances from my coworkers all morning and instead of giving me the normal self-esteem

266

boost, they are constant reminders I did it all for Elliot. By two o'clock there is still no sign of the Englishman and I ever so slightly start to relax. The feeling lasts until two-o-three when Marcus calls me into his office. I've hardly seen my boss in the week-and-a-half I've been here as I've been so caught up in the Shimmer campaign. I initially look forward to seeing him so I can tell him how much I love it here. That is until I walk into his office. On step two I stop dead in my tracks as I lay eyes on the great heartbreaker himself, Elliot Fielding, in the flesh, so close I could throw myself into his arms. Have you gathered how his appearance is affecting me?

Elliot looks amazing from his tasseled loafers right up to the navy blue sports coat he has casually paired with slightly faded Levi's. My body starts to release pheromones the very nanosecond I lay eyes on him. I feel so alive and turned on I'm afraid everyone in the entire building can feel the atmospheric change. When Elliot looks at me, it's all I can do to keep myself upright and dressed. It's been almost two weeks since I've seen him last but it feels more like two years.

Marcus smiles when I walk in and greets, "Mimi, come in! Of course you know Elliot."

I look at Elliot and force a smile, "Elliot, it's nice to see you again."

He takes my hand and (oh god, he kisses it!) and murmurs, "Mimi."

I'm torn between vastly conflicting emotions, I want to either scream, "Keep kissing me damn it!" or punch him in the mouth. In the end I simply sit down across from Marcus and wait to see why I have been summoned.

I don't have to wait long as my boss declares, "Mimi, I know you are aware that Elliot's next legal thriller is set in a public relations office." I nod my head all the while feeling the icy fingers of dread grip me. "He has spent a good amount of time in our Pipsy office," I nod my head. "And he feels that he could benefit from spending some time here, observing us as well." Then he asks, "Isn't that exciting?"

If he only knew how exciting it really was, but I merely nod my head again and ask, "How long will you be joining us, Elliot?"

He smiles like a tiger just released in a bird sanctuary and declares, "Until I've finished my research."

Hoping against hope this announcement is the only reason Marcus called me in, I stand up and smile, "Well, thanks for filling me in, Marcus." Then to Elliot I add, "Good luck with the book."

As I attempt to leave, my boss continues, "The reason I asked you in Mimi is I had hoped that you'd be willing to share your office with Elliot. We don't have a vacant spot for him at the moment and being the two of you have worked together in the past, well, I had hoped you wouldn't mind."

Mind sharing an office with Elliot Fielding?! It's like offering to let a drug addict baby-sit a stash of cocaine. Even though part of me is infuriated by Elliot's machinations, I am too aroused by the sight of him to acknowledge my anger. So I simply answer, "Of course I don't mind." To Elliot I add, "Shall I show you my office now?"

Elliot agrees and shakes hands with Marcus on the way out the door. When we're alone, he leans down and purrs in my ear, "You look gorgeous."

I don't answer as I'm afraid I will spontaneously combust if I so much as open my mouth. His scent alone is wreaking havoc on my equilibrium. I lead the way to my room at the end of the hall and once we get inside, I immediately close the vertical blinds facing the outside corridor. Then I close the door, lock it and jump into Elliot's arms before he knows what's hit him.

With my mouth on his I hiss, "How dare you! How dare you worm your way into my life again!"

Elliot kisses me back with matching intensity. He pulls my blouse out of my skirt and runs his hands up my bare torso. When he reaches my chest, he pinches me and growls, "This is how I dare!"

I have never in my nearly thirty-five years felt such extreme passion. Elliot unbuttons my shirt and pulls off my bra while I rip off his jacket and shirt, popping at least three buttons as I go. His mouth is all over nipping and kissing and loving me. Elliot pushes my skirt up to my waist as he lifts me onto the top of the desk. My whole body nearly splinters apart when I feel his insistent fingers tug at my panties. My hands move of their own accord to the waistband of his jeans. I slowly and deliberately release the buttons. I feel like I'm going to die if I don't have him right this second.

As I tug his jeans down, there is a knock on my door and I freeze mid-action. I somehow manage to take a breath and ask, "Yes?"

"It's Helena, I have the revised seating chart for the luncheon."

Elliot whispers, "Get rid of her."

I whisper back, "I can't. She's in charge of the project."

He demands, "Get rid of her."

Helena calls out, "Mimi, is something wrong?"

Elliot is not stopping his assault on me and I somehow manage to reply, "Can I meet you in your office in a minute, Helena?"

She answers, "Okay, I guess." at the same time that Elliot lays me back on the desk and consummates our union. I want to scream at him to stop, I want to rail at him for not asking me to marry him. I want to cry at the injustice of it all. But in the end I simply surrender to the exquisite pleasure splintering through my body.

Elliot holds me tight and declares over and over again his love for me. It is then I realize I will always belong to him and I will never be able to be more than Richard's friend. Even if Elliot goes through with his marriage to Beatrice, I will never feel this depth of emotion for another man and Richard is simply too good of a person to wind up with leftover love. Damn Elliot for doing this to me. Damn him for making me love him so much!

# Chapter 39

After my episode with Elliot two days ago, I pretty much move into Jocina's office with her. I need time away from the Englishman so I can try to regain my sanity. I tell myself over and over again that he is not available to me and I have to let him go. But apparently I refuse to believe this and continue to fantasize about a future together. Of course it doesn't help that I see him everywhere I go. Luckily, we were never alone again so there isn't a replay of the scene in my office.

Richard and I are having dinner tonight and I'm going to tell him we can never be more than friends. I've shed a tear or two over this and I won't blame him if he opts out of my offer of friendship all together. I would miss him beyond words, but it really isn't fair of me to expect him to be everything I want without returning the favor. My greatest fear is I'm going to wind up without either one of these men in my life. But basic humanity won't allow me to keep leading Richard on.

When Richard arrives at my apartment at seven-thirty, he looks wonderful, but my heart doesn't do any of the crazy flip-flopping it does when I lay eyes on Elliot. Richard kisses me hello and hands me a bouquet of pink tulips. He greets, "I would tell you that you look gorgeous but the truth is you look strung out. What's up?"

I laugh in spite of myself, "I was going to wait to tell you at dinner."

Richard gets very serious and rejoins, "Oh, no. I'm a firm believer that bad news should be shared in private." He walks over to my couch and plops down, "Spill it."

So I do. I tell him about my conversation with Elliot on the phone last week. I relay that Elliot came to New York early to see me. Then I give him the PG version of what happened in my office. I'm so shame-faced I can't even look him in the eye while I'm talking.

Finally, Richard cuts to the chase and asks, "Where do I stand in all of this?"

I screw up my courage and say, "You, Richard Bingham, have been a wonderful friend. I truly do love you and I think you're an amazing person. You make me laugh and heaven help you, Edith Bunker is mad about you, but I don't feel the same kind of love for you I do for Elliot."

When I look up, I realize that Richard has scooted so close to me our shoulders are touching. He looks at me and asks, "Can I just try a little something?"

With tears in my eyes, I nod my head and then he leans in and kisses me for all he's worth. It's sweet and tender and all together perfect except he isn't Elliot. When he finishes, he looks up at me with hope in his eyes and asks, "Did I change your mind?"

I shake my head sadly and announce, "You are the ideal

man and so help me, if I had any control over my emotions I would pick you. But I can't help it. I'm head over heels in love with that bastard Elliot."

Richard nods his head and offers, "Lucky bastard."

Miserably, I manage to say, "I'm sure that you don't even want to be my friend anymore."

He looks up with shock in his eyes, "Darling, if you had chosen me, your life would have be a bed of roses, no worries, no problems, no heartache." Then he shakes his head and adds, "But you've picked Elliot and lord knows, you need me now more than ever. I just don't see you getting through this without my help." Then he grabs my hand and declares, "No, my dear, I'm not going to abandon you now."

I burst into full blown tears of gratitude and love and wonder that I will be able to keep Richard in my life. I had simply never expected this degree of unselfishness from him and I am humbled by his decency. Scientists should study Richard Bingham in hopes of coming up with a serum that could be injected into substandard people to make them more like him.

Richard holds me while I cry, "BUT...you have to do something for me in return."

I snuffle, "Anything! I'll do anything, just name it."

Richard declares, "You have to find your replacement for me."

"Excuse me?"

He replies, "You heard me. I need you to scour the ends of the earth and find the perfect woman to take your place. As long as I can't have you, I want someone as close to you as can be found, deal?"

"Richard, you deserve someone a lot better than me. You deserve someone who isn't neurotic, emotional, and full of flaws. You deserve a bunion-free woman. I'm going to find you someone as far away from me as possible, a woman that will be worthy of your love."

He shakes his head, "That's not what I want. I want imperfect and quirky, gorgeous, curvy, and emotional. You have to find what my heart desires or the deal's off and I go back to putting the moves on you."

I rest my head on Richard's shoulder and agree, "Okay, you're on. But don't come running to me when you realize how full your hands are."

He teases, "I'm looking forward to those full hands, thank you very much. Now, what do we do about dinner?"

I ask, "Do you still want to go out?"

He confesses, "I'm afraid people will think I beat you if we go out with you looking like this." Then he smiles, "You're not one of those delicate ladylike criers, are you?"

I answer, "Nope." Then suggest, "Why don't we order in from that new Thai place on seventy-eighth?"

Richard agrees and scans the menu. I confide, "You know Edith Bunker is going to miss you like crazy."

He looks up and smiles, "But I'm not going anywhere. What's to miss?"

I roll my eyes, "Richard, it won't be the same for Edith and you know it. She's been after me to marry you since that day on your boat."

Richard hands me the phone and menu and declares,

"Here, you order." Then he sits down next to me and pulls my shoe off and starts to rub Edith Bunker. "Here's what I'm thinking. Just because you've chosen Elliot doesn't preclude me and Edith from having a relationship, does it?"

I start to giggle. "I can't imagine that you and my bunion are going to be able to carry on without involving me at some level, do you?"

So he counters, "How about this, Edith and I will have our love affair until you and Elliot get married, then we'll call it off."

I heartily agree, "Sounds like a plan to me." Richard and I spend the next couple of hours just hanging out and enjoying our dinner. Neither one of us brings up Elliot. We just fall into the easy companionship of good friends.

As I fall asleep that night, I give Jude and Hermione the thumbs up for their great scripting tonight. I know it had to be them because if it were Stan and Ollie there would have been a tornado or building fire to add drama to an already stressful situation.

# Chapter 40

I'm not at all surprised when Julio announces that I have a guest this morning. As it's Saturday and I'm not in the office, there is no way for Elliot to stalk me without actually showing up at my apartment. He arrives at my front door carrying a bag full of fresh fruit and muffins. Wearing a sheepish smile, his first words are, "I wasn't sure you were going to let me up."

With a resigned shrug of my shoulders, I reply, "What would be the point. What's done is done."

Elliot drops his bag in the kitchen and turns to look at me, "I'm going to tell Beatrice about us, Mimi. I want to help her, but I just can't stand the thought us not being together." Then he pulls me into his arms and just holds me.

When I finally speak, it's to say, "I told Richard last night that he and I could only be friends."

Elliot squeezes me tighter, "I love you so much. I promise that we're going to work this all out."

I ask, "So when are you going to break Beatrice's heart, before or after her appointment with the specialist?"

He answers, "I don't know when, but I'll find the right

time while she's still here in New York. Okay?"

I nod my head sadly at the thought. Poor Beatrice, I suppose this is better than actually killing her off though. I ask, "So what do you want to do today?"

Elliot replies, "First I'm going to feed you breakfast and then I thought we'd get out and enjoy this beautiful day. How does that sound?"

I concur that it sounds like a terrific plan. So after a fruit salad of fresh melon and pineapple and half of a bran muffin, I lace up my sneakers in hopes we'll get some good exercise. While walking hand in hand down Central Park, Elliot asks, "Do you think you want to stay in New York?"

I answer, "Honestly, I hadn't thought about it. The whole reason I came here was to get away from you. But now, I don't know. I mean, I love my job. It's a million times more exciting than PR in Pipsy, but of course my family isn't here and my house isn't here." Then I add, "And you aren't here."

He interrupts, "Don't you worry about me. If this is where you're going to be, this is where I'll be too. I'm not about to leave you again."

Walking along the park with Elliot feels like I've finally come home. We could be in a cornfield and I would feel the same thing. I'm where I belong as long as I'm next to him. We turn into the park at Seventy-Second by Strawberry Fields and stop a moment to remember how Joseph Collins wished us the same love that he shared with his wife. I guess he turned out to be our mascot after all.

Elliot and I explore new parts of the park today like the outdoor theater where they perform Shakespeare and the reservoir which is the running track for thousands of New Yorkers. Then we wind our way back to the boating pond where we rent a row boat for two hours. I have never been so happy in my whole life. There is a tiny niggling part of me that warns that my bubble will burst yet, but I ignore it. I feel that Jude and Hermione are writing me a happy ending and I'm not going to fight it.

Later when Elliot takes me home, we spend the night making love in a real bed, which is a highly novel experience considering that our previous encounters took place in a moving carriage and on the desk in my office. I tease him and announce that I'm still going to want him in an elevator and perhaps on top of the Empire State Building. I would have expected his uptight English self to have pooh-poohed those ideas right off but he merely raises his eyebrow and smiles. He even comes up with a couple locations of his own, The Tower of London and Buckingham Palace.

While we're lying in bed talking, Elliot declares, "You know, I think I should get to know Edith Bunker a little better."

I comment that he can try, but I warn that she is a fickle bitch so that he shouldn't feel bad if she snubs him. I don't tell him that she's been screaming all day, "You should be with Richard! How dare you leave Richard?"

Elliot reaches under the covers and grabs Edith and pulls her onto his lap where he proceeds to make her purr. He has magic fingers and even though that damn bunion of mine tries to resist, she becomes putty in his hands. When he's finished petting her I declare, "Well, that's it, Mr. Fielding, I now belong to you in full. Edith Bunker has given you rave reviews!"

I wake up the next morning snuggled deep in Elliot's arms. It's the most perfect place in the world to be and if I weren't overcome by a terrible wave of nausea, I would still be there and not hanging over the toilet for dear life. Stan and Ollie are back. I try to remember what I ate yesterday that might have given me food poisoning and it occurs that almost anything could be the culprit.

Elliot gets out of bed and joins me when he hears the first wave of retching. I am a violent vomiter. Even as a little girl I would hurl so forcefully I would break tiny capillaries all over my face. Elliot holds my hair back to keep it from getting in the way and after another grand upheaval, I appear to be done.

He helps me up and croons, "Poor baby, you've got a bug."

I half smile, "It doesn't feel like the flu. I think I might have a touch of food poisoning. How do you feel?"

He replies, "I feel great, so I can't imagine that it's food poisoning. We ate off of each other's plates all day."

He has a point. I ate everything he ate and vice versa. Maybe it is just a little twenty-four hour thing. All I know though is that I am currently ravenous having just emptied my stomach. Elliot tucks me back into bed and then goes to the kitchen to make me breakfast. In no time flat I'm eating honeydew melon with toast and sipping tea to settle my stomach. When I've cleaned my plate I'm inexplicably in the mood for an omelet and sausage and if you can believe it, buttered popcorn.

Once I'm sure that I'm not going to lose my breakfast too,

we get up, shower and get dressed for the day. Elliot and I walk to The Plaza, where he's staying, and by the time we get there I declare he has to feed me again. I don't want to waste time getting to another restaurant so we eat right there at one in the hotel. I don't warn Edith Bunker ahead of time, but I order a bunion with double the meat, double cheese, and double onions, but only one bun this time. I am both relieved and alarmed that I'm back on bunions, relieved I didn't turn on them forever and alarmed I started craving them before getting rid of Edith Bunker.

Elliot is trying to talk to me over lunch but I merely grunt in reply. I am solely focused on my delicious lunch. I initially balk that they're charging twenty-four dollars for a burger, but once I bite into it, I would gladly pay fifty. And the fries, I don't know what they did to the fries but I can't get enough of them. I think they are dipped in seasoned batter before deep frying and oh lord, they are spectacular.

Somewhere in the middle of the meal Elliot declares, "Mimi, if you don't stop groaning while you eat, I'm going to drag you out of here and up to my room."

I look up from my meal thoroughly intrigued by the idea but first I want to finish my lunch so I try to control myself, until they bring the desert cart. Elliot asks if I want anything. I have every intention of saying no until I see the most wicked looking brownie hot fudge sundae walk by. Actually, someone carries it, but it's still a dreamy, dreamy thing. I order one before I can stop myself.

Elliot smiles and groans, "You're teasing me on purpose aren't you?"

I try to explain that I'm not. I'm really just ravenously hungry but he doesn't believe me. So I set out to purposely torture him when my desert arrives. I lick whipped cream off my spoon with the concentration of a spoiled cat. I moan at the sheer pleasure of the homemade fudge sauce. And I close my eyes and savor every single drop of pure fat, French vanilla ice cream. What set out as a game has turned into intense enjoyment of the scrumptiousness before me. By the time I declare I couldn't possibly take one more bite, Elliot has already paid the check and is dragging me out of the restaurant. He whispers if I don't hurry, my fantasy of making love in an elevator might just be realized today. I purposefully slow my pace at the fascinating notion but he just pulls harder.

Remember how I said that I could never be a bulimic? Apparently I lied. I threw up again, not even an hour later. Elliot thinks I really do have the flu but I think that I just ate too much at lunch. Once I barf, the nausea passes and I want to eat again, this time its nachos and peach cobbler from room service. I discover it tastes best when I alternate bites, one bite of refried beans and cheese, one bit of peach cobbler with vanilla ice cream. After I finish my feast, we sit back to see what happens. Happily, I don't throw up but I am left feeling guilty about the hundreds of points that I've just consumed.

Elliot takes me home in a cab and we stay at my place as I have to work in the morning. I sleep like the dead and don't even move when the alarm goes off the next morning. Elliot nudges me and asks if I want him to call in sick for me, and I immediately snap to attention, "Good god, no! No one at work can know about us until everything is settled between you and Beatrice." As an afterthought I add, "In fact we should wait awhile even then, so it doesn't look like you were cheating on her."

He snuggles me, "How are you feeling?"

I smile and declare, "Starving! I must be all better." Elliot makes us breakfast while I shower and by eight-forty-two, we are sharing a cab into the office.

By Tuesday morning, it becomes abundantly clear that I don't have the flu and that I am in fact not a bulimic. I am pregnant. Yes, that's right, knocked up, bun in the oven, full on breeding. Of course I'm delighted as I'm making this baby with the man I love. But the timing is just crap. He is still engaged to another woman, I have just started a new job and he is still engaged to another woman! Did I mention he was engaged to another woman? I am guessing that this happened the night in the carriage because between you, me and the lamppost, I'm pretty certain we didn't use any protection. I mean, I know I didn't. It was just one of those spontaneous acts you are not supposed to engage in in the twenty-first century for a variety of reasons, this being one of them.

Muffy, Kevin, and Beatrice all arrive today and I don't plan on telling anyone my news, especially not Elliot. He has enough on his mind figuring out how he's going to break up with Beatrice without any additional pressure. The hardest part is going to be keeping it from everyone I work with. I am increasingly more nauseous and there are only so many incidences of food poisoning I can claim without making them suspicious.

I weigh in at noon today and break my vow not to tell

anyone about the b-a-b-y. I figure that Babs should really know so that I can find out what to do next as far as my diet is concerned. The good news is that Weight Watcher's has a plan for pregnant women, where I get to consume more points. The bad news is that it's only three to five extra points and my appetite is demanding at least double my current twenty-nine.

I'm meeting Muffy and Kevin at Elaine's at six-thirty for dinner so I leave the office early to get ready. When I walk into the restaurant, they are already there. It is so wonderful to see them that I throw myself into their arms. I realize how much I've missed seeing them on a daily basis and start to fantasize about going home. If only I could split my time between New York and Pipsy, I'd have the best of both worlds.

Muffy tells me that she and Tom have filed for divorce and being that we live in a no-fault state, she should be a free woman in three months. Then she announces she's quit her job at the country club. I look at her and Kevin and declare, "One of you has to work!"

Kevin replies, "We're both going to work. I'm financing Muff in opening her own tennis academy. We've already bought the property and we break ground the day after we get home."

I'm stunned, "This is unexpected. I mean, are you guys sure... I mean, what if, you know..."

My sister comes to my rescue, "We have already drawn up legal contracts that will protect both of us in case our relationship doesn't work."

Kevin contributes, "But just so you know, we're planning on it working."

I realize I sound pessimistic and someone in my shoes should just shut up and congratulate them, so that is exactly what I do. The plan is Muffy will run the actual fitness part of the club and Kevin will be in charge of the office end. They're going to open in Hilldale and offer specials that will make them a very competitive alternative to the country club.

Muff says, "The people who play at the club tend to be less competitive and just play socially. We're going to start tournaments in order to draw some of the more serious players to our facility as well."

Kevin chimes in, "That way it's not an either-or type of situation. They can do both."

Muffy adds, "Renée is going to be a huge help by joining and encouraging her snotty friends to do so as well. And Jonathan has agreed to do our PR. Oh Meems, we're so excited!"

I ask if they've come up with a name yet and Kevin says that they're thinking of "The Buff Muff." I ask if they don't think the name is highly provocative and they assure me that it's good subliminal advertising as apparently a buff muff is coveted by men and women alike. I just wonder what the junior league is going to say.

After dinner Kevin and Muffy decide to go out for a drink. They invite me along, but I can barely keep my eyes open, not to mention that I am not drinking. When I get back to my apartment I see the message light flashing. It's Elliot calling to tell me that he loves me and that everything is going to work out fine. I try to convince myself that he's right, but first I have to throw up my dinner.

# Chapter 41

Today is the big luncheon to launch "Pink" and while I should be thrilled that all of our hard work is about to pay off, I'm scared shitless as well. This is the first time that I will be face-to-face with Beatrice after officially stealing her fiancée and I feel lower than an eel's belly. Elliot hasn't broken up with her yet but vows to do the deed tonight.

Helena, Jocina, Imelda, and I don't even bother to go into the office this morning. We just head straight to grand ballroom at The Waldorf Astoria where the luncheon is being held. When I walk in at eight o'clock, the place is already a hive of activity. The tables look gorgeous with their pink linens and pink flower arrangements. The booths are all set up, and the stage we've erected is getting the final decorating touches, which essentially involve thousands of pink roses and tulle. I feel like I'm walking into an heiress's sweet sixteen party, but the effect is stunning.

The girls and I decided we will all wear white. The original plan was that we would dress in pink to match our theme, but upon further speculation we realized that we might look like a

Mary Kay convention; which in addition to being a competing cosmetics line to Shimmer, is also not the image we wish to portray.

My main function at the event is to make sure the celebrities get on stage at the right time and in the right order. It's not the most demanding job but I feel like it rivals the degree of execution needed to launch the space shuttle. My brain is simply not tuned into the task at hand.

By ten -fifteen the press starts to arrive to set up in the best locations to cover the event. By eleven the speakers have arrived and are doing initial interviews with the journalists. I notice that Beatrice arrives with Elliot and she is talking to the press as well. It occurs to me Elliot and I never considered the ramifications his breaking up with Beatrice would have. Every magazine in attendance is going to publish pictures and interviews with Elliot Fielding and his cancer-afflicted fiancée and by the time the story breaks, they will no longer be an item. Enter me, the Wicked Witch of the West who is responsible for stealing this admirable man from the woman he's loved for three years. Oh my god! Why hadn't we thought of this before now? I'm nauseous again. I frantically look around for the closest ladies room and when I realize it's too far away, I simply lean behind a large potted palm and unload my breakfast there.

There is no way Elliot is going to come out of this situation with any sympathy from the public eye and one guess what that will do to the sales of his next book. Then he'll grow to resent me and he'll stop loving me and I'll have to raise our child on my own. I want to go home and hide from the inevitable horror of it all but I can't. The very least I can do is stay and help to make sure the event is a success. I start to make deals with Stan and Ollie; write me a happy ending and I'll give half of my salary to breast cancer research. Who am I kidding? The pleas go more like, "Write me a happy ending and I'll do anything, anything at all, just write damn it, write!"

Helena comes over to me and tells me none too gently that I look like death warmed over and asks what's wrong. I mumble, "Food poisoning." And she asks if I've started picking out names for my food poisoning yet.

I look at her in shock but she just shakes her head and says, "No one knows. Go get a glass of orange juice, you'll feel better." I merely nod my head and do what she says. I'm afraid if I open my mouth I'll either puke on her or start crying.

By eleven-thirty, the guests start to arrive en masse and I assemble all of the celebrity speakers to inform them who they will be following in the line-up. As soon as they hear me announce the name of their predecessor, they need to make their way to stage left, where I will be waiting to meet them. I beg them to please not be in the bathroom when they are the next guest on stage. I mean the Golden Globes is a multi-million dollar production and they couldn't get Christine Lahti out of the potty in time to accept her award. I implore them to please learn from their contemporary's mistake.

Before going back to his table, Elliot leans in and whispers in my ear, "Remember, I love you, Mimi." I want to shout back, "But you're not going to when you see how badly this ends!" I don't though. I simply give him a pathetic smile and push him in the direction of his table.

The president of Shimmer opens the luncheon with a moving speech about the personal toll breast cancer has taken on her life. While she has not been afflicted with the disease herself, she still claims to be a survivor as her mother and her sister were both diagnosed with the disease and neither one of them won their battle. She is a survivor by default. She wishes more than anything there was someway to bring them back. As there isn't, she vows to do everything she can to keep other women from experiencing the pain she has suffered.

I am not the only one bawling through her speech. I am however the only one doing so near a microphone. People from the audience begin to look in my direction with kind and pitying eyes. They probably assume I have a similar story and their hearts are going out to me. If they only knew the truth, I imagine they would stone me with their rolls. I have a mad urge to run onto the stage and unburden myself of the truth. But thank the good lord, something stops me from doing this. It's Edith Bunker. She hisses, "Don't move!" And luckily I listen to her.

The first celebrity speaker is called to the stage and she also shares her heart breaking story of how breast cancer has touched her life. Then the second speaker, and so on and so on and so on until I'm sure there isn't a tear left in my head. My eyes are swollen, my nose is swollen and my lips are swollen. I look like I've been attacked by a swarm of bees. By the time Elliot is called, I'm about to beg him to stay with Beatrice and forget all about me. I'll raise my bastard child alone in Pipsy. My family will help take the place of his or her father.

When Elliot is announced the audience rises to their feet in thunderous applause. After all, he *is* their hero. He is the one that was man enough to stay with his sick girlfriend. He is the ultimate specimen! He walks to the microphone and the audience gradually starts to calm down.

Elliot smiles at the faces around the room and starts, "My experience with breast cancer has changed my life dramatically. While I have not been afflicted with the disease myself, it has taken its toll on two women that are very dear to me." I gasp and think, two women, who's the other? Elliot continues, "The first lady I loved who had it was also the same woman that I attribute my love of writing to. Without her, I have no idea what I would be doing with my life today. Her name was Henrietta Harding and she was my fifth grade teacher." The audience beams their approval. "Mrs. Harding introduced me to reading with an unparalleled enthusiasm and love of the written word. She and I continued to share our love for books long after I left her class. In fact we continued until she died three years ago. While Mrs. Harding was my favorite teacher for one year, Henrietta was my dear friend for over thirty." The audience is clapping wildly at Elliot's very touching story. I wondered why all of Elliot's book dedications have been to someone named Hen and now I know. My body manages to produce even more tears and I feel like the worst kind of villain ever.

When everyone calms down again, Elliot continues, "The second woman that I have loved with the disease is named Beatrice Hedges and she is here with me today." Elliot indicates Beatrice and she stands while the audience claps their approval. Beatrice does not sit back down, however. She walks straight to stage left and then proceeds past me to join Elliot. I wait with bated breath to see what she is doing. Helena looks at me with a panicked expression but I merely shrug my shoulders. I have absolutely no idea what to expect. Elliot looks surprised as well, but as soon as Beatrice gets to his side, he kisses her on the cheek and the crowd goes wild again. Where is Lee Harvey Oswald when you need him? Because more than anything, I wish someone would just shoot me now and put me out of my misery.

Beatrice steps in front of the microphone and starts to speak. She gives a small smile and announces, "I hope you will all forgive the intrusion. But I would like to be the one to share with you what happens next." Every person in the ballroom is holding their breath in anticipation when she continues, "I met Elliot shortly after Henrietta died and I was totally and completely enamored of him." She looks up at him adoringly and the audience applauds again. I have the sinking feeling that I really am going to be raising my child alone. Beatrice continues, "Elliot and I had only had three dates when I was diagnosed with breast cancer." She pauses before adding, "They were wonderful dates, but we both realized right away that we were only meant to be friends and nothing more."

What?! What is she talking about? Where is this going?

"I have allowed Elliot to sacrifice the last three years of his life to my cause because I was selfish and afraid to face my battle alone." Everyone is looking at her in shock and she continues, "I even went so far as to accept his proposal of marriage. But the truth is while I love him and will always cherish him for the sacrifices he has made on my behalf, I am not in love with him." Elliot looks like you could knock him over with a feather. Beatrice turns to him and smiles, "Elliot Fielding, you and I both deserve a grand passion and I think it's about time we find one. The biggest thing that cancer has taught me is that life is a gift, a very precious gift and we are obligated to make the most of it." Now she takes his hand and continues, "While we are meant for other people, I want you to know I would not have had the strength to be here today without all of your love and support. For all of that and so much more, I will never be able to repay you. But my greatest hope is that someday you will forgive me for taking so much from you when it wasn't mine to take." Beatrice stands on her tiptoes and kisses Elliot's cheek and then she gives him a hug. The audience is back on their feet encouraging this strange and wonderful moment.

I stand and stare at them as though I'm watching a movie and not real life. Did everything actually just work out here? Who wrote this? Jude, Hermione, are you back? I don't know what to do, so I simply join the crowd and clap and clap and clap until my hands feel like they're going to fall off.

As Beatrice walks off the stage, she stops in front of me and takes my hand, "I'm so sorry, Mimi. I never meant to come between the two of you. Be good to him." And then she walks away. How did she know about us? Neither one of us told her. Then I watch as she walks back to her table where Kevin is waiting for her with open arms. She steps into them at the same time he catches my eye and gives me a thumbs up. Well I'll be. This is why Kevin wanted to be in New York to support Beatrice. I'm feeling about a million emotions run through me right now but the predominant one is love. Love for Kevin, love for Elliot and even love for Beatrice. It took amazing courage to do what she just did and I realize she is a woman that I would be honored to have as a friend.

Elliot walks off the stage and right into my arms. I hug him fiercely and then come to my senses, "Elliot, people are taking pictures. We have to stop."

He declares, "Like hell!" Then he drops down on one knee and asks, "Mimi Finnegan, will you marry me?"

I simply nod my head and start to cry again and answer, "Of course I will."

Then Elliot stands up and whispers in my ear, "We better hurry before everyone finds out about the baby."

I look up at him in shock and ask, "How did you know about the baby?"

He smiles, "Hmmm, let me think, throwing up, ravenously hungry, extremely emotional, all the signs are there." Elliot leans down and kisses me with a passion that is tinged with something new. It's laced with promise and hope for our future together.

When we finally break apart I can still hear the thunderous applause from the audience and I wonder what we're missing. But then I look up and realize that they are all clapping for me and Elliot. That's when I know that Stan and Ollie have finally been sent packing because I have my happy ending.

# Chapter 42

Renée and Laurent insist we use their back yard for our reception. With the super human efforts of the Finnegan family, we have planned our wedding in a record two months and are blessed with a beautiful day that only mid-October can guarantee. Last night at the rehearsal dinner, Kevin and Muffy announced their engagement and Ginger and Jonathan shared the news that they are pregnant with triplets. Elliot and I took the opportunity to tell the family we were going to split our time between Pipsy and New York City. After the wedding we are going to go house hunting in both places and find new homes for ourselves. All in all life couldn't be more wonderful.

The wedding ceremony itself is emotional and joyful and full of wonderful moments like when Camille dropped rose petals down the aisle and then turned around to pick them up again. Laurent tried to tell her to leave them but she screamed out at the top of her two-year-old lungs, "But Mommy said I have to pick up my messes!" And then Kevin couldn't find the rings when the priest asked for them. He eventually remembered that he put them in his sock for safe keeping.

When he bent over to retrieve them the congregation started to applaud.

My bridesmaids are of course my sisters and Marge. I think Marge was a little surprised that I asked her, but delighted all the same. She has vowed to get me through my pregnancy all the while keeping me within the thirty pound weight gain that I'm allowed.

Kevin is our best man and Jonathan, Richard and one of Elliot's friends from England round out their numbers. At least fifty of Elliot's friends and family make the trip from England to be with us on our day. Even Beatrice has come and she's not alone. When she got home, she discovered that her washing machine had been leaking the whole time she was away. Her hardwood floors were in desperate shape and the man that the insurance company sent out to appraise the damage also happened to be her grand passion. By all signs they are madly in love.

Richard didn't bring a date as he assures me that he is holding me to our bargain that I will be in charge of finding my replacement in his affections. I already have a few candidates in mind and conveniently all three ladies are here at the wedding. I will be introducing them to my friend at the reception and then we wait to see if one of them is the one. Of course Richard and Elliot are both on their best behavior today but there's an underlying tension between them that alerts me to the fact they should still not be left alone.

Edith Bunker continues to plague my life and as I am about to gain twenty to thirty pounds instead of losing ten, I imagine that she will be around for a good while longer. The good news is that she finally gave up on her love for Richard and has dedicated herself totally to Elliot.

I've got to get to the reception now, but don't worry; I'll let you know how it turns out with Richard, Fiona, Bethanne, and Ellie. My money is on one of them but I don't want to say who in case I'm wrong.

# About the Author

While attending the University of Illinois, in Chicago, Whitney Dineen, began a career as a plus-size model. After modeling in New York City, she and her husband, Jimmy, moved to Los Angeles. In addition to modeling, Whitney spent the California years supplying some of Hollywood's biggest stars with her delicious cookies and candies (see more at WhitneysGoodies.com.) Whitney and her husband currently live in the beautiful Pacific Northwest where they spend their time raising their daughters, free-range chickens and organic vegetables.

Whitney loves to hear from her readers! You can contact her via her website WhitneyDineen.com.

Made in the USA
San Bernardino, CA
14 May 2015